THE MYSTERY OF
ANGELINA FROOD

THE DR. THORNDYKE MYSTERIES

The Red Thumb Mark (1907)

The Eye of Osiris (1911)
published in the USA as *The Vanishing Man*

The Mystery of 31, New Inn (1912)

A Silent Witness (1914)

Helen Vardon's Confession (1922)

The Cat's Eye (1923)

The Mystery of Angelina Frood (1924)

The Shadow of the Wolf (1925)

The D'Arblay Mystery (1926)

A Certain Dr Thorndyke (1927)

As a Thief in the Night (1928)

Mr Pottermack's Oversight (1930)

Pontifex, Son and Thorndyke (1931)

When Rogues Fall Out (1932)
published in the U.S.A. as *Dr. Thorndyke's Discovery*

Dr Thorndyke Intervenes (1933)

For the Defence: Dr Thorndyke (1934)

The Penrose Mystery (1936)

Felo de se? (1937)
published in the U.S.A. as *Death at the Inn*

The Stoneware Monkey (1938)

Mr Polton Explains (1940)

The Jacob Street Mystery (1942)
published in the U.S.A. as *The Unconscious Witness*

THE MYSTERY OF ANGELINA FROOD

R. AUSTIN FREEMAN

A Dr. Thorndyke Novel

WILDSIDE PRESS

Published by Wildside Press LLC.
www.wildsidebooks.com

CHAPTER I

THE DOPER'S WIFE

It takes a good deal to surprise a really seasoned medical practitioner, and still more to arouse in him an abiding curiosity. But at the time when I took charge of Dr. Humphrey's practice in Osnaburgh-street, Regent's Park, I was far from being a seasoned practitioner, having, in fact, been qualified little more than a year, in which short period I had not yet developed the professional immunity from either of the above mental states. Hence the singular experience which I am about to relate not only made a deep impression on me at the time, but remained with me for long after as a matter of curious speculation.

It was close upon midnight, indeed an adjacent church clock had already struck the third quarter, when I laid aside my book and yawned profoundly, without prejudice to the author who had kept me so long from my bed. Then I rose and stretched myself, and was in the act of knocking the long-extinct ashes out of my pipe when the bell rang. As the servants had gone to bed, I went out to the door, congratulating myself on having stayed up beyond my usual bedtime, but wishing the visitor at the devil all the same. The opening of the door gave me a view of a wet street with a drizzle of rain falling, a large closed car by the kerb, and a tallish man on the doorstep, apparently about to renew his attack on the bell.

"Dr. Pumphrey?" he asked; and by that token I gathered that he was a stranger.

"No," I answered; "he is out of town, but I am looking after his practice."

"Very well," he said, somewhat brusquely. "I want you to come and see a lady who has been suddenly taken ill. She has had a rather severe shock."

"Do you mean a mental or a physical shock?" I asked.

"Well, I should say mental," he replied, but so inconclusively that I pressed him for more definite particulars.

"Has she sustained any injuries?" I inquired.

"No," he answered, but still indecisively. "No; that is, so far as I know. I think not."

"No wound, for instance?"

"No," he replied, promptly and very definitely, from which I was disposed to suspect that there was an injury of some other kind. But it was of no use guessing. I hurried back into the surgery, and, having snatched up the emergency bag and my stethoscope, rejoined my visitor, who forthwith hustled me into the car. The door slammed, and the vehicle moved off with the silent, easy motion of a powerful engine.

We started towards Marylebone-road and swept round into Albany-street, but after that I lost my bearings: for the fine rain had settled on the windows so that it was difficult to see through them, and I was not very familiar with the neighbourhood. It seemed quite a short journey, but a big car is very deceptive as to distance. At any rate, it occupied but a few minutes, and during that time my companion and I exchanged hardly a word. As the car slowed down I asked:

"What is this lady's name?"

"Her name," he replied, in a somewhat hesitating manner, "is—she is a Mrs. Johnson."

The manner of the reply suggested a not very intimate acquaintance, which seemed odd under the circumstances, and I reflected on it rapidly as I got out of the car and followed my conductor. We seemed to be in a quiet bystreet of the better class, but it was very dark, and I had but a glimpse as I stepped from the car to the gate of the house. Of the latter, all that I was able to note was that it appeared to be of a decent, rather old-fashioned type, standing behind a small front garden, that the windows were fitted with jalousie shutters, and that the number on the door was 43.

As we ascended the steps the door opened, and a woman was dimly discernible behind it. A lighted candle was on the hall table, and this my conductor picked up, requesting me to follow him up the stairs. When we arrived at the first floor landing, he halted and indicated a door which was slightly ajar.

"That is the room," said he; and with that he turned and retired down the stairs.

I stood for a few moments on the dark landing, deeply impressed by the oddity of the whole affair, and sensible of a growing suspicion, which was not lessened when, by the thin line of light from within the room, I observed on the door-jamb one or two bruises as if the door had been forced from without. However, this was none of my business, and thus reflecting, I was about to knock at the door when four fingers appeared round the edge of it and drew it further open, and a man's head became visible in the opening.

The fingers and the head were alike such as instantly to rivet the attention of a doctor. The former were of the kind known as "clubbed fingers," fingers with bulbous ends, of which the nails curved over like nut-shells. The head, in form like a great William pear, presented a long, coffin-shaped face with high cheekbones, deepset eyes with narrow, slanting eye-slits, and a lofty, square forehead surmounted by a most singular mop of mouse-coloured hair which stood straight up like the fur of a mole.

"I am the doctor," said I, having taken in these particulars in an instantaneous glance, and having further noted that the man's eyes were reddened and wet. He made no reply, but drew the door open and retired, whereupon I entered the room, closing the door behind me, and thereby becoming aware that there was something amiss with the latch.

The room was a bedroom, and on the bed lay a woman, fully clothed, and apparently in evening dress, though the upper part of her person was concealed by a cloak which was drawn up to her chin. She was a young woman—about twenty-eight, I judged—comely, and, in fact, rather handsome, but deadly pale. She was not, however, unconscious, for she looked at me listlessly, though with a certain attention. In some slight embarrassment, I approached the bed, and, as the man had subsided into a chair in a corner of the room, I addressed myself to the patient.

"Good evening, Mrs. Johnson. I am sorry to see you looking so ill. What is the matter? I understand that you have had some kind of shock."

As I addressed her, I seemed to detect a faint expression of surprise, but she replied at once, in a weak voice that was little more than a whisper: "Yes. I have had rather an upset. That is all. They need not really have troubled you."

"Well, you don't look very flourishing," said I, taking the wrist that was uncovered by her mantle, "and your hand is as cold as a fish."

I felt her pulse, checking it by my watch, and meanwhile looking her over critically. And not her alone. For on the wall opposite me was a mirror in which, by a little judicious adjustment of position, I was able to observe the other occupant of the room while keeping my back towards him; and what I observed was that he was sitting with his elbows on his knees, and his face buried in his hands.

"Might one inquire," I asked, as I put away my watch, "what kind of shock it is that you are suffering from?"

The faintest trace of a smile stole across her pale face as she answered: "That isn't really a medical question, Doctor, is it?"

"Perhaps it isn't," I replied, though, of course, it was.

But I thought it best to waive the question, as there seemed to be some reservation; and, noting this latter fact, I again considered her attentively. Whatever her condition was, and whatever it might be due to, I had to form my opinion unassisted, for I could see that no information would be furnished; and the question that I had to settle was whether her state was purely mental, or whether it was complicated by any kind of physical injury. The waxen pallor of her face made me uneasy, and I found it difficult to interpret the expression of the set features. Some strong emotion had left its traces; but whether that emotion was grief, horror, or fear, or whether the expression denoted bodily pain, I could not determine. She had closed her eyes, and her face was like a death mask, save that it lacked the serenity of a dead face.

"Are you in any pain!" I asked, with my fingers still on the thready pulse. But she merely shook her head wearily, without opening her eyes.

It was very unsatisfactory. Her appearance was consistent with all kinds of unpleasant possibilities, as was also the strange atmosphere of secrecy about the whole affair. Nor was the attitude of that ill-favoured man whom I could see in the glass, still sitting hunched up with his face buried in his hands, at all reassuring. And gradually my attention began to focus itself upon the cloak which covered the woman's body and was drawn around her neck up to her chin. Did that cloak conceal anything? It seemed incredible, seeing that they had sent for a doctor. But the behaviour of everybody concerned was incredibly irrational. I produced my stethoscope, which was fitted with a diaphragm that enabled one to hear through the clothing, and, drawing the cloak partly aside, applied the chest-piece over the heart. On this the patient opened her eyes and made a movement of her hand towards the upper part of the cloak. I listened carefully to her heart—which was organically sound, though a good deal disordered in action—and moved the stethoscope once or twice, drawing aside the cloak by degrees. Finally, with a somewhat quick movement, I turned it back completely.

"Why," I exclaimed, "what on earth have you been doing to your neck?"

"That mark?" she said in a half-whisper. "It is nothing. It was made by a gold collar that I wore yesterday. It was rather tight."

"I see," said I, truthfully enough; for the explanation of her condition was now pretty clear up to a certain point.

Of course, I did not believe her. I did not suppose that she expected me to. But it was evidently useless to dispute her statement or make any comment. The mark upon her neck was a livid bruise made by some cord or band that had been drawn tight with considerable force; and it was not more than an hour old. How or by whom the injury had been inflicted was not, in a medical sense, my concern. But I was by no means clear that I had not some responsibilities in the case other than the professional ones.

At this moment the man in the corner uttered a deep groan and exclaimed in low, intense tones, "My God! My God!" Then, to my extreme embarrassment, he began to sob audibly.

It was excessively uncomfortable. I looked from the woman—into whose ghastly face an expression of something like disgust and contempt had stolen—to the huddled figure in the glass. And as I looked, the man plunged one hand into his pocket and dragged out a handkerchief, bringing with it a little paper packet that fell to the floor. Something in the appearance of that packet, and especially in the hasty grab to recover it and the quick, furtive glance towards me that accompanied the action, made a new and sinister suggestion—a suggestion that the man's emotional, almost hysterical state supported, and that lent a certain unpleasant congruity to the otherwise inexplicable circumstances. That packet, I had little doubt, contained cocaine. The question was how did that fact—if it were a fact—bear on my patient's condition.

I inspected her afresh, and felt her pulse again. In the man's case the appearances were distinctive enough. His nerves were in rags, and even across the room I could see that the hand that held the handkerchief shook as if with a palsy. But in the woman's condition there was no positive suggestion of drugs; and something in her face—a strong, resolute face despite its expression of suffering—and her quiet, composed manner when she spoke, seemed to exclude the idea. However, there was no use in speculating. I had got all the information I was likely to get, and all that remained for me to do was to administer such treatment as my imperfect understanding of the case indicated. Accordingly I opened my emergency bag, and, taking out a couple of little bottles and a measure-glass, went over to the washstand and mixed a draught in the tumbler, diluting it from the water-bottle.

In crossing the room, I passed the fireplace, where, on and above the mantelpiece, I observed a number of signed photographs, apparently of actors and actresses, including two of my patient, both of which were in character costume and unsigned. From which it seemed probable that my patient was an actress; a probability that was strengthened by the hour at which I had been summoned and by certain other appearances in the room with which Dr. Pumphrey's largely theatrical practice had made me familiar. But, as my patient would have remarked, this was not a medical question.

"Now, Mrs. Johnson," I said, when I had prepared the draught—and as I spoke she opened her eyes and looked at me with a slightly puzzled expression—"I want you to drink this."

She allowed me to sit her up enough to enable her to swallow the draught; and as her head was raised, I took the opportunity to glance at the back of her neck, where I thought I could distinctly trace the crossing of the cord or band that had been drawn round it. She sank back with a sigh, but remained with her eyes open, looking at me as I repacked my bag.

"I shall send you some medicine," I said, "which you must take regularly. It is unnecessary for me to say," I added, addressing the man, "that Mrs. Johnson must be kept very quiet, and in no way agitated."

He bowed, but made no reply; and I then took my leave.

"Good night, Mrs. Johnson," I said, shaking her cold hand gently. "I hope you will be very much better in an hour or two. I think you will if you keep quite quiet and take your medicine."

She thanked me in a few softly spoken words and with a very sweet smile, of which the sad wistfulness went to my heart. I was loath to leave her, in her weak and helpless state, to the care of her unprepossessing companion, encompassed by I knew not what perils. But I was only a passing stranger, and could do no more than my professional office.

As I approached the door—with an inquisitive eye on its disordered lock and loosened striking-box—the man rose, and made as if to let me out. I wished him good-night, and he returned the salutation in a pleasant voice, and with a distinctly refined accent, quite out of character with his uncouth appearance. Feeling my way down the dark staircase, I presently encountered my first acquaintance, who came to the foot of the stairs with the candle.

"Well," he said, in his brusque way, "how is she?"

"She is very weak and shaken," I replied. "I want to send her some medicine. Shall I take the address, or are you driving me back?"

"I will take you back in the car," said he, "and you can give me the medicine."

The car was waiting at the gate, and we went out together. As I turned to close the gate after me, I cast a quick glance at the house and its surroundings, searching for some distinctive feature in case recognition of the place should be necessary later. But it was a dark night, though the rain had now ceased, and I could see no more than that the adjoining house seemed to have a sort of corner turret, crowned with a small cupola, and surmounted by a weather-vane.

During the short journey home not a word was spoken, and when the car drew up at Dr. Pumphrey's door and I let myself in with the key, my companion silently followed me in. I prepared the medicine at once, and handed it to him with a few brief instructions. He took it from me, and then asked what my fee was.

"Do I understand that I am not required to continue the attendance?" I asked.

"They will send for you, I suppose, if they want you," he replied. "But I had better pay your fee for this visit as I came for you."

I named the fee, and, when he had paid it, I said: "You understand that she will require very careful and tender treatment while she is so weak?"

"I do," he answered; "but I am not a member of the household. Did you make it clear to Mr.—her husband?"

I noted the significant hesitation, and replied: "I told him, but as to making it clear to him, I can't say. His mental condition was none of the most lucid. I hope she has someone more responsible to look after her."

"She has," he replied; and then he asked: "You don't think she is in any danger, I hope?"

"In a medical sense," I answered, "I think not. In other respects you know better than I do."

He gave me a quick look, and nodded slightly. Then, with a curt "good-night," he turned and went out to the car.

When he was gone, I made a brief record of the visit in the day-book, and entered the fee in the cash column. In the case of the experienced Dr. Pumphrey, this would have been the end of the transaction. But, new as I was to medical practice, I was unable to take this matter-of-fact view of its incidents. My mind still surged with surprise, curiosity, and a deep concern for my fair patient. Filling my pipe, I sat down before the gas fire to think over the mystery to which I had suddenly become a party.

What was it that had happened in that house T Obviously, something scandalous and sinister. The secrecy alone made that manifest. Not only had the whereabouts of the house been withheld from me, but a false name had been given. I realized that when my late visitor stumbled over the name and substituted "her husband," He had forgotten what name it was that he had given on the spur of the moment. I understood, too, the look of surprise that my patient had given when I addressed her by that false name. Clearly, something had happened which had to be hushed up if possible.

What was it? The elements of the problem, and the material for solving it, were the mark on the woman's neck, the condition of the door, and a packet which I felt morally certain contained cocaine. I considered these three factors separately and together.

The mark on the neck was quite recent. Its character was unmistakable. A cord or band had been drawn tight and with considerable violence, either by the woman herself, or by some other person: that is to say, it was a case either of attempted suicide or attempted murder. To which of these alternatives did the circumstances point?

There was the door. It had been broken in, and had therefore been locked on the inside. That was consistent with suicide, but not inconsistent with murder. Then, by whom had it been broken in? By a murderer to get at his victim? Or by a rescuer? And if the latter, was it to avert suicide or murder?

Again, there was the drug—assumed, but almost certain.

What was the bearing of that? Could these three persons be a party of "dopers," and the tragedy the outcome of an orgy of drug-taking? I rejected this possibility at once. It was not consistent with the patient's condition nor with her appearance or manner; and the man who had fetched me and brought me back was a robust, sane-looking man who seemed quite beyond suspicion.

I next considered the persons. There were three of them: two men and a woman. Of the men, one was a virile, fairly good-looking man of perhaps forty; the other—the husband—was conspicuously unprepossessing, physically degenerate and mentally, as I judged, a hysterical poltroon. Here there seemed to be the making of trouble, especially when one considered the personal attractiveness of the woman.

I recalled her appearance very vividly. A handsome woman, not, perhaps, actually beautiful—though she might have been that if the roses of youth and health had bloomed in those cheeks that I had seen blanched with that ghastly pallor. But apart from mere comeliness, there was a suggestion of a pleasing, gracious personality. I don't know how it had been conveyed to me, excepting by the smile with which she had thanked me and bidden me farewell: a smile that had imparted a singular sweetness to her face. But I had received that impression, and also that she was a woman of decided character and intelligence.

Her appearance was rather striking. She had a great mass of dark hair, parted in the middle, and drawn down over the temples, nearly covering the ears; darkish grey eyes, and unusually strong, black, level eyebrows, that almost met above the straight, shapely nose. Perhaps it was those eyebrows that gave the strength and intensity to her expression, aided by the compressed lips—though this was probably a passing condition due to her mental state.

My cogitations were prolonged well into the small hours, but they led to nothing but an open verdict. At length I rose with a slight shiver, and, dismissing the topic from my mind, crept up to bed.

But both the persons and the incident refused to accept their dismissal. For many days afterwards I was haunted by two faces; the one, ugly, coffin-shaped, surmounted by a shock of soft, furry, mouse-coloured hair; the other, sweet, appealing, mutely eloquent of tragedy and sorrow. Of course, I received no further summons; and the whereabouts of the house of mystery remained a secret until almost the end of my stay in Osnaburgh-street. Indeed, it was on the very day before Dr. Pumphrey's return that I made the discovery.

I had been making a visit to a patient who lived near Regent's Park, and on my way back had taken what I assumed to be a short cut. This led me into a quiet, old fashioned residential street, of which the houses stood back behind small front gardens. As I walked along the street I seemed to be aware of a faint sense of familiarity which caused me to observe the houses with more than usual attention. Presently I observed a little way ahead on the opposite side a house with a corner turret topped by a cupola, which bore above it a weather-vane. I crossed the road as I approached it, and looked eagerly at the next house. Its identity was unmistakable. My attention was immediately attracted by the jalousies with which the windows were fitted, and on looking at the front door I observed that the number was forty-three.

This, then, was the house of mystery, perhaps of crime.

But whatever that tragedy had been, its actors were there no longer. The windows were curtainless and blank; an air of Spring-cleaning and preparation pervaded the premises, and a bill on a little notice-board announced a furnished house to let, and invited inquiries. For a moment, I was tempted to accept that invitation. But I was restrained by a feeling that it would be in a way a breach of confidence. The names of those persons had been purposely withheld from me, doubtless for excellent reasons, and professional ethics seemed to forbid any unauthorized pryings into their private affairs. Wherefore, with a valedictory glance at the first-floor window, which I assumed to be that of the room that I had entered, I went on my way, telling myself that, now, the incident was really closed, and that I had looked my last on the persons who had enacted their parts in it.

In which, however, I was mistaken. The curtain was down on the first act, but the play was not over. Only the succeeding acts were yet in the unfathomed future. "Coming events cast their shadows before them," but who can interpret those shadows, until the shapes which cast them loom up, plain and palpable, to mock at their own unheeded premonitions?

CHAPTER II

RE-ENTER "MR. JOHNSON"

It was a good many months before the curtain rose on the second act of the drama of which this narrative is the record. Rather more than a year had passed, and in that time certain changes had taken place in my condition, of which I need refer only to the one that, indirectly, operated as the cause of my becoming once more a party to the drama aforesaid. I had come into a small property, just barely sufficient to render me independent, and to enable me to live in idleness, if idleness had been my hobby. As it was not, I betook myself to Adam-street, Adelphi, to confer with my trusty medical agent, Mr. Turcival, and from that conference was born my connexion with the strange events which will be hereafter related.

Mr. Turcival had several practices to sell, but only one that he thought quite suitable. "It is a death vacancy," said he, "at Rochester. A very small practice, and you won't get much out of it, as the late incumbent was an old man and you are a young man—and you look ten years younger since you shaved off that fine beard and moustache. But it is going for a song, and you can afford to wait; and you couldn't have a more pleasant place to wait in than Rochester. Better go down and have a look at it. I'll write to the local agents, Japp and Bundy, and they will show you the house and effects. What do you say?"

I said "yes," and so favourably was I impressed that the very next day found me in a first-class compartment en route for Rochester, with a substantial portmanteau in the guard's van.

At Dartford it became necessary to change, and as I sauntered on the platform, waiting for the Rochester train, my attention was attracted to a man who sat, somewhat wearily and dejectedly, on a bench, rolling a cigarette. I was impressed by the swift dexterity with which he handled the paper and tobacco, a dexterity that was explained by the colour of his fingers, which were stained to the hue of mahogany. But my attention was quickly diverted from the colour of the fingers to their shape. They were clubbed fingers. At the moment when I observed the fact I was looking over his shoulder from behind, and could not see his face. But I could see that he had a large, pear-shaped head, surmounted by an enormous cap, from beneath which a mass of mouse-coloured hair stuck out like untidy thatch.

I suppose I must have halted unconsciously, for he suddenly looked round, casting at me a curious, quick, furtive, suspicious glance. He evidently did not recognize me—naturally, since my appearance was so much changed; but I recognized him instantly. He was "Mr.—, her husband." And his appearance was not improved since I had last seen him. Inspecting him from the front, I observed that he was sordidly shabby and none too clean, and that his large, rough boots were white with dust as if from a long tramp on the chalky Kentish roads.

When the train came in, I watched him saunter to a compartment a few doors from my own, rolling a fresh cigarette as he went: and at each station when we stopped, I looked out of the window to see where he got out. But he made no appearance until the train slowed down at Rochester when I alighted quickly and strolled towards his compartment. It had evidently been well filled, for a number of passengers emerged before he appeared, contesting the narrow doorway with a stout workman. As he squeezed past, the skirt of his coat caught and was drawn back, revealing a sheath-knife of the kind known to seamen as "Green River," attached to a narrow leather belt. I did not like the look of that knife. No landsman has any legitimate use for such a weapon. And the fact that this man habitually carried about him the means of inflicting lethal injuries—for it had no other purpose—threw a fresh light, if any were needed, on the sinister events of that memorable night in the quiet house near Regent's Park.

As I had to look after my luggage, I lost sight of him; and when having deposited my portmanteau in the cloak room, I walked out across the station approach and looked up and down the street, he was nowhere to be seen. Dimly wondering what this man might be doing in Rochester, and whether his handsome wife were here, too—assuming her to be still in existence—I turned and began to saunter slowly westward. I had walked but two or three hundred yards when the door of a tavern which I was approaching opened, and a man emerged, licking his lips with uncommon satisfaction, and rolling a cigarette. It was my late fellow-traveller. He stood by the tavern door, looking about him, and glancing at the people on the footway. Just as I was passing him, he approached me and spoke.

"I wonder," said he, "if you happen to know a Mrs. Frood who lives somewhere about here."

"I am afraid I don't," I replied, thankful to be able to tell the truth—for I should have denied knowledge of her in any case. "I am a stranger to the town at present."

He thanked me and turned away, and I walked on, but no longer at a saunter, wondering who Mrs. Frood might be and keeping an eye on the numbers of the houses on the opposite side of the street.

A few minutes walk brought into view the number I was seeking, painted in the tympanum of a handsome Georgian portico appertaining to one of a pair of pleasant old redbrick houses. I halted to inspect these architectural twins before crossing the road. Old houses always interest me, and these two were particularly engaging, as their owners apparently realized, for they were in the pink of condition, and the harmony of the quiet green woodwork and the sober red brick was no chance effect. Moreover they were painted alike to carry out the intention of the architect, who had evidently designed them to form a single composition; to which end he had very effectively placed, between the twin porticoes, a central door which gave access to a passage common to the two houses and leading, no doubt, to the back premises.

Having noted these particulars, I crossed the road and approached the twin which bore beside its doorway a brass plate, inscribed "Japp and Bundy, Architects and Surveyors." In the adjoining bay window, in front of a green curtain, was a list of houses to let; and as I paused for a moment to glance at this, a face decorated with a pair of colossal tortoiseshell-rimmed spectacles, rose slowly above the curtain, and then, catching my eye, popped down again with some suddenness.

I ascended the short flight of steps to the open street door, and entering the hall, opened the office door and walked in. The owner of the spectacles was perched on a high stool at a higher desk with his back to me, writing in a large book. The other occupant of the office was a small, spare, elderly man, with a pleasant wrinkly face and a cockatoo-like crest of white hair, who confronted me across a large table on which a plan was spread out. He looked up interrogatively as I entered, and I proceeded at once to announce myself.

"I am Dr. Strangeways," said I, drawing a bundle of papers from my pocket. "Mr. Turcival—the medical agent, you know—thought I had better come down and settle things up on the spot. So here I am."

"Precisely," said my new acquaintance, motioning me to a chair—it was a shield-back Heppelwhite, I noticed—"I agree with Mr. Turcival. It is all quite plain sailing. The position is this: Old Dr. Partridge died about three weeks ago, and the executor of his will, who lives in Northumberland, has instructed us to realize his estate. We have valued the furniture, fittings, and effects, have added a small amount to cover the drugs and instruments and the goodwill of the practice, and this is the premium. It is practically just the value of the effects."

"And the lease of the house?"

"Expired some years ago and we allowed Dr. Partridge to remain as a yearly tenant, which he preferred. You could do the same or you could have a lease, if you wished."

"Is the house your property?" I asked.

"No; but we manage it for the owner, a Mrs. Frood."

"Oh, it belongs to Mrs. Frood, does it?"

He looked up at me quickly, and I noticed that the gentleman at the desk had stopped writing. "Do you know Mrs. Frood?" he asked.

"No; but it happens that a man who came down by my train asked me a few minutes ago if I could give him her address. Fortunately I couldn't."

"Why fortunately?"

The question brought me, up short. My prejudice against the man was due to my knowledge of his antecedents, which I was not prepared to disclose. I therefore replied evasively:

"Well, I wasn't very favourably impressed by his appearance. He was a shabby-looking customer. I suspected that he was a cadger of some kind."

"Indeed! Now, what sort of a person was he? Could you describe him?"

"He was a youngish man—from thirty-five to forty, I should say—apparently well educated but very seedy and not particularly clean. A queer-looking man, with a big, pear-shaped head and a mop of hair like the fur of a Persian cat. His fingers are clubbed at the ends, and stained with tobacco to the knuckles. Do you know him?"

"I rather suspect I do. What do you say, Bundy?"

Mr. Bundy grunted. "Hubby, I ween," said he.

"You don't mean Mrs. Frood's husband?" I exclaimed.

"I do. And it is, as you said, very fortunate that you were not able to give him her address, as she is unable to live with him and is at present unwilling to let him know her whereabouts. It is an unfortunate affair. However, to return to your business; you had better go up and have a look at the house and see what you think of it. You might just walk up with Dr. Strangeways, Bundy."

Mr. Bundy swung round on his stool, and, taking off his spectacles, stuck in his right eye a gold-rimmed monocle, through which he inspected me critically. Then he hopped off the stool, and, lifting the lid of the desk, took out a velour hat and a pair of chamois gloves, the former of which he adjusted carefully on his head before a small mirror, and, having taken down a labelled key from a key-board and provided himself with a smart, silver-mounted cane, announced that he was ready.

As I walked along the picturesque old street at Mr. Bundy's side, I reverted to my late fellow passenger and my prospective landlady.

"I gather," said I, "that Mrs. Frood's matrimonial affairs are somewhat involved."

"So do I," said Bundy. "Seems to have made a regular mucker of it. I don't know much about her, myself, but Japp knows the whole story. He's some sort of relative of hers; uncle or second cousin or something of the kind. But Japp is a bit like the sailor's parrot: he doesn't let on unnecessarily."

"'What sort of a woman is Mrs. Frood?" I asked.

"Oh, quite a tidy sort of body. I've only seen her once or twice; haven't been here long myself: tallish woman, lot of black hair; thick eyebrows; rather squeaky voice. Not exactly my idea of a beauty, but Frood seems quite keen on her."

"By the way, how comes it that he doesn't know her address? She's a Rochester woman, isn't she?"

"No. I don't know where she comes from. London, I think. This property was left to her by an aunt who lived here: a cousin of Japp's. Angelina came down here a few weeks ago on the q.t. to get away from hubby, and I fancy she's been keeping pretty close."

"She's living in lodgings, then, I suppose?"

"Yes; at least she lives in a set of offices that Japp furnished for her, and the lady who rents the rest of the house looks after her. As a matter of fact, the offices are next door to ours; but you had better consider that information as confidential, at any rate while hubby is in the neighbourhood. This is your shanty."

He halted at the door of a rather small, red brick house, and while I was examining the half-obliterated inscription on the brass plate, he thrust the key into the lock and made ineffectual efforts to turn it. Suddenly there was a loud click from within, followed by the clanking of a chain and the drawing of bolts. Then the door opened slowly, and a long-faced, heavy-browed, elderly woman surveyed us with a gloomy stare.

"Why didn't you ring the bell?" she demanded, gruffly. "Had a key," replied Bundy, extracting it, and flourishing it before her face.

"And what's the good of a key when the door was bolted and chained?"

"But, naturally, I couldn't see that the door was bolted and chained."

"I suppose you couldn't with that thing stuck in your eye. Well, what do you want?"

"I have brought this gentleman, Dr. Strangeways, to see you. He has seen your portraits in the shop windows and wished to be introduced. Also he wants to look over the house. He thinks of taking the practice."

"Well, why couldn't you say that before?" she demanded.

"Before what?" he inquired blandly.

She made no reply other than a low growl, and Bundy continued:

"This lady, Dr. Strangeways, is the renowned Mrs. Dunk, more familiarly known as La Giaconda, who administered the domestic affairs of the late Dr. Partridge, and is at present functioning as custodian of the premises." He concluded the presentation by a ceremonious bow and a sweep of his hat, which Mrs. Dunk acknowledged by turning her back on him and producing a large bunch of keys, with which she proceeded to unlock the doors that opened on the hall.

"The upstairs rooms are unlocked," she said, adding: "If you want me you can ring the bell," and with this she retired to the basement stairs and vanished.

My examination of the rooms was rather perfunctory, for I had made up my mind already. The premium was absurdly small, and I could see that the house was furnished well enough for my immediate needs. As to the practice, I had no particular expectations.

"Better have a look at the books," said Bundy when we went into the little surgery, "though Mr. Turcival has been through them, and I daresay he has told you all about the practice."

"Yes," I answered, "he told me that the practice was very small and that I probably shouldn't get much of it, as Partridge was an old man and I am a young one. Still, I may as well glance through the books."

Bundy laid the day book and ledger on the desk and placed a stool by the latter, and I seated myself and began to turn over the leaves and note down a few figures on a slip of paper, while my companion beguiled the time by browsing round the surgery, taking down bottles and sniffing at their contents, pulling out drawers and inspecting the instruments and appliances. A very brief examination of the books served to confirm Mr. Turcival's modest estimate of the practice, and when I had finished, I closed them and turned round to report to Mr. Bundy, who was, at the moment, engaged in "sounding" the surgery clock with the late Dr. Partridge's stethoscope.

"I think it will do," said I. "The practice is negligible, but the furniture and fittings are worth the money, and I daresay I shall get some patients in time. At any rate, the premises are all in going order."

"You are not dependent on the practice, then?" said he.

"No. I have enough just barely to exist on until the patients begin to arrive. But what about the house?"

"You can have a lease if you like, or you can go on with the arrangement that Partridge had. If I were you, I should take the house on a three years' agreement with the option of a lease later if you find that the venture turns out satisfactorily."

"Yes," I agreed, "that seems a good arrangement. And when could I have possession?"

"You've got possession now if you agree to the terms. Say yes, and I'll draft out the agreement when I get back. You and Mrs. Frood can sign it this evening.

You give us a cheque and we give you your copy of the document, and the thing is d-u-n, done."

"And what about this old woman?"

"La Giaconda Dunkibus? I should keep her if I were you. She looks an old devil, but she's a good servant. Partridge had a great opinion of her, so Japp tells me, and you can see for yourself that the house is in apple-pie order and as clean as a new pin."

"You think she would be willing to stay?"

Bundy grinned (he was a good deal given to grinning, and he certainly had a magnificent set of teeth). "Willing?" he exclaimed. "She's going to stay whether you want her or not. She has been here the best part of her life and nothing short of a torpedo would shift her. You'll have to take her with the fixtures, but I don't think you'll regret it."

As Bundy was speaking, I had been, half-unconsciously, looking him over, interested in the queer contrast between his almost boyish appearance and gay irresponsible manner on the one hand, and, on the other, his shrewdness, his business capacity, and his quick, decisive, evidently forceful character.

To look at, he was just a young "nut," small, spruce, dandified, and apparently not displeased with himself. His age I judged to be about twenty-five, his height about five feet six. In figure, he was slight, but well set-up, and he seemed active and full of life and energy. He was extraordinarily well turned-out. From his close-cropped head, with the forelock "smarmed" back in the correct "nuttish" fashion, so that his cranium resembled a large black-topped filbert, to his immaculately polished and remarkably small shoes, there was not an inch of his person that had not received the most careful attention. He was clean-shaved; so clean that on the smooth skin nothing but the faint blue tinge on cheek and chin remained to suggest the coarse and horrid possibilities of whiskers. And his hands had evidently received the same careful attention as his face; indeed, even as he was talking to me, he produced from his pocket some kind of ridiculous little instrument with which he proceeded to polish his fingernails.

"Shall I ring the bell?" he asked after a short pause, "and call up the spirit of the Dunklett from the vasty deep? May as well let her know her luck."

As I assented he pressed the bell-push, and in less than a minute Mrs. Dunk made her appearance and stood in the doorway, looking inquiringly at Bundy, but uttering no sound.

"Dr. Strangeways is going to take the practice, Mrs. Dunk," said Bundy, "inclusive of the house, furniture, and all effects, and he is also prepared to take you at a valuation."

As the light of battle began to gleam in Mrs. Dunk's eyes, I thought it best to intervene and conduct the negotiations myself.

"I understand from Mr. Bundy," said I, "that you were Dr. Partridge's housekeeper for many years, and it occurred to me that you might be willing to act in the same capacity for me. What do you say?"

"Very well," she replied. "When do you want to move in?"

"I propose to move in at once. My luggage is at the station."

"Have you checked the inventory?" she asked.

"No, I haven't, but I suppose nothing has been taken away?"

"No," she answered. "Everything is as it was when Dr. Partridge died."

"Then we can go over the inventory later. I will have my things sent up from the station, and I shall come in during the afternoon to unpack."

She agreed concisely to this arrangement, and, when we had settled a few minor details, I departed with Bundy to make my way to the station and thereafter to go in search of lunch.

"You think," said I, as we halted opposite the station approach, "that we can get everything completed today?"

"Yes," he replied, "I will get the agreement drawn up in the terms that we have just settled on, and will make an appointment with Mrs. Frood. You had better look in at the office about half-past six."

He turned away with a friendly nod and a flash of his white teeth, and bustled off up the street, swinging his smart cane jauntily, and looking, with his trim, well-cut clothes, his primrose-coloured gloves, and his glistening shoes, the very type of cheerful, prosperous, self-respecting and self-satisfied youth.

CHAPTER III

ANGELINA FROOD

Punctually at half-past six I presented myself at the office of Messrs. Japp and Bundy. The senior partner was seated at a writing-table covered with legal-looking documents, and, as I entered, he looked up with a genial, wrinkly smile of recognition, and then turned to his junior.

"You've got Dr. Strangeways's agreement ready, haven't you, Bundy?" he asked.

"Just finished it five minutes ago," was the reply. "Here you are."

Bundy swung round on his stool and held out the two copies. "Would you mind going through it with Dr. Strangeways?" said Japp. "And then you might go with him to Mrs. Frood's and witness the signatures. I told her you were coming."

Bundy pulled out his watch, and glared at it through his great spectacles.

"By Jove!" he exclaimed, "I'm afraid I can't. There's old Baldwin, you know. I've got to be there at a quarter to seven."

"So you have," said Japp, "I had forgotten that. You had better be off now. I'll see to Dr. Strangeways, if he isn't in a hurry for a minute or two."

"I'm not in a hurry at all," said I. "Don't put yourself out for me."

"Well, if you really are not," said Japp, "I'll just finish what I am doing, and then I'll run in with you and get the agreement completed. You might look through it while you are waiting and see that it is all in order."

Bundy handed me the agreement, and, as I sat down to study it, he removed his spectacles, hopped off his perch, brought forth his hat, gloves, and stick, and, having presented his teeth for my inspection, took his departure.

I read through the agreement carefully to ascertain that it embodied the terms agreed on verbally and compared the two copies. Then, while Mr. Japp continued to turn over the leaves of his documents, I let my thoughts stray from the trim, orderly office to the house of mystery in London and the strange events that had befallen there on that rainy night more than a year ago. Once more I called up before the eyes of memory the face of my mysterious patient, sweet and gracious in spite of its deathly pallor. Many a time, in the months that had passed, had I recalled it: so often that it seemed, in a way, to have become familiar. In a few minutes I was going to look upon that face again—for there could be no reasonable doubt that my prospective landlady was she. I looked forward expectantly, almost with excitement, to the meeting. Would she recognize me? I wondered. And if she did not, should I make myself known? This was a difficult question, and I had come to no decision upon it when I was aroused from my reverie by a movement on the part of Mr. Japp, whose labours had apparently come to an end. Folding up the documents and securing them in little bundles with red tape, he deposited them in a cupboard with his notes, and from the same receptacle took out his hat.

"Now," said he, "if you find the agreement in order, we will proceed to execute it. Are you going to pay the premium now?"

"I have my cheque-book with me," I replied. "When we have signed the agreement, I will settle up for everything."

"Thank you," said he. "I have prepared a receipt which is, practically, an assignment of the furniture and effects and of all rights in the practice."

He held the door open and I passed out. We descended the steps, and passing the central door common to the two houses, ascended to that of the adjoining house, where Mr. Japp executed a flourish on a handsome brass knocker. In a few moments the door was opened by a woman whom I couldn't see very distinctly in the dim hall, especially as she turned about and retired up the stairs. Mr. Japp advanced to the door of the front room and rapped with his knuckles, whereupon a high, clear, feminine voice bade him come in. He accordingly entered, and I followed.

The first glance disposed of any doubts that I might have had. The lady who stood up to receive us was unquestionably my late patient, though she looked taller than I had expected. But it was the well-remembered face, less changed, indeed, than I could have wished, for it was still pale, drawn, and weary, as I could see plainly enough in spite of the rather dim light; for, although it was not yet quite dark, the curtains were drawn and a lamp lighted on a small table, beside which was a low easy-chair, on which some needlework had been thrown down.

Mr. Japp introduced me to my future landlady, who bowed, and having invited us to be seated, took up her needlework and sat down in the easy-chair.

"You are not looking quite up to the mark," Japp observed, regarding her critically, as he turned over the papers.

"No," she admitted, "I think I am a little run down."

"H'm," said Japp. "Oughtn't to get run down at your age. Why, you are only just wound up. However, you've got a doctor for a tenant, so you will be able to take out some of the rent in medical advice. Let me see, I told you what the terms of the agreement were, but you had better look through it before you sign."

He handed her one of the documents, which she took from him, and, dropping her needlework in her lap, leaned back in her chair to read it. Meanwhile, I examined her with a good deal of interest and curiosity, wondering how she had fared and what had happened to her in the months that had elapsed since I had last seen her. The light was not very favourable for a minute inspection, for the lamp on the table was the sole luminary, and that was covered by a red silk shade. But I was confirmed in my original impression of her. She was more than ordinarily good-looking, and rather striking in appearance, and I judged that under happier conditions she might have appeared even more attractive. As, it was, the formally parted dark hair, the strongly marked, straight eyebrows, the firm mouth, rather compressed and a little drawn down at the corners, and the pale complexion imparted to her face a character that was somewhat intense, sombre, and even troubled. But, for this I could fully account from my knowledge of her circumstances, and I was conscious of looking on her with a very sympathetic and friendly eye.

"This is quite satisfactory to me," she said at length, in the clear, high-pitched voice to which Bundy had objected, "and if it is equally so to Dr. Strangeways, I suppose I had better sign."

She laid the paper on the table, and, taking the fountain-pen that Japp proffered, signed her name, Angelina Frood, in a bold, legible hand, and then returned the pen to its owner; who forthwith affixed his signature as witness and spread out the duplicate for me to sign. When this also was completed, he handed me the copy signed by Mrs. Frood and the receipt for the premium, and I drew a cheque for the amount and delivered it to him.

"Many thanks," said he, slipping it into a wallet and pocketing it. "That concludes our business and puts you finally in possession. I wish you every success in your practice. By the way, I mentioned to Mrs. Frood that you had seen her husband and that you know how she is placed; and she agreed with me that it was best that you should understand the position in case you should meet him again."

"Certainly," Mrs. Frood agreed. "There is no use in trying to make a secret of it. He came down with you from London, Mr. Japp tells me."

"Not from London," said I. "He got in at Dartford." Here Mr. Japp rose and stole towards the door. "Don't let me interrupt you," said he, "but I must get back to the office and hear what Bundy has to report. Don't get up. I can let myself out."

He made his exit quietly, shutting the door after him, and as soon as he was gone Mrs. Frood asked:

"Do you mean that he changed into your train at Dartford?"

"No," I answered. "I think he came to Dartford on foot. He looked tired and his boots were covered with white dust."

"You are very observant, Dr. Strangeways," she said.

"I wonder what made you notice him so particularly?"

"He is rather a noticeable man," I said, and then, deciding that it was better to be quite frank, I added: "But the fact is I had seen him before."

"Indeed!" said she. "Would you think me very inquisitive if I asked where you had seen him?"

"Not at all," I answered. "It was a little more than a year ago, about twelve o'clock at night, in a house near Regent's Park, to which I was taken in a closed car to see a lady."

As I spoke she dropped her needlework and sat up, gazing at me with a startled and rather puzzled expression. "But," she said, "you are not the doctor who came to see me that night?"

"I am, indeed," said I.

"Now," she exclaimed, "isn't that an extraordinary thing? I had a feeling that I had seen you somewhere before. I seemed to recognize your voice. But you don't look the same. Hadn't you a beard then?"

"Yes, I am but the shaven and shorn remnant of my former self, but I am your late medical attendant."

She looked at me with an odd, reflective, questioning expression, but without making any further comment. Presently she said:

"You were very kind and sympathetic though you were so quiet. I wonder what you thought of it all."

"I hadn't much to go on beyond the medical facts," I replied evasively.

"Oh, you needn't be so cautious," said she, "now that the cat is out of the bag."

"Well," I said, "it was pretty obvious that there had been trouble of some kind. The door had been broken open, there was one man in a state of hysterics, another man considerably upset and rather angry, and a woman with the mark on her neck of a cord or band—"

"It was a knitted silk necktie, to be accurate. But you put the matter in a nutshell very neatly; and I see that you diagnosed what novelists call 'the eternal triangle.' And to a certain extent you were right; only the triangle was imaginary. If you don't mind, I will tell you just what did happen. The gentleman who came for you was a Mr. Fordyce, the lessee of one or two provincial theatres—I was on the stage then; but perhaps you guessed that."

"As a matter of fact, I did."

"Well, Mr. Fordyce had an idea of producing a play at one of his houses, and was going to give me a leading part. He had been to our house once or twice to talk the matter over with Nicholas (my husband) and me, and we were more or less friendly. He was quite a nice, sober kind of man, and perfectly proper and respectful. On this night he had been at the theatre where I had an engagement, and, as it was a wet night, he drove me home in his car, and was coming in to have a few words with us about our business. He wanted to see a photograph of me in a particular costume, and when we arrived home I ran upstairs to fetch it. There I found Nicholas, who had seen our arrival from the window, and was in a state of furious jealousy. Directly I entered the room, he locked the door and flew at me like a wild beast. As to what followed, I think you know as much as I do, for I fainted, and when I recovered Nicholas was sobbing in a corner, and Mr. Fordyce was standing by the door, looking as black as thunder."

"Had your husband been jealous of Mr. Fordyce previously?"

"Not a bit. But on this occasion he was in a very queer state. I think he had been drinking, and taking some other things that were bad for him—"

"Such as cocaine," I suggested.

"Yes. But, dear me! What a very noticing person you are, Dr. Strangeways! But you are quite right. It was the cocaine that was the cause of the trouble. He was always a difficult man; emotional, excitable, eccentric, and not very temperate, but after he had acquired the drug habit he went to the bad completely. He became slovenly, and even dirty in his person, frightfully emotional, and gave up work of all kind, so that but for my tiny income and my small earnings we should have starved."

"So you actually supported him?"

"Latterly I did. And I daresay, if I had remained on the stage, we should have done fairly well, as I was supposed to have some talent, though I didn't like the life. But, of course, after this affair, I didn't dare to live with him. He wasn't safe. I should have been constantly in fear of my life."

"Had he ever been violent before?"

"Not seriously. He had often threatened horrible things, and I had looked on his threats as mere vapourings, but this was a different affair. I must have had a really narrow escape. So the very next day, I went into lodgings. But that didn't answer. He wouldn't agree to the separation, and was continually dogging me and making a disturbance. In the end, I had to give up my engagement and go off, leaving no address."

"I suppose you went back to your people?"

"No," she replied. "As a matter of fact, I haven't any people. My mother died when I was quite a child, and I lost my father when I was about seventeen. He died on the Gold Coast, where he held an appointment as District Commissioner."

"Ah," said I, "I thought you were in some way connected with West Africa. I noticed the zodiac ring on your finger when you were signing the agreement. When I was newly qualified I took a trip down the West Coast as a ship's surgeon, and bought one of those rings at Cape Coast."

"They are quaint little things, aren't they?" she remarked, slipping the ring off her finger and handing it to me. "I don't often wear it, though. It is rather clumsy, and it doesn't fit very well; and I don't care much for rings."

I turned the little trinket over in my hand and examined it with reminiscent interest. It was a roughly wrought band of yellow native gold, with the conventional signs of the zodiac worked round it in raised figures. Inside I noticed that the letters A. C. had been engraved.

"It was given to you before you were married, I presume," said I, as I returned it to her.

"Yes," she replied, "those are the initials of my maiden name—Angelina Carthew." She took the ring from me, but instead of replacing it on her finger, dropped it into a little pouch-like purse with metal jaws, which she had taken from her pocket.

"Your position is a very disagreeable one," said I, reverting to the main topic. "I wonder that you haven't applied for a judicial separation. There are ample grounds for making the application."

"I suppose there are. But it wouldn't help me really, even if it were granted. I shouldn't get rid of him."

"You could apply to the police if he molested you."

"No doubt. But that doesn't sound very restful, does it?"

"I am afraid it doesn't. But it would be better than being constantly molested without having any remedy or refuge."

"Perhaps it would," she agreed doubtfully, and then, with a faint smile, she added: "I suppose you are wondering what on earth made me marry him?"

"Well," I replied, "it appears to me that his good fortune was more remarkable than his personal attractions."

"He wasn't always like he is now," said she. "I married him nearly ten years ago, and he was fairly presentable then. His manners were quite nice and he had certain accomplishments that rather appealed to a young girl—I was only eighteen and rather impressionable. He was then getting a living by writing magazine stories—love stories, they were, of a highly emotional type—and occasional verses. They were second-rate stuff, really, but to me he seemed a budding genius. It was not until after we were married that the disillusionment came, and then only gradually as his bad habits developed."

"By the way, what do you suppose he has come down here for? What does he want? I suppose he wishes you to go back to him?"

"I suppose he does. But, primarily, I expect he wants money. It is a horrible position," she added, with sudden passion. "I hate the idea of hiding away from him when I suspect that the poor wretch has come down to his last few shillings. After all, he is my husband; and I am not so deadly poor now."

"He seemed to have the wherewith to provide a fair supply of tobacco, to say nothing of the cocaine and a 'modest quencher' at the tavern," I remarked drily. "At any rate, I hope he won't succeed in finding out where you live."

"I hope not," said she. "If he does, I shall have to move on, as I have had to do several times already, and I don't want to do that. I have only been here a little over two months, and it has been very pleasant and peaceful. But you see, Dr. Strangeways, that, if I am to follow Mr. Japp's advice, I shall inflict on you a very unpromising patient. There is no medical treatment for matrimonial troubles."

"No," I agreed, rising and taking up my hat, "but the physical effects may be dealt with. If I am appointed your medical advisor, I shall send you a tonic, and if I may look in now and again to see how you are getting on, I may be able to help you over some of your difficulties."

"It is very kind of you," she said, rising and shaking my hand warmly; and, accepting my suggestion that she had better not come to the street door, she showed me out into the hall and dismissed me with a smile and a little bow.

When I reached the bottom of the steps, I stood irresolutely for a few moments and then, instead of making my way homeward, turned up the street towards the cathedral and the bridge, walking slowly and reflecting profoundly on the story I had just heard. It was a pitiful story; and the quiet, restrained manner of the telling made it the more impressive. All that was masculine in me rose in revolt against the useless, inexcusable wrecking of this poor woman's life. As to the man, he was, no doubt, to be pitied for being the miserable, degenerate wretch that he was. But he was doomed beyond any hope of salvation. Such wretches as he are condemned in the moment of their birth; they are born to an inheritance of misery and dishonour. But it is infamous that in their inevitable descent into the abyss—from which no one can save them—they should have the power to drag down with them sane and healthy human beings who were destined by nature to a life of happiness, of usefulness, and honour. I thought of the woman I had just left—comely, dignified, energetic, probably even talented. What was her future to be? So far as I could see, the upas shadow of this drug-sodden wastrel had fallen upon her, never to be lifted until merciful death should dissolve the ill-omened union.

This last reflection gave my thoughts a new turn. What was this man's purpose in pursuing her? Was he bent merely on extorting money or on sharing her modest income? Or was there some more sinister motive? I recalled his face; an evil, sly, vindictive face. I considered what I knew of him; that he had undoubtedly made one attempt to murder this woman, and that, to my knowledge, he carried about his person the means of committing murder. For what purpose could he have provided himself with that formidable weapon? It might be merely as a means of coercion, or it might be as a means of revenge.

Thus meditating, I had proceeded some distance along the street when I observed, on the opposite side, an old, three-gabled house which looked like some kind of institution. A lamp above the doorway threw its light on a stone tablet on which I could see an inscription of some length, and, judging this to be an ancient almshouse, I crossed the road to inspect it more closely. A glance at the tablet told me that this was the famous rest-house established in the sixteenth century by worthy Richard Watts, to give a night's lodging and entertainment to six poor travellers, with the express proviso that the said travellers must be neither rogues nor proctors. I had read through the quaint inscription and was speculating, as many others have speculated, on the nature of Richard Watts's grievance against proctors as a class, when the door opened suddenly and a man rushed out with such impetuosity that he nearly collided with me. I had moved out of his way when he halted and addressed me excitedly.

"I say, governor, can you tell me where I can find a doctor?"

"You have found one," I replied. "I am a doctor. What is the matter?"

"There's a bloke in here throwing a fit," he answered, backing into the doorway and holding the door open for me. I entered, and followed him down a passage to a largish, barely furnished room, where I found four men and a woman, who looked like a hospital nurse, standing around and watching anxiously a man who lay on the floor.

"Here's a doctor, matron," said my conductor, as he ushered me in.

"Well, Simmonds," said the matron, "you haven't wasted much time."

"No, mum," replied Simmonds, "I struck it lucky. Caught him just outside."

Meanwhile I had stepped up to the prostrate man, and at the first glance I recognized him. He was Mrs. Frood's husband. And, whatever he might be "throwing," it was not a fit—in the ordinary medical sense; that is to say, it was not epilepsy or apoplexy; nor was it a fainting fit of an orthodox kind. If the patient had been a woman one would have called it a hysterical seizure, and I could give it no other name, though I was not unmindful of the paper packet that I had seen on that former occasion. But the emotional element was obvious. The man purported to be insensible, and manifestly was not. The tightly closed eyes, the everted lips—showing a row of blackened teeth—the clutching movements of the clawlike hands—all were suggestive of at least half-conscious simulation. I stood for a while, stooping over him and watching him intently, and as I did so the bystanders watched me. Then I felt his pulse, and found it, as I had expected, quick, feeble, and irregular; and finally, producing my stethoscope, listened to his heart with as little disturbance of his clothing as possible.

"Well, doctor," said the matron, "what do you think of him?"

"He is decidedly ill," I replied. "His heart is rather jumpy, and not very strong. Too much tobacco, I fancy, and perhaps some other things that are not very good, and possibly insufficient food."

"He told me, when he came in," said the matron, "that he was practically destitute."

"Ah," murmured Simmonds, "I expect he's been blowing all his money on Turkish baths," whereupon the other poor travellers sniggered softly, and were immediately extinguished by a reproving glance from the matron.

"Do you know what brought this attack on?" I asked.

"Yes," she replied; "he had a little dispute with Simmonds, here, and suddenly became violently excited, and then he fell down insensible, as you see him. It was all about nothing."

"I jest arsked 'im," said Simmonds, "if 'e could give me the name of the cove what done 'is 'air, 'cos I thought I'd like to 'ave mine done in the same fashionable style. That seemed to give 'im the fair pip. 'E jawed me something chronic, until I got shirty and told 'im if 'e didn't shut 'is face I'd give 'im a wipe acrost the snout. Then blow me if 'e didn't start to throw a fit."

While this lucid explanation was proceeding I noticed that the patient was evidently listening intently, though he continued to twitch his face, exhibit his unlovely teeth, and wriggle his fingers. He was apparently waiting for my verdict with some anxiety.

"The question is," said the matron, "what is to be done with him? Do you think he is in any danger?"

As she spoke, we drifted towards the door, and when we were in the passage, out of earshot, I said:

"The best place for that man is the infirmary. There is nothing much the matter with him but dope. He has been dosing himself with cocaine, and he has probably got some more of the stuff about him. He is in no danger now, but if he takes any more he may upset himself badly."

"It is rather late to send him to the infirmary," she said, "and I don't quite like to do it. Poor fellow, he seems fearfully down on his luck, and he is quite a superior kind of man. Do you think it would be safe for him to stay here for the night if he had a little medicine of some kind?"

"It would be safe enough," I replied, "if you could get possession of his coat and waistcoat and lock them up until the morning."

"Oh, I'll manage that," said she; "and about the medicine?"

"Let Simmonds walk up with me—I have taken Dr. Partridge's practice—and I will give it to him."

We re-entered the supper-room and found the conditions somewhat changed. Whether it was that the word "infirmary" had been wafted to the patient's attentive ears, I cannot say; but there were evident signs of recovery. Our friend was sitting up, glaring wildly about him, and inquiring where he was; to which questions Simmonds was furnishing answers of a luridly inaccurate character. When I had taken another look at the patient, and received a vacant stare of almost aggressive unrecognition, I took possession of the facetious Simmonds, and, having promised to look in in the morning, wished the matron good-night and departed with my escort; who entertained me on the way home with picturesque, unflattering, and remarkably shrewd comments on the sufferer.

I had made up a stimulant mixture, and handed it to Simmonds when I remem-bered Mrs. Frood and that Simmonds would pass her house on his way back. For an instant, I thought of asking him to deliver her medicine for me; and then, with quite a shock, I realized what a hideous blunder it would have been. Evidently, the poor travellers gave their names, and if the man, Frood, had given his correctly, the coincidence of the names would have impressed Simmonds instantly, and then the murder would have been out, and the fat would have been in the fire properly. It was a narrow escape, and it made me realize how insecure was that unfortunate lady's position with this man lurking in the town. And, realizing this, I determined to trust the addressed bottle to nobody, but to leave it at the house myself. Accord-ingly, having made up the medicine and wrapped it neatly in paper, I thrust it into my pocket, and, calling out to Mrs. Dunk that I should be back to supper in about half an hour, I set forth, and in a few minutes arrived at the little Georgian doorway and plied the elegant brass knocker. The door was opened—rather incautiously, I thought—by Mrs. Frood herself.

"I am my own bottle-boy, you see, Mrs. Frood," said I, handing her the medicine. "I thought it safer not to send an addressed packet under the circumstances."

"But how good of you!" she exclaimed. "How kind and thoughtful! But you shouldn't have troubled about it tonight."

"It was only a matter of five minutes' walk," said I, "and besides, there was something that I thought you had better know," and hereupon I proceeded to give her a brief account of my recent adventures and the condition of her precious husband. "Is he subject to attacks of this kind?" I asked.

"Yes," she answered. "When he is put out about anything in some ways he is rather like a hysterical woman. But, you see, I was right. He is penniless. And that—now I come to think of it—makes it rather odd that he should be here. But won't you come in for a moment?"

I entered and shut the door. "Why is it odd?" I asked.

"Because he would be getting some money tomorrow. I make him a small allowance; it is very little, but it is as much as I can possibly manage; and it is paid monthly, on the fifteenth of the month. But he has to apply for it personally at the bank or send an accredited messenger with a receipt; and as tomorrow is the fifteenth, the question is, why on earth is he down here now? I mean that it is odd that he should not have waited to collect the allowance before coming to hunt me up."

"If he is in communication with your banker," said I, "he could, I suppose, get a letter forwarded to you?"

"No," she replied; "the banker who pays him is the London agent of Mr. Japp's banker, and he doesn't know on whose behalf the payments are made. I had to make that arrangement, or he would have bombarded me with letters."

"Well," I said, "you had better keep close for a day or two. If his search for you is unsuccessful, he may get discouraged and raise the siege. I will let you know what his movements are, so far as I can."

She thanked me once more with most evident sincerity, and as I made my way to the door, she let me out with a cordial and friendly shake of the hand.

CHAPTER IV

DEALS WITH CHARITY AND ARCHAEOLOGY

Immediately after breakfast on the following morning I made my way to Mr. Richard Watts's establishment, where I learned that all the poor travellers had departed with the exception of my patient, who had been allowed to stay pending my report on him.

"I shall be glad to see the back of him, poor fellow," said the matron, "for, of course, we have no arrangements for dealing with sick men."

"Do you often get cases of illness here?" I asked.

"I really don't know," she answered. "You see, I am only doing temporary duty here while the regular matron is away. But I should think not, though little ailments are apt to occur in the case of a poor man who has been on the road for a week or so."

"This man is on tramp, is he'" said I.

"Well, no," she replied. "It seems, from what he tells me, that his wife has left him, and he had reason to believe that she was staying in this town. So he came down here to try to find her. He supposed that Rochester was a little place where everybody knew everybody else, and that he would have no difficulty in discovering her whereabouts. But all his inquiries have come to nothing. Nobody seems to have heard of her. I suppose you don't happen to know the name—Frood?"

"I only came here yesterday, myself," was my evasive reply. "I am a stranger to the town. But is he certain that she is here?"

"I don't think he is. At any rate, he seems inclined to give up the search for the present, and he is very anxious to get back to London. But I don't know how he is going to manage it. He isn't fit to walk."

"Well," I said, "if it is only the railway fare that stands in the way, that difficulty can be got over. I will pay for his ticket; but I should like to be sure that he really goes."

"Oh, I'll see to that," she said, with evident relief. "I will go with him to the station, and get his ticket and see him into the train. But you had better just have a look at him, and see that he is fit to go."

She conducted me to the supper-room, where our friend was sitting in a Windsor armchair, looking the very picture of misery and dejection.

"Here is the doctor come to see you, Mr. Frood," the matron said cheerfully, "and he is kind enough to say that, if you are well enough to travel, he will pay your fare to London. So there's an end of your difficulties."

The poor devil glanced at me for an instant, and then looked away; and, to my intense discomfort, I saw that his eyes were filling.

"It is indeed good of you, Sir," he murmured, shakily, but in a very pleasant voice and with a refined accent; "most good and kind to help a lame dog over a stile in this way. I don't know how to thank you."

Here, as he showed a distinct tendency to weep, I replied hastily:

"Not at all. We've all got to help one another in this world. And how are you feeling? Hand is still a little bit shaky, I see."

I put my finger on his wrist and then looked him over generally. He was a miserable wreck, but I judged that he was as well as he was ever likely to be.

"Well," I said, "you are not in first-class form, but you are up to a short railway journey. I suppose you have somewhere to go to in London?"

"Yes," he replied, dismally, "I have a room. It isn't in the Albany, but it is a shelter from the weather."

"Never mind," said I. "We must hope for better times. The matron is going to see you safely to the station and comfortably settled in the train—and"—here I handed her a ten shilling note—"you will get Mr. Frood's ticket, matron, and you had better give him the change. He may want a cab when he gets to town."

He glowered sulkily at this arrangement—I suspect he had run out of cigarettes—but he thanked me again, and, when I had privately ascertained the time of the train which was to bear him away, I wished him adieu.

"I suppose," said I, "there is no likelihood of his hopping out at Strood to get a drink and losing the train?"

The matron smiled knowingly. "He will start from Strood," said she. "I shall take him over the bridge in the tram and put him into the London express there. We don't want him back here tonight."

Much relieved by the good lady's evident grasp of the situation, I turned away up the street and began to consider my next move. I had nothing to do this morning, for at present there was not a single patient on my books with the exception of Mrs. Frood; and it may have been in accordance with the prevailing belief that to persons in my condition, an individual, familiarly known as "the old gentleman," obligingly functions as employment agent, that my thoughts turned to that solitary patient. At any rate they did. Suddenly, it was borne in on me that I ought, without delay, to convey to her the glad tidings of her husband's departure. Whether the necessity would have appeared as urgent if her personal attractions had been less, I will not presume to say; nor whether had I been more self-critical, I should not have looked with some suspicion on this intense concern respecting the welfare of a woman who was almost a stranger to me. As it was, it appeared to me that I was but discharging a neighbourly duty when I executed an insinuating rat-tat on the handsome brass knocker which was adorned—somewhat inappropriately, under the circumstances—with a mask of Hypnos.

After a short interval, the door was opened by a spare, middle-aged woman of melancholic aspect, with tow-coloured hair and a somewhat anemic complexion, who regarded me inquiringly with a faded blue eye.

"Is Mrs. Frood at home?" I asked briskly.

"I am afraid she is not," was the reply, uttered in a dejected tone. "I saw her go out some time ago, and I haven't heard her come back. But I'll just see, if you will come in a moment."

I entered the hall and listened with an unaccountable feeling of disappointment as she rapped on the door first of the front room, and then of the back.

"She isn't in her rooms there," was the dispirited report, "but she may be in the basement. I'll call out and ask."

She retired to the inner hall and gave utterance to a wail like that of an afflicted seagull. But there was no response; and I began to feel myself infected by her melancholy.

"I am sorry you have missed her, Sir," said she; and then she asked: "Are you her doctor, Sir?"

I felt myself justified in affirming that I was, whereupon she exclaimed:

"Ah, poor thing! It is a comfort to know that she has someone to look after her. She has been looking very sadly of late. Very sadly, she has."

I began to back cautiously towards the door, but she followed me up and continued: "I am afraid she has had a deal of trouble; a deal of trouble, poor dear. Not that she ever speaks of it to me. But I know. I can see the lines of grief and sorrow—like a worm in the bud, so to speak, Sir—and it makes my heart ache. It does, indeed."

I mumbled sympathetically and continued to back towards the door.

"I don't see very much of her," she continued in a plaintive tone. "She keeps herself very close. Too close, I think. You see, she does for herself entirely. Now and again, when she asks me, which is very seldom, I put a bit of supper in her room. That is all. And I do think that it isn't good for a young woman to live so solitary; and I do hope you'll make her take a little more change."

"I suppose she goes out sometimes," said I, noting that she was out at the present moment.

"Oh, yes," was the reply. "She goes out a good deal. But always alone. She never has any society."

"And what time does she usually come in?" I asked, with a view to a later call.

"About six; or between that and seven. Then she has her supper and puts the things out on the hall table. And that is the last I usually see of her."

By this time I had reached the door and softly unfastened the latch.

"If you should see her," I said, "you might tell her that I shall look in this evening about half-past seven."

"Certainly, Sir," she replied. "I shall see her at lunch-time, and I will give her your message."

I thanked her, and, having now got the door open, I wished her good morning, and retreated down the steps.

As I was in the act of turning away, my eye lighted on the adjacent bay window, appertaining to the office of Messrs. Japp and Bundy, and I then perceived' above the green curtain the upper half of a human face, including a pair of tortoiseshell-rimmed spectacles; an apparition which informed me that Mr. Bundy had been—to use Sam Weller's expression—"a-twigging of me." On catching my eye, the face rose higher, disclosing a broad grin; whereupon, without any apparent reason, I felt myself turning somewhat red. However, I mounted the official steps, and, opening the office door, confronted the smiler and his more sedate partner.

"Ha!" said the former, "you drew a blank, doctor. I saw the lovely Angelina go out about an hour ago. Whom did you see?"

"The lady of the house, I presume; a pale, depressed female."

"I know," said Bundy. "Looks like an undertaker's widow. That's Mrs. Gillow. Rhymes with willow—very appropriate, too," and he began to chant in an absurd, Punch-like voice: "Oh, all round my hat I'll wear the green—"

"Be quiet, Bundy," said Mr. Japp, regarding his partner with a wrinkly and indulgent smile.

Bundy clapped his hand over his mouth and blew out his cheeks, and I took the opportunity to explain: "I called on Mrs. Frood to let her know that her husband is leaving the town."

"Leaving the town, is he?" said Mr. Japp, elevating his eyebrows and thereby causing his forehead to resemble a small Venetian blind. "Do you know when?"

"He goes this morning by the ten-thirty express to London."

"Hooray!" ejaculated Bundy, with a flourish of his arms that nearly capsized his stool. He recovered himself with an effort, and then, fixing his eyes on me, proceeded to whistle the opening bars of "O! Thou that tellest good tidings to Zion!"

"That'll do, Bundy," said Mr. Japp. Then turning to me, he asked: "Where did you learn these good tidings, Doctor?'"

I gave them a brief account of the happenings of the previous night and this morning's sequel, to which they listened with deep attention. When I had finished Mr. Japp said: "You have done a very great kindness to my friend Mrs. Frood. It will be an immense relief to her to know that she can walk abroad without the danger of encountering this man. Besides, if he had stayed here he would probably have found her out."

"He might even have found her at home," said Bundy, "and that would have been worse. So I propose a vote of thanks to the doctor—with musical honours. *For-hor he's a jolly good fell—*"

"There, that'll do, Bundy, that'll do," said Mr. Japp. "I never saw such a fellow. You'll have the neighbours complaining."

Bundy leaned towards me confidentially and remarked in a stage whisper, glancing at his partner: "Fidgetty old cove; regular old killjoy." Then, with a sudden change of manner, he asked: "What about that wall job, Japp? Are you going to have a look at them?"

"I can't go at present," said Japp. "Bulford will be coming in presently and I must see him. Have you got anything special to do?"

"Only old Jeff'son's lease, and that can wait. Shall I trot over and see what sort of mess they are making of things?"

"I wish you would," said Japp; whereupon Mr. Bundy removed his spectacles, stuck in his monocle, extracted from the desk his hat and gloves which he assumed with the aid of the looking-glass, and took his stick from the corner. Then he looked at me reflectively and asked:

"Are you interested in archaeology, Doctor?"

"Somewhat," I replied. "Why do you ask?"

"Because we are putting some patches in the remains of the city wall. It isn't much to look at, and there isn't a great deal of the original Roman work left; but if you would care to have a look at it you might walk up there with me."

I agreed readily, being, as I have said, somewhat at a loose end, and we set forth together, Bundy babbling cheerfully as we went.

"I have often thought," said he, "that there must have been something rather pleasant and restful about the old walled cities, particularly after curfew when the gates were shut—that is, provided you were inside at the time."

"Yes," said I. "An enclosed precinct has a certain agreeable quality of seclusion that you can't get in an open town or village. When I was a student, I lived for a time in chambers in Staple Inn, and it was, as you say, rather pleasant, when one came home at night, and the porter had let one in at the wicket, to enter and find the gates closed, the courts all quiet and empty, and to know that all traffic was stopped and all strangers shut out until the morning. But it doesn't appear to be in accordance with modern taste, for those old Chancery Inns have nearly all gone, and there is no tendency to replace them with anything similar."

"No," Bundy agreed, stopping to look up at an old timber house, "taste in regard to buildings, if there is any—Japp says there isn't—has changed completely in the last hundred years or so. Look at this alley we are in now. Every house has got a physiognomy of its own. But when we rebuild it, we shall fill it up with houses that will look as if they had been bought in packets like matchboxes."

Gossiping thus, we threaded our way through all sorts of queer little alleys and passages. At length Bundy stopped at a wooden gate in a high fence, and, pushing it open, motioned for me to enter; and as I did so he drew out the key which was in the lock and put it in his pocket.

The place which we had entered was a space of waste land, littered with the remains of some old houses that had been demolished and enclosed on three sides by high fences. The fourth side was formed by a great mass of crumbling rubble, patched in places with rough masonry and brickwork, and showing in its lower part the remains of courses of Roman bricks. It rose to a considerable height, and was evidently of enormous thickness, as could be seen where large areas of the face had crumbled away, exposing great cavities, in which wall-flowers, valerian and other rock-haunting plants, had taken up their abode. On one of these a small gang of men were at work, and it was evident that repairs on a considerable scale were contemplated, for there were several large heaps of rough stone and old bricks, and in a cart-shed in a corner of the space were a large number of barrels of lime.

As we entered, the foreman came forward to meet us, and Bundy handed him the key from the gate.

"Better keep it in your pocket," said he. "Mr. Japp is rather particular about keys that he has charge of. He doesn't like them left in doors or gates. How are the men getting on?"

"As well as you can expect of a lot of casuals like these," was the reply. "There isn't a mason or a bricklayer among them, excepting that old chap that's mixing the mortar. However, it's only a rough job."

We walked over to the part of the old wall where the men were at work, and the appearances certainly justified the foreman's last remark. It was a very rough job. The method appeared to consist in building up outside the cavity a primitive wall of unhewn stone with plenty of mortar, and, when it had risen a foot or two, filling up the cavity inside with loose bricks, lumps of stone, shovelfuls of liquid mortar, and chunks of lime.

I ventured to remark that it did not look a very secure method of building, upon which Bundy turned his monocle on me and smiled knowingly.

"My dear Doctor," said he, "you don't appear to appreciate the subtlety of the method. The purpose of these activities is to create employment. That has been clearly stated by the town council. But if you want to create employment you build a wall that will tumble down and give somebody else the job of putting it up again."

Here, as a man suddenly bore down on us with a bucket of mortar, Bundy hopped back to avoid the unclean contact, and nearly sat down on a heap of smoking lime.

"You had a narrow escape that time, mister," remarked the old gentleman who presided over the mortar department, as Bundy carefully dusted his delicate shoes with his handkerchief; "that stuff would 'ave made short work of them fine clothes of yourn."

"Would it?" said Bundy, dusting his shoes yet more carefully and wiping the soles on the turf.

"Ah," rejoined the old man; "terrible stuff is quicklime. Eats up everything same as what fire does." He rested his hands on his shovel, and, assuming a reminiscent air, continued: "There was a pal o' mine what was skipper of a barge. A iron barge, she was, and he had to take on a lading of lime from some kilns. The stuff was put aboard with a shoot. Well, my pal, he gets 'is barge under the shoot and then 'e goes off, leavin' 'is mate to see the lime shot into the hold. Well, it seems the mate had been takin' some stuff aboard, too. Beer, or p'raps whisky. At any rate, he'd got a skinful. Well, presently the skipper comes back, and he sees 'em a-tippin' the trucks of lime on to the shoot, and he sees the barge's hold beginning to fill, but 'e don't see 'is mate nowhere. He goes aboard, down to the cabin, but there ain't no signs of the mate there, nor yet anywheres else. Well, they gets the barge loaded and the hatch-covers on, and everything ready for sea; and still there ain't no signs of the mate. So my pal, rememberin' that the mate—his name was Bill—rememberin' that Bill seemed a bit squiffy, supposed he must 'ave gone overboard. So 'e takes on a fresh hand temporary and off 'e goes on 'is trip.

"Well, they makes their port all right and brings up alongside the wharf, but owing to a strike among the transport men they can't unload for about three weeks. However, when the strike is over, they rigs a whip and a basket and begins to get the stuff out. All goes well until they get down to the bottom tier. Then one of the men brings up a bone on his shovel. 'Hallo!' says the skipper, 'what's bones a-doin' in a cargo of fresh lime?" He rakes over the stuff on the floor and up comes a skull with a hole in the top of it. 'Why, blow me,' says the skipper, 'if that don't look like Bill. He warn't as thin in the face as all that, but I seem to know them teeth.' Just then one of the men finds a clay pipe—and the skipper reckernizes it at once. 'That there's Bill's pipe,' sez he, 'and them bones is Bill's bones,' 'e sez. And so they were. They found 'is belt-buckle and 'is knife, and 'is trouser buttons and the nails out of 'is boots. And that's all there was left of Bill. He must have tumbled down into the hold and cracked his nut, and then the first truckful of lime must 'ave covered 'im up. So, if you sets any value on them 'andsome shoes o' yourn, don't you go a-treadin' in quick lime."

Bundy looked down anxiously at his shoes, and, having given them an additional wipe, he moved away from the dangerous neighbourhood of the lime and we went together to examine the ancient wall.

"That was rather a tall yarn of the old man's," remarked Bundy. "Is it a fact that lime is as corrosive as he made out?"

"I don't really know very much about it," I replied. "There is a general belief that it will consume almost anything but metal. How true that is I can't say, but I remember that at the Crippen trial one of the medical experts—I think it was Pepper—said that if the body had been buried in quicklime it would have been entirely consumed—excepting the bones, of course. But it is difficult to believe that a body could disappear completely in three weeks, or thereabouts, as our friend said. How fine this old wall looks with those clumps of valerian and wallflowers growing on it! I suppose it encircled the town completely at one time?"

"Yes," he replied, "and it is a pity there isn't more of it left, or at least one or two of the gateways. A city gate is such a magnificent adornment. Think of the gates of Canterbury and Rye, and especially at Sandwich, where you actually enter the town through the barbican; and think of what Rochester must have been before all the gates were pulled down. But you must hear Japp on the subject. He's a regular architectural Jeremiah. By the way, what did you think of Mrs. Frood? You saw her last night, didn't you?"

"Yes. I was rather taken with her. She is very nice and friendly and unaffected, and good-looking, too. I thought her distinctly handsome."

"She isn't bad-looking," Bundy admitted. "But I can't stand her voice. It gets on my nerves. I hate a squeaky voice."

"I shouldn't call it squeaky," said I. "It is a high voice, and rather sing-song; and it isn't, somehow, quite in keeping with her appearance and manner."

"No," said Bundy, "that's what it is. She's too big for a voice like that."

I laughed at the quaint expression. "People's voices," said I, "are not like steamers' whistles, graduated in pitch according to their tonnage. Besides, Mrs. Frood is not such a very big woman."

"She is a good size," said he. "I should call her rather tall. At any rate, she is taller than I am. But I suppose you will say that she might be that without competing with the late Mrs. Bates."

"Comparisons between the heights of men and women," I said cautiously, "are rather misleading," and here I changed the subject, though I judged that Bundy was not sensitive in regard to his stature, for while he was cleaning the lime from his shoes I had noticed that he wore unusually low heels. Nor need he have been, for though on a small scale, he was quite an important-looking person.

"Don't you think," he asked, after a pause, "that it is rather queer that the man Frood should have gone off so soon. He only came down yesterday, and he can't have made much of a search for Madame."

"The queer thing is that he should have come down on that particular day," I replied. "It seems that he draws a monthly allowance on the fifteenth. That was what made him so anxious to get back; but it is odd that he didn't put off his visit here until he had collected the money."

"If he had run his wife to earth, he could have collected it from her," said Bundy. "I wonder how he found out that she was here."

"He evidently hadn't very exact information," I said, "nor did he seem quite certain that she really was here. And his failure to get any news of her appears to have discouraged him considerably. It is just possible that he has gone back to get more precise information if he can, when he has drawn his allowance."

"That is very likely," Bundy agreed; "and it is probable that we haven't seen the last of him yet."

"I have a strong suspicion that we haven't," said I.

"If he is sure she is here, and can get enough money together to come and spend a week here, he will be pretty certain to discover her whereabouts. It is a dreadful position for her. She ought to get a judicial separation."

"I doubt if she could," said he. "You may be sure he would contest that application pretty strongly, and what case would she have in support of it? He is an unclean blighter; he doesn't work; he smokes and drinks too much, and you say he takes drugs. But he doesn't seem to be violent or dangerous or threatening, or to be on questionable terms with other women—at least, I have never heard anything to that effect. Have you?"

"No," I answered—I had said nothing to him or Japp about the London incident. "He seems to have married the only woman in the world who would look at him."

Bundy grinned. "An unkind cut, that, Doctor," said he; "but I believe you're right. And here we are, back at the official premises. Are you coming in?"

I declined the invitation, and as he skipped up the steps I turned my face homewards.

CHAPTER V

JOHN THORNDYKE

The sexual preferences or affinities of men and women have always impressed me as very mysterious and inexplicable. I am referring to the selective choice of individuals, not to the general attraction of the sexes for one another. Why should a particular pair of human beings single one another out from the mass of their fellows as preferable to all others? Why to one particular man does one particular woman and no other become the exciting cause of the emotion of love? It is not a matter of mere physical beauty or mental excellence, for if it were men and women would be simply classifiable into the attractive and the non-attractive; whereas we find in practice that a woman who may be to the majority of men an object of indifference, is to some one man an object of passionate love; and vice-versa. Nor is love necessarily accompanied by any delusions as to the worth of its object, for it will persist in spite of the clear recognition of personal defects and in conscious conflict with judgment and reason.

The above reflections, with others equally profound, occupied my mind as I sat on a rather uncomfortable little rush-seated chair in the nave of Rochester Cathedral; whither I had proceeded in obedience to orders from Mrs. Dunk, to attend the choral afternoon service; and they were occasioned by the sudden recognition—not without surprise—of the very deep impression that had been made on me by my patient, Mrs. Frood. For the intensity of that impression I could not satisfactorily account. It is true that her circumstances were interesting and provocative of sympathy. But that was no reason for the haunting of my thoughts by her, of which I was conscious. She was not a really beautiful woman, though I thought her more than commonly good-looking; and she had evidently made no particular impression on Bundy. Yet, though I had seen her but three times, including my first meeting with her a year ago, I had to recognize that she had hardly been out of my thoughts since, and I was aware of looking forward with ridiculous expectancy to my proposed visit to her this evening.

Thus, speculations on the meaning of this preoccupation mingled themselves with other speculations, as, for instance, on the abrupt changes of intention suggested by half of an Early English arch clapped up against a Norman pier; and as my thoughts rambled on, undisturbed by a pleasant voice, intoning with soothing unintelligibility somewhere beyond the stone screen, I watched with languid curiosity the strangers who entered and stole on tiptoe to the nearest vacant chair. Presently, however, as the intoning voice gave place to the deep, pervading hum of the organ, a visitor entered who instantly attracted my attention.

He was obviously a personage—a real personage; not one of those who have achieved greatness by the free use of their elbows, or have had it thrust upon them by influential friends. This was an unmistakable thoroughbred. He was a tall man, very erect and dignified in carriage, and in spite of his iron-grey hair, evidently strong, active, and athletic. But it was his face that specially riveted my attention: not merely by reason that it was a handsome, symmetrical face, inclining to the Greek type, with level brows, a fine, straight nose, and a shapely mouth, but rather on account of its suggestion of commanding strength and intelligence. It was a strangely calm—even immobile—face; but yet it conveyed a feeling of attentiveness and concentration, and especially of power.

I watched the stranger curiously as he stepped quietly to a seat not far from me, noting how he seemed to stand out from the ordinary men who surrounded him, and wondering who he was. But I was not left to wonder very long. A few moments later another visitor arrived, but not a stranger this time; for in this newcomer I recognized an old acquaintance, a Dr. Jervis, whom I had known when I was a student and when he had taken temporary charge of my uncle's practise. Since then, as I had learned, he had qualified as a barrister and specialized in legal medicine as the coadjutor of the famous medical jurist, Dr. John Thorndyke.

For a few moments Jervis stood near the entrance looking about the nave, as if in search of someone. Then, suddenly, his eye lighted on the distinguished stranger, and he walked straight over to him and sat down by his side; from which, and from the smile of recognition with which he was greeted, I inferred that the stranger was none other than Dr. Thorndyke himself.

Jervis had apparently not seen, or at least not recognized me, but, as I observed that there was a vacant chair by his side, I determined to renew our acquaintance and secure, if possible, a presentation to his eminent colleague. Accordingly, I crossed the nave, and, taking the vacant chair, introduced myself, and was greeted with a cordial hand-shake.

The circumstances did not admit of conversation, but presently, when the anthem appeared to be drawing to a close, Jervis glanced at his watch and whispered to me: "I want to hear all your news, Strangeways, and to introduce you to Thorndyke; and we must get some tea before we go to the station. Shall we clear out now?"

As I assented he whispered to Thorndyke, and we all rose and filed silently towards the door, our exit covered by the concluding strains of the anthem. As soon as we were outside Jervis presented me to his colleague, and suggested an immediate adjournment to some place of refreshment. I proposed that they should come and have tea with me, but Jervis replied: "I'm afraid we haven't time today. There is a very comfortable teashop close to the Jasperian gatehouse. You had better come there and then perhaps you can walk to the station with us."

We adopted this plan, and when we had established ourselves on a settle by the window of the ancient, low-ceiled room and given our orders to a young lady in a becoming brown costume, Jervis proceeded to interrogate.

"And what might you be doing in Rochester, Strangeways?"

"Nominally," I replied, "I am engaged in medical practice. Actually, I am a gentleman at large. I have taken a death vacancy here, and I arrived yesterday morning."

"Any patients?" he inquired.

"Two at present," I answered. "One I brought down with me and returned empty this morning. The other is his wife."

"Ha," said Jervis, "a concise statement, but obscure. It seems to require amplification."

I accordingly proceeded to amplify, describing in detail my journey from town and my subsequent dealings with my fellow-traveller. The circumstances of Mrs. Frood, being matters of professional confidence, I was at first disposed to suppress; but then, reflecting that my two friends were in a position to give expert opinions and advice, I put them in possession of all the facts that were known to me, excepting the Regent's Park incident, which I felt hardly at liberty to disclose.

"Well," said Jervis, when I had finished, "if the rest of your practice develops on similar lines, we shall have to set up a branch establishment in your neighbourhood. There are all sorts of possibilities in this case. Don't you think so, Thorndyke?"

"I should hardly say 'all sorts,'" was the reply. "The possibilities seem to me to be principally of one sort; extremely disagreeable for the poor lady. She has the alternatives of allowing herself to be associated with this man—which seems to be impossible—or of spending the remainder of her life in a perpetual effort to escape from him; which is an appalling prospect for a young woman."

"Yes," agreed Jervis, "it is bad enough. But there seems to me worse possibilities with a fellow of this kind; a drinking, drug-swallowing, hysterical degenerate. You never know what a man of that type will do."

"You always hope that he will commit suicide," said Thorndyke; "and to do him justice, he does fairly often show that much perception of his proper place in nature. But, as you say, the actions of a mentally and morally abnormal man are incalculable. He may kill himself or he may kill somebody else, or he may join with other abnormals to commit incomprehensible and apparently motiveless political crimes. But we will hope that Mr. Frood will limit his activities to sponging on his wife."

The conversation now turned from my affairs to those of my friends, and I ventured to inquire what had brought them to Rochester.

"We came down," said Jervis, "to watch an inquest for one of our insurance clients. But after all it has had to be adjourned for a fortnight. So we may have the pleasure of seeing you again."

"We won't leave it to chance," said I. "Let us settle that you come to lunch with me, if that will be convenient. You can fix your own time."

My two friends consulted, and, having referred to their timetable, accepted the invitation for one o'clock on that day fortnight; and when I had "booked the appointment," we finished our tea and sallied forth, making our way over the bridge to Strood Station, at the main entrance to which I wished them adieu.

As I turned away from the station and sauntered slowly along the shore before recrossing the bridge, I recalled the conversation of my two colleagues with a certain vague discomfort. To both of them, it was evident, the relations of my fair patient and her husband presented sinister possibilities, although I had not informed them of the actual murderous attack; and though the more cautious reticent Thorndyke had seemed to minimize them, his remarks had expressed what was already in my own mind, accentuated by what I knew. These nervy, abnormal men are never safe to deal with. Their unstable emotions may be upset in a moment and then no one can tell what will happen. It was quite possible that Frood had come to Rochester with the perfectly peaceable intention of inducing his wife to return to him. But this was far from certain, and I shuddered to think of what might follow a refusal on her part. I did not like that knife. I have a sane man's dislike of lethal weapons of all kinds; but especially do I dislike them in the hands of those whose self-control is liable to break down suddenly.

It was true that this man had not succeeded in finding his wife, and even seemed to have given up the search. But I felt pretty certain that he had not. Somehow, he had discovered that she was in the town, and from the same source he might get further information; and, in any case, I felt no doubt that he would renew the pursuit, and that, in the end, he would find her. And then—but at this point I found myself opposite the house and observed Mrs. Gillow standing on the doorstep, fumbling in her pocket for the latch-key. She had just extracted it, and was in the act of inserting it into the latch when I crossed the road and made my presence known. She greeted me with a wan smile as I ascended the steps, and, having by this time got the door open, admitted me to the hall.

"I gave Mrs. Frood your message at lunch-time, sir," said she, in a depressed tone, "and I believe she has come in." Here, having closed the street door, she rapped softly with her knuckles at that of the front room, whereupon the voice to which Bundy objected so much called out: "Come in, Mrs. Gillow."

The latter threw the door open. "It is the doctor, Madam," said she; and on this announcement, I walked in.

"I didn't hear you knock," said Mrs. Frood, rising, and holding out her hand.

"I didn't knock," I replied. "I sneaked in under cover of Mrs. Gillow."

"That was very secret and cautious of you," said she.

"You make me feel like a sort of feminine Prince Charlie, lying perdu in the robbers' cavern; whereas, I have actually been taking my walks abroad and brazenly looking in the shop windows. But I have kept a sharp lookout, all the same."

"There really wasn't any need," said I. "The siege is raised.

"You don't mean that my husband has gone?" she exclaimed.

"I do, indeed," I answered; and I gave her a brief account of the events of the morning, suppressing my unofficial part in the transaction.

"Do you think," she asked, "that the matron paid his fare out of her own pocket?"

"I am sure she didn't," I answered hastily. "She touched some local altruist for the amount; it was only a few shillings, you know."

"Still," she said, "I feel that I ought to refund those few shillings. They were really expended for my benefit."

"Well, you can't," I said with some emphasis. "You couldn't do it without disclosing your identity, and then you would have some philanthropist trying to effect a reconciliation. Your cue is to keep yourself to yourself for the present."

"For the present!" she echoed. "It seems to me that I have got to be a fugitive for the rest of my natural life. It is a horrible position, to have to live in a state of perpetual concealment, like a criminal, and never dare to make an acquaintance."

"Don't you know anyone in Rochester?" I asked.

"Not a soul," she replied, "excepting Mr. Japp, who is a relative by marriage—he was my aunt's brother-in-law—his partner, and Mrs. Gillow and you. And you all know my position."

"Does Mrs. Gillow know the state of affairs?" I asked in some surprise.

"Yes," she answered, "I thought it best to tell her, in confidence, so that she should understand that I want to live a quiet life."

"I suppose you haven't cut yourself off completely from all your friends?" said I.

"Very nearly. I haven't many friends that I really care about much, but I keep in touch with one or two of my old comrades. But I have had to swear them to secrecy—though it looks as if the secret had leaked out in some way. Of course they all know Nicholas—my husband."

"And I suppose you have been able to learn from them how your husband views the separation?"

"Yes. Of course he thinks I have treated him abominably, and he evidently suspects that I have some motive for leaving him other than mere dislike of his unpleasant habits. The usual motive, in fact."

"What Sam Weller would call a 'priory attachment'?" I suggested.

"Yes. He is a jealous and suspicious man by nature. I had quite a lot of trouble with him in that way before that final outbreak, though I have always been most circumspect in my relations with other men. Still, a woman doesn't complain of a little jealousy. Within reason, it is a natural, masculine failing."

"I should consider a tendency to use a knitted silk necktie for purposes which I need not specify as going rather beyond ordinary masculine failings," I remarked drily; on which she laughed and admitted that perhaps it was so. There was a short pause; then, turning to a fresh subject, she asked: "Do you think you will get any of Dr. Partridge's practice?"

"I suspect not, or at any rate very little; and that reminds me that I have not yet inquired as to my patient's condition. Are you any better?"

As I asked the question, I looked at her attentively, and noted that she was still rather pale and haggard, so far as I could judge by the subdued light of the shaded lamp, and that the darkness under the eyes remained undiminished.

"I am afraid I am not doing you much credit," she replied, with a faint smile. "But you can't expect any improvement while these unsettled conditions exist. If you could induce my respected husband to elope with another woman you would effect an immediate cure."

"I am afraid," said I, "that is beyond my powers, to say nothing of the inhumanity to the other woman. But we must persevere. You must let me look in on you from time to time, just to keep an eye on you."

"I hope you will," she replied, energetically. "If it doesn't weary you to listen to my complaints and gossip a little, please keep me on your visiting list. With the exception of Mr. Japp, you are the only human creature that I hold converse with. Mrs. Gillow is a dear, good creature, but instinct warns me not to get on conversational terms with her. She's rather lonely, too."

"Yes; you might find it difficult to turn the tap off. I am always very cautious with housekeepers and landladies."

She darted a mischievous glance at me. "Even if your landlady happens to be your patient?" she asked.

I chuckled as I remembered our dual relationship.

"That," said I "is an exceptional case. The landlady becomes merged in the patient, and the patient tends to become a friend."

"The doctor," she retorted, "tends very strongly to become a friend, and a very kind and helpful friend. I think you have been exceedingly good to me—a mere waif who has drifted across your horizon."

"Well," I said, "if you think so, far be it from me to contradict you. One may as well pick up gratefully a stray crumb of commendation that one doesn't deserve to set off against the deserved credit that one doesn't get. But I should like to think that all my good deeds in the future will be as agreeable in the doing."

She gave me a prim little smile. "We are getting monstrously polite," she remarked, upon which we both laughed.

"However," said I, "the moral of it all is that you ought to have a friendly medical eye kept on you, and, as mine is the eye that happens to be available, and as you are kind enough to accept the optical supervision, I shall give myself the pleasure of looking in on you from time to time to see how you are and to hear how the world wags. What is the best time to find you at home?"

"I am nearly always at home after seven o'clock, but perhaps that is not very convenient for you. I don't know how you manage your practice."

"The fact is," said I, "that at present you are my practice, so I shall adapt my visiting round to your circumstances, and make my call at, or after, seven. I suppose you get some exercise?"

"Oh, yes. Quite a lot. I walk out in the country, and wander about Chatham and Gillingham and out to Frindsbury. I have been along the Watling Street as far as Cobham. Rochester itself I rather avoid for fear of making acquaintances, though it is a pleasant old town in spite of the improvements."

As she spoke of these solitary rambles the idea floated into my mind that, later on, I might perchance offer to diminish their solitude. But I quickly dismissed it. Her position was, in any case, one of some delicacy—that of a young woman living apart from her husband. It would be an act the very reverse of friendly to compromise her in any way; nor would it tend at all to my own professional credit. A doctor's reputation is nearly as tender as a woman's.

Our conversation had occupied nearly three quarters of an hour, and, although I would willingly have lingered, it appeared to me that I had made as long a visit as was permissible. I accordingly rose, and, having given a few words of somewhat perfunctory professional advice, shook hands with my patient and let myself out.

CHAPTER VI

THE SHADOWS DEEPEN

The coming events, whose premonitory shadows had been falling upon me unnoted since I came to Rochester, were daily drawing nearer. Perhaps it may have been that the deepening shadows began dimly to make themselves felt; that some indistinct sense of instability and insecurity had begun to steal into my consciousness. It may have been so. But, nevertheless, looking back, I can see that when the catastrophe burst upon me it found me all unsuspicious and unprepared.

Nearly a fortnight had passed since my meeting with my two friends in the Cathedral, and I was looking forward with some eagerness to their impending visit. During that fortnight little seemed to have happened, though the trivial daily occurrences were beginning to acquire a cumulative significance not entirely unperceived by me. My promise to Mrs. Frood had been carried out very thoroughly: for at least every alternate evening had found me seated by the little table with the red-shaded lamp, making the best pretence I could of being there in a professional capacity.

It was unquestionably indiscreet. The instant liking that I had taken to this woman should have warned me that here was one of those unaccountable "affinities" that are charged with such immense potentialities of blessing or disaster. The first impression should have made it clear to me that I could not safely spend much time in her society. But unfortunately the very circumstance that should have warned me to keep away was the magnet that drew me to her side.

However, there was one consoling fact: if the indiscretion was mine, so by me alone were the consequences supported. Our relations were of the most unexceptionable kind; indeed, she was not the sort of woman with whom any man would have taken a liberty. As to my feelings towards her, I could not pretend to deceive myself, but similarly, I had no delusions as to her feelings towards me. She welcomed my visits with that frank simplicity that is delightful to a friend and hopeless to a lover. It was plain to me that the bare possibility of anything beyond straightforward, honest friendship never entered her head. But this very innocence and purity, while at once a rebuke and a reassurance, but riveted my fetters the more firmly.

Such as our friendship was (and disregarding the secret reservation on my side), it grew apace; indeed, it sprang into existence at our first meeting. There was between us that ease and absence of reserve that distinguishes the intercourse of those who like and understand one another. I never had any fear of unwittingly giving offence. In our long talks and discussions, we had no need of choosing our words or phrases or of making allowances for possible prejudices. We could say plainly what we meant with the perfect assurance that it would be neither misunderstood nor resented. In short, if my feelings towards her could only have been kept at the same level as hers towards me, our friendship would have been perfect.

In the course of these long and pleasant gossiping visits, I observed my patient somewhat closely, and, quite apart from the personal affinity, I became more and more favourably impressed. She was a clever woman, quick and alert in mind, and evidently well informed. She seemed to be kindly, and was certainly amiable and even-tempered, though not in the least weak or deficient in character. Probably, in happier circumstances, she would have been more gay and vivacious, for, though she was habitually rather grave and even sombre, there were occasional flashes of wit that suggested a naturally lively temperament.

As to her appearance—to repeat in more detail what I have already said—she was a rather large woman, very erect and somewhat stately in bearing; distinctly good-looking (though of this I was not, perhaps, a very good judge). Her features were regular, but not in any way striking. Her expression was, as I have said, a little sombre and severe, the mouth firmly set and slightly depressed at the corners, the eyebrows black, straight, and unusually well-marked and nearly meeting above the nose. She had an abundance of black, or nearly black, hair, parted low on the forehead and drawn back loosely, covering the ears and temples, and she wore a largish coil nearly on the top of the head; a formal, matronly style that accentuated the gravity of her expression.

Such was Angelina Frood as I looked on her in those never-to-be-forgotten evenings; as she rises before the eyes of memory as I write, and as she will remain in my recollection so long as I live.

In this fortnight one really arresting incident had occurred. It was just a week after my meeting with Dr. Thorndyke, when, returning from a walk along the London Road as far as Gad's Hill, I stopped on Rochester Bridge to watch a barge which had just passed under, and was rehoisting her lowered mast. As I was leaning on the parapet, a man brushed past me, and I turned my head idly to look at him. Then, in an instant, I started up; for though the man's back was towards me, there was something unmistakably familiar in the gaunt figure, the seedy clothes, the great cloth cap, the shock of mouse-coloured hair, and the thick oaken stick that he swung in his hand. But I was not going to leave myself in any doubt on the subject. Cautiously I began to retrace my steps, keeping him in view but avoiding overtaking him, until he reached the western end of the bridge, when he halted and looked back. Then any possible doubt was set at rest. The man was Nicholas Frood. I don't know whether he saw me; he made no sign of recognition; and when he turned and walked on, I continued to follow, determined to make sure of his destination.

As I had hoped and expected, he took the road to the right, leading to the river bank and the station. Still following him, I noted that he walked at a fairly brisk pace and seemed to have recovered completely from his debility—if that debility had not been entirely counterfeit. Opposite the pier he turned into the station approach, and when from the corner I had watched him enter the station, I gave up the pursuit, assuming that he was returning to London.

But how long had he been in Rochester? What had he been doing, and what success had he had in his search? These were the questions that I asked myself as

I walked back over the bridge. Probably he had come down for the day; and since he was returning, it was reasonable to infer that he had had no luck. As I entered the town and glanced up at the great clock that hangs out across the street from the Corn Exchange, like a sort of horological warming-pan, I saw that it was close upon eight. It was a good deal after my usual time for calling on Mrs. Frood, but the circumstances were exceptional and I felt that it was necessary to ascertain whether anything untoward had occurred. I was still debating what I should do when, as I came opposite the house, I saw Mrs. Gillow coming out of the door. Immediately I crossed the road and accosted her.

"Have you seen Mrs. Frood this evening, Mrs. Gillow?" I asked, after passing the usual compliments.

"Yes, sir," was the reply. "I left her only a few minutes ago working at one of the drawings that she does for Mr. Japp. She seems better this evening—brighter and more cheerful. I think your visits have done her good, sir. It is a lonely life for a young woman—having no one to talk to all through the long evenings. I'm always glad to hear your knock, and so, I think, is she."

"I'm pleased to hear you say so, Mrs. Gillow," said I. "However, as it is rather late, and she has something to occupy her, I don't think I will call this evening."

With this I took my leave and went on my way in better spirits. Evidently all was well so far. Nevertheless, the reappearance of this man was an uncomfortable incident. It was clear that he had not given up the pursuit, and, seeing that Rochester was only some thirty miles from London, it would be quite easy for him to make periodical descents on the place to continue the search. There was no denying that Mrs. Frood's position was extremely insecure, and I could think of no plan for making it less so, excepting that of leaving Rochester, for a time at least, a solution which ought to have commended itself to me, but did not.

Perhaps it was this fact that decided me not to say anything about the incident. The obvious thing was to have told her and put her on her guard. But I persuaded myself that it would only make her anxious to no purpose; that she could not prevent him from coming nor could she take any further measures for concealment. And then there was the possibility that he might never come again.

So far as I know, he never did. During the rest of the week I perambulated the town hour after hour, looking into the shops, scanning the faces of the wayfarers in the streets and even visiting the stations at the times when the London trains were due; but never a glimpse did I catch of that ill-omened figure.

And all the time, the shadows were deepening, and that which cast them was drawing nearer.

It was nearly a week after my meeting with Nicholas Frood that an event befell at which I looked askance at the time and which was, as it turned out, the opening scene of a new act. It was on the Saturday. I am able to fix the date by an incident, trivial enough in itself, but important by reason of its forming thus a definite point of departure. My visitors were due on the following Monday, and it had occurred to me that I had better lay in a little stock of wine; and as Mr. Japp was an old resident who knew everybody in the town, I decided to consult him as to the choice of a wine merchant.

It was a little past mid-day when I arrived at the office, and as I entered I observed that some kind of conference was in progress. A man, whom I recognized as the foreman of the gang who were working on the old wall, was standing sheepishly with his knuckles resting on the table; Bundy had swung round on his stool and was glaring owlishly through his great spectacles, while Mr. Japp was sitting bolt upright, his forehead in a state of extreme corrugation and his eyes fixed severely on the foreman.

"I suppose," said Bundy, "you left it in the gate?"

"I expect Evans did," replied the foreman. "You see, I had to call in at the office, so I gave the key to Evans and told him to go on with the other men and let them in. When I got there the gate was open and the men were at work, and I forgot all about the key until it was time to come away and lock up. Then I asked Evans for it, and he said he'd left it in the gate. But when I went to look for it it wasn't there. Someone must have took it out."

"Doesn't seem very likely," said Bundy. "However, I suppose it will turn up. It had one of our wooden labels tied to it. Shall I give him the duplicate to lock up the place?"

"You must, I suppose," said Japp; "but it must be brought straight back and given to me. You understand, Smith? Bring it back at once, and deliver it to me or to Mr. Bundy. And look here, Smith. I shall offer ten shillings reward for that key; and if it is brought back and I have to pay the reward you will have to make it up among you. You understand that?"

Smith indicated grumpily that he understood; and when Bundy had handed him the duplicate key, he took his departure in dudgeon.

When he had gone I stated my business, and Bundy pricked up his ears.

"Wine, hey?" said he, removing his spectacles and assuming his monocle. "Tucker will be the man for him, won't he, Japp? Very superior wine merchant is Tucker. Old and crusted; round and soft; rare and curious. I'd better pop round with him and introduce him, hadn't I? You'll want to taste a few samples, I presume, Doctor?"

"I'm not giving a wholesale order," said I, smiling at his enthusiasm. "A dozen or so of claret and one or two bottles of port is all I want."

"Still," said Bundy, "you want to know what the stuff's like. Not going to buy a pig in a poke. You'll have to taste it, of course. I'll help you. Two heads are better than one. Come on. You said Tucker, didn't you, Japp?"

"As a matter of fact," said Japp, wrinkling his face up into an appreciative smile, "I didn't say anything. But Tucker will do; only he won't let you taste anything until you have bought it."

"Won't he!" said Bundy. "We shall see. Come along, Doctor."

He dragged me out of the office and down the steps, and we set forth towards the bridge; but we had not walked more than a couple of hundred yards when he suddenly shot up a narrow alley and beckoned to me mysteriously. I followed him up the alley, and as he halted I asked:

"What have you come here for?"

"I want you," he replied impressively, "to take a look at this wall."

I scrutinized the wall with minute attention but failed to discover any noteworthy peculiarities in it.

"Well," I said, at length, "I don't see anything unusual about this wall."

"Neither do I," he replied, looking furtively down the alley.

"Then, what the deuce—" I began.

"It's all right," said he. "She's gone. That damsel in the pink hat. I just popped up here to let her pass. The fact is," he explained, as he emerged cautiously into the High Street, glancing up and down like an Indian on the war-path, "these women are the plague of my life; always trying to hook me for teas or bazaars or garden fetes or some sort of confounded foolishness; and that pink-hatted lady is a regular sleuth-hound."

We walked quickly along the narrow pavement, Bundy looking about him warily, until we reached the wine-merchant's premises, into which my companion dived like a harlequin and forthwith proceeded to introduce me and my requirements. Mr. Tucker was a small, elderly man; old and crusted and as dry as his own Amontillado; but he was not proof against Bundy's blandishments. Before I had had time to utter a protest, I found myself in a dark cavern at the rear of the shop, watching Mr. Tucker fill a couple of glasses from a mouldy-looking cask.

"Ha!" said Bundy, sipping the wine with a judicial air. "H'm. Yes. Not so bad. Slightly corked, perhaps."

"Corked!" exclaimed Tucker, staring at Bundy in amazement. "How can it be corked when it is just out of the cask?"

"Well, bunged, then," Bundy corrected.

"I never heard of wine being bunged," said Tucker. "There's no such thing."

"Isn't there? Well, then, it can't be. Must be my fancy. What do you think of it, Doctor?"

"It seems quite a sound claret," said I, inwardly wishing my volatile friend at the devil, for I felt compelled, by way of soothing the wine merchant's wounded feelings, to order twice the quantity that I had intended. We had just completed the transaction, and were crossing the outer shop when the doorway became occluded by two female figures, and Bundy uttered a half-suppressed groan. I drew aside to make way for the newcomers—two ladies whom polite persons would have described as middle-aged, on the assumption that they contemplated a somewhat extreme degree of longevity—and I was aware that Bundy was endeavouring to take cover behind me. But it was of no use. One of them espied him instantly and announced her discovery with a little squeak of ecstasy.

"Why, it's Mr. Bundy. I do declare! Now, where *have* you been all this long time? It's ages and ages and ages since you came to see us, isn't it, Martha? Let me see, now, when was it?" She fixed a reflective eye on her companion, while Bundy smiled a sickly smile and glanced wistfully at the open door.

"I know," she exclaimed, triumphantly. "It was when we had the feeble-minded children to tea, and Mr. Blote showed them the gold fish trick—at least he tried to, but the glass bowl stuck in the bag under his coat-tails and wouldn't come out; and when he tried to pull it out it broke—"

"I think you are mistaken, Marian," the other lady interrupted. "It wasn't the feeble-minded tea. It was after that, when we helped the Jewbury-Browns to get up that rumble sale—"

"Jumble sale, you mean, dear," her companion corrected.

"I mean rummage sale," the lady called Martha insisted, severely. "If you will try to recall the circumstances, you will remember that the jumble sale took place after—"

"Not after," the other lady corrected. "It was before—several days before, I should say, speaking from a somewhat imperfect memory. If you will try to recollect, Martha, dear—"

"I recollect quite distinctly," the lady called Martha interposed, a little haughtily. "There was the feeble-minded tea—that was on a Tuesday—or was it a Thursday—no, it was a Tuesday, or at least—well, at any rate, it was some days before the jum—rum—"

"Not at all," the other lady dissented emphatically. At this point, catching the eye of the lady called Marian, I crept by slow degrees out on the threshold and turned an expectant eye on Bundy. The rather broad hint took immediate effect, for the lady said to her companion: "I am afraid, Martha, dear, you are detaining Mr. Bundy and his friend. *Good-bye*, Mr. Bundy. Shall we see you next Friday evening? We are giving a little entertainment to the barge-boys. We are inviting them to come and bring their mouth-organs and get up a little informal concert. *Do* come if you can. We shall be *so* delighted. *Good-bye*."

Bundy shook hands effusively with the two ladies and darted out after me, seizing my arm and hurrying me along the pavement.

"Bit of luck for me, Doctor, having you with me. If I had been alone and unprotected I shouldn't have escaped for half-an-hour; and I should have been definitely booked for the barge-boys' pandemonium. Hallo! What's Japp up to? Oh, I see. He's sticking up the notice about that key. I ought to have done that. Japp writes a shocking fist. I must see if it is possible to make it out."

As we approached the office I glanced at the sheet of paper which Mr. Japp had just affixed to the window, and was able to read the rather crabbed heading, "Ten Shillings Reward." The rest of the inscription being of no interest to me, I wished Bundy adieu and went on my way, leaving him engaged in a critical inspection of the notice. Happening to look back a few moments later, I saw him still gazing earnestly at the paper, all unconscious of a lady in a pink hat who was tripping lightly across the road and bearing down on him with an alluring smile.

Threading my way among the foot-passengers who filled the narrow pavements, I let my thoughts ramble idly from subject to subject; from the expected visit of my two friends on the following Monday to the alarming character of the local feminine population. But always they tended to come back to my patient, Mrs. Frood. I had seen her on the preceding night and had been very ill-satisfied with her appearance. She had been paler than usual—more heavy-eyed and weary-looking; and she had impressed me as being decidedly low-spirited. It seemed as though the continual uncertainty and unrest, the abiding threat of some intolerable action on the part of her worthless husband, were becoming more than she could endure; and unwillingly I was beginning to recognize that it was my duty, both as her doctor and as her friend, to advise her to move, at least for a time, to some locality where she would be free from the constant fear of molestation.

The question was: when should I broach the subject?

And that involved the further question: when should I make my next visit? Inclination suggested the present evening, but discretion hinted that I ought to allow a decent interval between my calls; and thus oscillating between the two, I found myself in a state of indecision which lasted for the rest of the day. Eventually discretion conquered, and I decided to postpone the visit and the proposal until the following evening.

The decision was reached about the time I should have been setting forth to make the visit, and no sooner had that time definitely passed than I began to regret my resolution and to be possessed by a causeless anxiety. Restlessly I wandered from room to room; taking up books, opening them and putting them down again, and generally displaying the typical symptoms of an acute attack of fidgets until Mrs. Dunk proceeded with a determined air to lay the supper, and drew my attention to it with an emphasis which it was impossible to disregard.

I had just drawn the cork of a bottle of Mr. Tucker's claret when the doorbell rang, an event without precedent in my experience. Silently I replaced the newly-extracted cork and listened. Apparently it was a patient, for I heard the street door close and footsteps proceed to the consulting-room. A minute later Mrs. Dunk opened the dining-room door and announced:

"Mrs. Frood to see you, sir."

With a slight thrill of anxiety at this unexpected visit, I strode out, and, crossing the hall, entered the somewhat dingy and ill-lighted consulting-room. Mrs. Frood was seated in the patients' chair, but she rose as I entered and held out her hand; and as I grasped it, I noticed how tall she looked in her outdoor clothes. But I also noticed that she was looking even more pale and haggard than when I had seen her last.

"There is nothing the matter, I hope?" said I.

"No," she answered; "nothing much more than usual; but I have come to present a petition."

I looked at her inquiringly, and she continued:

"I have been sleeping very badly, as you know. Last night I had practically no sleep at all, and very little the night before; and I feel that I really can't face the prospect of another sleepless night. Would you think it very immoral if I were to ask you for something that would give me a few hours' rest?"

"Certainly not," I answered, though with no great enthusiasm, for I am disposed to take hypnotics somewhat seriously. "You can't go on without sleep. I will give you one or two tablets to take before you go to bed. They will secure you a decent night's rest, and then I hope you will feel a little brighter."

"I hope so," she said, with a weary sigh.

I looked at her critically. She was, as I have said, pale and haggard; but there seemed to be something more; a certain wildness in her eyes and a suggestion or fear.

"You are not looking yourself at all tonight," I said. "What is it?"

"I don't know," she answered. "The same old thing, I suppose. But I do feel rather miserable. I seem to have come to the end of my' endurance. I look into the future and it all seems dark. I am afraid of it. In fact, I seem to have—you'll think me very silly, I know—but I have a sort of presentiment of evil. Of course, it's all nonsense. But that is what I feel."

"Is there any reason for this presentiment?" I asked uneasily; for my thoughts flew at once to that ill-omened figure that I had seen on the bridge. "Has anything happened to occasion these forebodings?"

"Oh, nothing in particular," she replied. But she spoke without looking at me—an unusual thing for her to do—and I found in her answer something ambiguous and rather evasive. Could it be that she had seen her husband on that day when I had followed him? Or had he been in the town again—this very day, perhaps? Or was there something yet more significant, something even more menacing? That this deep depression of spirits, these forebodings, were not without some exciting cause I felt the strongest suspicion. But whatever the cause might be, she was evidently unwilling to speak about it.

While I was speculating thus, I found myself looking her over with a minute attention of which I was not conscious at the time; noting little trivial details of her appearance and belongings with an odd exactness of observation. My eyes travelled over the little handbag, stamped with her initials, that rested on her lap; her dainty, high-heeled shoes with their little oval buckles of darkened bronze; the small brooch at her throat with the large opal in the middle and the surrounding circle of little pearls, and even noted that one of the pearls was missing and that the vacant place corresponded to the figure three on a clock-dial. And then they would come back to her face; to the set mouth and the downcast eyes with their expression of gloomy reverie.

I was profoundly uneasy and was on the point of opening the subject of her leaving the town. Then I decided that I would see her on the morrow and would go into the matter then. Accordingly I went into the surgery and put a few tablets of sulphonal into a little box, and having stuck one of Dr. Partridge's labels on it, wrote the directions and then wrapped it up and sealed it.

"There," I said, giving it to her, "take a couple of those tablets and go to bed early, and let me find you looking a little more cheerful tomorrow."

She took the packet and dropped it into her bag. "It is very good of you," she said warmly. "I know you don't like doing it, and that makes it the more kind. But I will do as you tell me. I have just to go in to Chatham, but when I get back I will go to bed quite early."

I walked with her to the door, and when I had opened it she stopped and held out her hand. "Good night," she said, "and thank you so very much. I expect you will find me a great deal better tomorrow." She pressed my hand slightly, made me a little bow, smiled, and, turning away, passed out; and I now noticed that the haze which had hung over the town all the afternoon had thickened into a definite fog. I stepped out on to the threshold and watched her as she walked quickly down the street, following the erect, dignified figure wistfully with my eyes as it grew more and more shadowy and unsubstantial until it faded into the fog and vanished. Then I went in to my solitary supper, with an unwonted sense of loneliness; and throughout the long evening I turned over again and again our unsatisfying talk and wondered afresh whether that presentiment of evil was but the product of insomnia and mental fatigue, or whether behind it was some sinister reality.

CHAPTER VII

MRS. GILLOW SOUNDS THE ALARM

Nine o'clock on the following morning found me still seated at the breakfast table, with the debris of the meal before me and the Sunday paper propped up against the coffee-pot. It was a pleasant, sunny morning at the end of April. The birds were twittering joyously in the trees at the back of the house, a premature bluebottle perambulated the window-pane, after an unsuccessful attempt to crawl under the dish-cover, and somewhere in the town an optimistic bell-ringer was endeavouring to lure unwary loiterers out of the sunshine into the shadow of the sanctuary.

It was all very agreeable and soothing. The birds were delightful in the exuberance of their spirits; even the bluebottle was a harbinger of summer; and the solo of the bellringer, softened by distance, impinged gently on the appreciative ear, awakening a grateful sense of immunity. The sunshine and the placid sounds were favourable to reflection, which the Sunday paper was powerless to disturb. As my eye roamed inattentively down the inconsequent column of printers' errors, my mind flitted, beelike, from topic to topic; from my vague professional prospects to the visitors whom I was expecting on the morrow and from them to the rather disturbing incident of the previous evening. But here my thoughts had a tendency to stick; and I was just considering whether the proprieties admitted of my making a morning call on Mrs. Frood, with a view to clearing up the obscurity, when the street-door bell rang. The unusual sound at such an unlikely time caused me to sit up and listen with just a tinge of uneasy expectancy. A few moments later Mrs. Dunk opened the door, and having stated concisely and impassively, "Mrs. Gillow," retired, leaving the door ajar. I started up in something approaching alarm, and hurried across to the consulting-room, where I found Mrs. Gillow standing by the chair with anxiety writ large on her melancholy face.

"There's nothing amiss, I hope, Mrs. Gillow?" said I.

"I am sorry to say there is, sir," she replied. "I hope you'll excuse me for disturbing you on a Sunday morning, but I thought, as you were her doctor, and a friend, too, and I may say—"

"But what has happened?" I interrupted impatiently.

"Why, sir, the fact is that she went out last night and she hasn't come back."

"You are quite sure she hasn't come back?"

"Perfectly. I saw her just before she went out, and she said she was coming to see you, to get something to make her sleep, and then she was just going into Chatham, and that she would be back soon, so that she could go to bed early. I sat up quite late listening for her, and before I went to bed I went down and knocked at both her doors, and as I didn't get any answer, I looked into both rooms. But she wasn't in either, and her little supper was untouched on the table in the sitting-room. I couldn't sleep a wink all night for worrying about her, and the first thing this morning I went down, and, when I found the door unbolted and unchained, I went into her rooms again. But there was no sign of her. Her supper was still there, untouched, and her bed had not been slept in."

"Did you look downstairs?" I asked.

"Yes. She usually kept the door of the basement stairs locked, I think, but it was unlocked this morning, so I went down and searched all over the basement; but she wasn't there."

"It is very extraordinary, Mrs. Gillow," I said, "and rather alarming. I certainly understood that she was going home as soon as she had been to Chatham. By the way, do you know what she was going to Chatham for?"

"I don't, sir. She might have been going there to do some shopping, but it was rather late, though it was Saturday night."

"You don't know, I suppose, whether she took any things with her—though she couldn't have taken much, as she had only a little handbag with her when she came here."

"She hasn't taken any of her toilet things," said Mrs. Gillow, "because I looked over her dressing-table, and all her brushes and things were there; and, as you say, she couldn't have taken much in that little bag. What do you think we had better do, sir?"

"I think," said I, "that, in the first place, I will go and see Mr. Japp. He is a relative and knows more about her than we do, and, of course, it will be for him to take any measures that may seem necessary. At any rate, I will see him and hear what he says."

"Don't you think we ought to let the police know?" she asked.

"Well, Mrs. Gillow," I said, "we mustn't be too hasty. Mrs. Frood had reasons for avoiding publicity. Perhaps we had better not busy ourselves too much until we are quite certain that she has gone. She may possibly return in the course of the day."

"I am sure I hope so," she replied despondently. "But I am very much afraid she won't. I have a presentiment that something dreadful has happened to her."

"Why do you say that?" I asked. "Have you any reason for thinking so?"

"I have no actual reason," she answered, "but I have always thought that there was something behind her fear of meeting her husband."

Having no desire to discuss speculative opinions, I made no direct reply to this. Apparently Mrs. Gillow had no more to tell, and as I was anxious to see Mr. Japp and hear if he could throw any light on the mystery, I adjourned the discussion on which she would have embarked and piloted her persuasively towards the door. "I shall see you again later, Mrs. Gillow," I said, "and will let you know if I hear anything. Meanwhile, I think you had better not speak of the matter to anybody."

As soon as she was gone I made rapid preparations to go forth on my errand, and a couple of minutes later was speeding down the street at a pace dictated rather by the agitation of my mind than by any urgency of purpose. Although, by an effort of will, I had preserved a quiet, matter-of-fact demeanour while I was talking to Mrs. Gillow, her alarming news had fallen on me like a thunderbolt; and even now, as I strode forward swiftly, my thoughts seemed numbed by the suddenness of the catastrophe. That something terrible had happened I had little more doubt than had Mrs. Gillow, and a good deal more reason for my fears; for that last interview with the missing woman, looked back upon by the light of her unaccountable disappearance, now appeared full of dreadful suggestions. I had thought that she looked frightened, and she admitted to a presentiment of evil. Of whom or of what was she afraid? And what did she mean by a presentiment? Reasonable people do not have gratuitous presentiments; and I recalled her evasive reply when I asked if she had any reasons for her foreboding of evil. Now, there was little doubt that she had; that the shadow of some impending danger had fallen on her and that she knew it.

As I approached the premises of Japp and Bundy, I was assailed by a sudden doubt as to whether Mr. Japp lived there; and this doubt increased when I had executed two loud knocks at the door without eliciting any response. I was just raising my hand to make a third attack when I became aware of Bundy's head rising above the curtain of the office window; and even in my agitation I could not but notice its extremely dishevelled state. His hair—usually "smarmed" back neatly from the forehead and brushed over the crown of his head—now hung down untidily over his face like a bunch of rat's tails, and the unusualness of his appearance was increased by the fact that he wore neither spectacles nor the indispensable monocle. The apparition, however, was visible but for a moment, for even as I glanced at him he made a sign to me to wait and forthwith vanished.

There followed an interval of about a minute, at the end of which the door opened and I entered, discovering Bundy behind it in a dressing-gown and pyjamas, but with his hair neatly brushed and his monocle duly adjusted.

"Sorry to keep you waiting, Doc," said he. "Fact is, your knock woke me. The early bird catches the worm in his pyjamas."

"I apologize for disturbing your slumbers," said I, "but I wanted to see Japp. Isn't he in?"

"Japp doesn't live here," said Bundy, motioning to me to follow him upstairs. "He used to, but the house began to fill up with the business stuff and we had to make a drawing office and a store-room, so he moved off to a house on Boley Hill, and now I live here like Robinson Crusoe."

"Do you mean that you do your own cooking and housework?"

"Lord, no," he replied. "I get most of my meals at Japp's place. Prepare my own breakfast sometimes—I'm going to now: and I make tea for us both. Got a little gas-stove in the kitchen. And a charlady comes in every day to wash up and do my rooms. If you are not in a hurry, I'll walk round with you to Japp's house."

"I am in rather a hurry," said I; "at least—well, I don't know why I should be; but I am rather upset. The fact is, a very alarming thing has happened. I have just heard of it from Mrs. Gillow. It seems that Mrs. Frood went out last evening and has not come back."

Bundy whistled. "She's done a bolt," said he. "I wonder why. Do you think she can have run up against hubby in the town?"

"I don't believe for a moment that she has gone away voluntarily," said I. "She came to see me last night to get a sedative because she couldn't sleep, and she said that she was going home as soon as she had been to Chatham, and that she was going to take her medicine and go to bed early."

"That might have been a blind," suggested Bundy; "or she might have run up against her husband in Chatham."

I shook my head impatiently. "That is all nonsense, Bundy. A woman doesn't walk off into space in that fashion. Something has happened to her, I feel sure. I only hope it isn't something horrible; one doesn't dare to think of the possibilities that the circumstances suggest."

"No," said Bundy, "and it's better not to. Great mistake to let your imagination run away with you. Don't you worry, Doc. She'll probably turn up all right, or send Japp a line to say where she has gone to."

"Devil take it, Bundy!" I exclaimed irritably, "you are talking as if she were just a cat that had strayed away. If you don't care a hang what becomes of her, I do. I am extremely alarmed about her. How soon will you be ready?"

"I'll run and get on my things at once," he replied, with a sudden change of manner. "You must excuse me, old chap. I didn't realize that you were so upset. I'll be with you in a few minutes and then we will start. Japp will be able to give me some breakfast."

He bustled off—to the next room, as I gathered from the sound—and left me to work off my impatience by gazing out of the window and pacing restlessly up and down the barely-furnished sitting-room. But, impatient as I was, the rapidity with which he made his toilet surprised me, for in less than ten minutes he reappeared, spick and span, complete with hat, gloves, and stick, and announced that he was ready.

"I am not usually such a sluggard," he said, as we walked quickly along the street, "but yesterday evening I got a novel. I ought not to read novels. When I do, I am apt to make a single mouthful of it; and that is what I did last night. I started the book at nine and finished it at two this morning; and the result is that I am as sleepy as an owl even now."

In illustration of this statement he gave a prodigious yawn and then turned up the steep little thoroughfare, where be presently halted at the door of a small, old-fashioned house and rang the bell. The door was opened by a middle-aged servant, from whom he learned that Mr. Japp was at home, and to whom Bundy communicated his needs in the matter of breakfast. We found Mr. Japp seated by the dining-room window, studying a newspaper with the aid of a large pipe, and Bundy proceeded to introduce me and the occasion of my visit in a few crisp sentences.

Mr. Japp's reception of the news was very different from his partner's. Starting up from his chair and taking his pipe from his mouth, he gazed at me for some seconds in silent dismay.

"I suppose," he said at length, "there is no mistake. It is really certain that she did not come back last night?"

"I am afraid there is no doubt of the fact," I replied, and I gave him the details with which Mrs. Gillow had furnished me.

"Dear! dear!" he exclaimed. "I don't like the look of this at all. What the deuce can have happened to her?"

Here Bundy repeated the suggestion that he had made to me, but Japp shook his head. "She wouldn't have gone off without letting me or the doctor know. Why should she? We are friends, and she knew she could trust us. Besides, the thing isn't possible. A middle-class woman can't set out like a tramp without any luggage or common necessaries. There's only one possibility," he added after a pause. "She might have seen Nicholas prowling about and gone straight to the station and taken a train to London. One of her woman friends would have been able to put her up for the night."

"Or," suggested Bundy, "she might even have gone up to town with Nick himself if he met her and threatened to make a scene."

"Yes," said Japp doubtfully, "that is, I suppose, possible. But it isn't in the least likely. For that matter, nothing is likely. It is a most mysterious affair, and very disturbing, very disturbing, indeed."

"The question is," said I, "what is to be done? Do you think we ought to communicate with the police?"

"Well, no," he replied; "not immediately. If we don't hear anything, say tomorrow, I suppose we shall have to. But we had better not be precipitate. If we go to the police, we shall have to tell them everything. Let us give her time to communicate, in case she has had to make a sudden retirement—a clear forty-eight hours, as it is a weekend. But we had better make some cautious inquiries meanwhile. I suggest that we walk up to the hospital. They know me pretty well there, and I could just informally ascertain whether any accidents had been admitted, without giving any detailed reasons for the inquiry. Are you coming with us, Bundy?"

"Yes," replied Bundy, who, having been provided with a light breakfast, was despatching it with lightning speed; "I shall be ready by the time you have got your boots on."

A few minutes later we set forth together, and made our way straight to the hospital. Bundy and I waited outside while Japp went in to make his inquiries; and, as we walked up and down, my imagination busied itself in picturing the hideous possibilities suggested by a somewhat extensive experience of the casualty department of a general hospital. Presently Japp emerged, shaking his head.

"She is not there," said he. "There were no casualties of any kind admitted last night or since."

"Is there no other hospital?" I asked.

"None but the military hospital," he replied. "All the casualties from the district would be brought here. So we seem to be at the end of our resources, short of inquiring at the police-station; and even if that were advisable, it would be useless, for if—anything had happened—anything, I mean, that we hope has not happened—Mrs. Gillow would have heard. She will be sure to have had something about her by which she could have been identified."

"She had," said I. "The little box that I gave her had her name and my address on it."

"Then," said Japp. "I don't see that we can do anything more. We can only wait until tomorrow evening or Tuesday morning, and if we don't get any news of her by then, notify the police."

Unwillingly I had to admit that this was so; and when I had walked back with the partners to Mr. Japp's house, I left them and proceeded to report to Mrs. Gillow and to ascertain whether, in the meantime, she had received any tidings of her missing tenant.

It was with more of fear than hope that I plied the familiar knocker, but the eager, expectant face that greeted me when the door opened, while it relieved the one, banished the other. She had heard nothing, and when I had communicated my own unsatisfactory report she groaned and shook her head.

"You are quite sure," I said, after an interval of silence, "that she did not return from Chatham?"

"I don't see how she could have done," was the reply.

"You see, it was like this: I was going to see my sister at Frindsbury, and as I came down to the hall, Mrs. Frood opened her door and spoke to me. She had her hat on then, and she told me she was coming to you, and then going on to Chatham, but that she would be back pretty soon, and was going to bed early. I went out, leaving her at her room door, and took the tram to Frindsbury, and I got back home about a quarter to ten. Her sitting-room door was open, and I could see that she hadn't gone to bed, because her lamp was alight and her supper tray was on the table and hadn't been touched. I knocked at her bedroom door, but there was no answer, so I went upstairs and sat up listening for her, and before I went to bed I went down again, as I told you."

"What time was it when you went out?" I asked.

"About a quarter past eight. I told her I was going to Frindsbury, and that I should be home before ten, and I asked her not to bolt the door if she came in before me."

"Then," said I, "she must have gone out directly after you, because it was only a little after half-past eight when she called on me; and presumably she went straight on to Chatham. If we only knew what she was going there for we might be able to trace her. Did she know anybody at Chatham?"

"So far as I know," replied Mrs. Gillow, "she didn't know anybody here but you and Mr. Japp. I can't imagine what she could have been going to Chatham for."

After a little further talk, I took my leave and walked homeward in a very wretched frame of mind. Tormented as I was with a gnawing anxiety, inaction was intolerable. Yet there was nothing to be done; nothing but to wait in the feeble hope that the morning might bring some message of relief, and with a heavy foreboding that the tidings, when they came, would be evil tidings. But I found it impossible to wait passively at home. At intervals during the day I went forth to wander up and down the streets; and some impulse which I hardly dared to recognize directed my steps again and again to the wharves and foreshore that lie by the bend of the river between Rochester and Chatham.

On the following morning I betook myself as early as I decently could to the office of Japp and Bundy. No letter had arrived by the early post, nor, when I repeated my visit later, was there any news, either by post or telegram, or from Mrs. Gillow. I paid a furtive visit to the police-station and glanced nervously over the bills on the notice-board, and I made another perambulation of the waterside districts, which occupied me until it was time for me to repair to the station to meet the train by which my friends were expected to arrive, and did, in fact, arrive.

As we walked from the station to my house Jervis looked at me critically from time to time. After one of these inspections he remarked:

"I don't know whether it is my fancy, Strangeways, but it seems to me that the cares of medical practice are affecting your spirits. You look worried."

"I am worried," I replied. "There has been a very disturbing development of that case that I was telling you about."

"The doper, you mean?"

"His wife. She has disappeared. She went out on Saturday night and has not been seen since."

"That sounds rather ominous," said Jervis. "I presume the circumstances—if you know them—could be communicated without any breach of confidence."

"They will have to be made fully public if she doesn't turn up by this evening," I replied, "and I am only too glad of the chance to talk the matter over with you," and forthwith I proceeded to give a circumstantial account of the events connected with the disappearance, not omitting any detail that seemed to have the slightest bearing. And I now felt justified in relating my experience when I was acting for Dr. Pumphrey. The narrative was interrupted by our arrival at my house, but when we had taken our places at the table it was continued and listened to with intense interest by my two friends.

"Well," said Jervis, when I had finished, "it has an ugly look, especially when one considers it in connexion with that affair in London. But there is something to be said for your friend Bundy's suggestion. Don't you think so, Thorndyke?"

"Something, perhaps," Thorndyke agreed, "but not much; and if no letter arrives tonight or tomorrow morning, I should say it is excluded. This lady seems to have had complete confidence in Strangeways and in Mr. Japp. She could depend on their secrecy if she had to move suddenly to a fresh locality; and she seems to have been a responsible person who would not unnecessarily expose them to anxiety about her safety. Moreover, she would know that, if she kept them in the dark, they must unavoidably put the police on her track, which would be the last thing that she would wish."

"Can you make any suggestion as to what has probably happened?" I asked.

"It is not of much use to speculate," replied Thorndyke.

"If we exclude a voluntary disappearance, an accident or sudden illness, as we apparently can, there seems to remain only the possibility of crime. But to the theory of crime—of murder, to put it bluntly—there is a manifest objection. So far as the circumstances are known to us, a murder, if it had occurred, would have been an impromptu murder, committed in a more or less public place. But the first indication of a murder of that kind is usually—the discovery of the body. Here, however, thirty-six hours have elapsed, and no body has come to light. On the other hand, we have to bear in mind that there is a large, tidal river skirting the town. Into that river the missing lady might have fallen accidentally, or have been thrown, dead or alive. But it is not very profitable to speculate. We can neither form any opinion nor take any action until we have some further facts."

I must confess that, as I listened to Thorndyke thus calmly comparing the horrible possibilities, I experienced a dreadful sinking of the heart, but yet I realized that this passionless consideration of the essential evidence was more to the point, and promised more result than any amount of unskilful groping under the urge of emotion and personal feeling. And, realizing this, I formed the bold resolution of enlisting Thorndyke's aid in a regular, professional capacity, and began to cast about for the means of introducing the rather delicate subject. But while I was reflecting, the opportunity, was gone, at least for the present. Lunch had virtually come to an end, for Mrs. Dunk had silently and with iron visage just placed the port and the coffee on the table and retired, when, Jervis, who had observed her with evident interest, inquired: "Does that old Sphinx do the cooking, Strangeways?"

"She does everything," I answered. "I have suggested that she should get some help, but she just growled and ignored the suggestion."

"Well," said Jervis, "she doesn't give you much excuse for growling. She has turned out a lunch that would have done credit to Delmonico's. Are you coming to the inquest with us? We shall have to be starting in a few minutes."

"I may as well," said I. "Then I can bring you back to tea. And I want to make a proposal, which we can discuss as we go along. It is with regard to the case of Mrs. Frood."

As my two friends looked at me inquiringly but made no remark, I poured out the coffee and continued: "You see, Mrs. Frood was my patient, and, in a way, my friend; in fact, with the exception of Japp, I was the only friend she had in the place. Consequently I take it as my duty to ascertain what has happened to her, and, if she has come to any harm, to see that the wrongdoers are brought to account. Of course, I am not competent to investigate the case myself, but I am in the position to bear any costs that the investigation would entail."

"Lucky man," said Jervis. "And what is the proposal?"

"I was wondering," I replied, a little nervously, "whether I could prevail on you to undertake the case."

Jervis glanced at his senior, and the latter replied:

"It is just a little premature to speak of a 'case.' The missing lady may return or communicate with her friends. If she does not, the inquiry will fall into the hands of the police; and there is no reason to suppose that they will not be fully competent to deal with it. They have more means and facilities than we have. But if the inquiry should become necessary, and the police should be unsuccessful, Jervis and I would be prepared to render you any assistance that we could."

"On professional terms," I stipulated.

Thorndyke smiled. "The financial aspects of the case," said he, "can be considered when they arise. Now, I think, it is time for us to start."

As we walked down to the building where the inquest was to be held, we pursued the topic, and Thorndyke pointed out my position in the case.

"You notice, Strangeways," said he, "that you are the principal witness. You are the last person who saw Mrs. Frood before her disappearance, you heard her state her intended movements, you knew her circumstances, you saw and examined her husband, and you alone can give an exact description of her as she was at the time when she disappeared. I would suggest that, during the inquest, which will not interest you, you might usefully try to reconstitute that last interview and make full notes in writing of all that occurred with a very careful and detailed description of the person, clothing, and belongings of the missing lady. The police will want this information, and so shall I, if I am to give any consideration to the case."

On this suggestion I proceeded to act as soon as we had taken our places at the foot of the long table occupied by the coroner and the jury, detaching myself as well as I could from the matter of the inquest; and by the time that the deliberations were at an end and the verdict agreed upon, I had drafted out a complete set of notes and made two copies, one for the police and one for Thorndyke.

As soon as we were outside the court I presented the latter copy, which Thorndyke read through.

"This is *admirable*, Strangeways," said he, as he placed it in his note-case. "I must compliment you upon your powers of observation. The description of the missing lady is remarkably clear and exhaustive. And now I would suggest that you call in at Mr. Japp's office on our way back, and ascertain whether any letter has been received. If there has been no communication we shall have to regard the appearances as suspicious, and calling for investigation."

Secretly gratified at the interest which Thorndyke seemed to be developing in the mystery, I conducted my friends up the High-street until we reached the office, which I entered, leaving my colleagues outside. Mr. Japp looked up from a letter which he was writing, and Bundy, who had been peeping over the curtain, revolved on his stool and faced me.

"Any news?" I asked.

Japp shook his head gloomily. "Not a sign," said he.

"I shall wait until the first post is in tomorrow morning, and then, if there are no tidings of her, I shall go across to the police station. Perhaps you had better come with me, as you are able to give the particulars that they will want."

"Very well," I said, "I will look in at half-past nine," and with this I was turning away when Bundy inquired: "Are those two toffs outside friends of yours?" and, on my replying in the affirmative, he continued: "They seem to be taking a deuce of an interest in Japp's proclamation. You might tell them that if they happen to have found that key, the money is quite safe. I will see that Japp pays up."

I promised to deliver the message, and, as Bundy craned up to make a further inspection of my colleagues, I departed to join the latter.

"There is no news up to the present," I said, "but Japp proposes to wait until tomorrow morning for a last chance before applying to the police."

"Was that Japp who was inspecting us through that preposterous pair of barnacles?" Jervis asked.

"No," I answered. "That was Bundy. He suspects you of having found that key and of holding on to it until you are sure of the reward."

"What key is it?" asked Jervis. "The key of the strong-room? They seem to be in a rare twitter about it."

"No; it is just a gate-key belonging to a piece of waste land where they are doing some repairs to the old city wall. And, by the way, thereby hangs a tale; a horrible and tragic tale of a convivial bargee, which ought to have a special interest for a pair of medical jurists"—and here I related to them the gruesome story that was told to Bundy and me by the old mortar-mixer.

They both chuckled appreciatively at the denouement, and Jervis remarked:

"It would seem that the late Bill was a rather inflammable gentleman. The yarn recalls the tragic end of Mr. Krook in 'Bleak House,' only that Krook went one better than Bill, for he managed to combust himself in an hour or two without any lime at all."

The story and the comment brought us to my house, which we had no sooner entered than Mrs. Dunk, who seemed to have been lying in wait for us, made her appearance with the tea; and while we were disposing of this refreshment Thorndyke reverted to the case of my missing patient.

"As I am to keep an eye on this ease," said he, "I shall want to be kept in touch with it. Of course, the actual investigation—if there has to be one—will need to be conducted on the spot, which is not possible to me. What I suggest is that you write out a detailed account of everything that is known to you in connexion with it. Don't select your facts. Put down everything in any way connected with the case and say all you know about the person concerned—Mrs. Frood herself and everybody who was acquainted with her. Send this statement to me and keep a copy. Then, if any new fact becomes known, let me have it and make a note of it for your own information. You are on the spot and I shall look to you for the data; and if I want any of them amplified or confirmed I shall communicate with you.

"There is one other matter. Do not confide to anyone that you have consulted me or that I am interested in the case; neither to Mr. Japp, to the police, nor to anybody else whatsoever; and I advise you to keep your own interest in the mystery to yourself as far as possible."

"What is the need of this secrecy?" I asked, in some surprise.

"The point is," replied Thorndyke, "that when you are investigating a crime you are playing against the criminal. But if the criminal is unknown to you, you are playing against an unseen adversary. If you are visible to him he can watch your moves and reply to them. Obviously your policy is to keep out of sight and make your moves unseen. And remember that as long as you do not know who the criminal is, you don't know who he is not. Anyone may be the criminal, or may be his unconscious agent or coadjutor. If you make confidences they may be innocently passed on to the guilty parties. So keep your own counsel rigorously. If there has been a crime, that crime has local connexions and probably a local origin. The solution of the mystery will probably be discovered here. And if you intend to take a hand in the solution let it be a lone hand; and keep me informed of everything that you do or observe; and for my part, I will give you all the help I can."

By the time we had finished our tea and our discussion the hour of my friends' departure was drawing nigh. I walked with them to the station, and when I bade them farewell I received a warm invitation to visit them at their chambers in the Temple; an invitation of which I determined to avail myself on the first favourable opportunity.

CHAPTER VIII

SERGEANT COBBLEDICK TAKES A HAND

Punctually at half-past nine on the following morning I presented myself at the office, and, if I had indulged in any hopes of favourable news—which I had not—they would have been dispelled by a glance at Mr. Japp's troubled face.

"I suppose you have heard nothing?" I said, when we had exchanged brief greetings.

He shook his head gloomily as he opened the cupboard and took out his hat.

"No," he answered, "and I am afraid we never shall."

He sighed heavily, and, putting on his hat, walked slowly to the door. "It is a dreadful affair," he continued, as we went out together. "How she would have hated the idea of it, poor girl! All the horrid publicity, the posters, the sensational newspaper paragraphs, the descriptions of her person and belongings. And then, at the end of it all, God knows what horror may come to light. It won't bear thinking of."

He trudged along at my side with bent head and eyes cast down, and for the remainder of the short journey neither of us spoke. On reaching the police-station we made our way into a small, quiet office, the only tenant of which was a benevolent-looking, bald-headed sergeant, who was seated at a high desk, and, who presented that peculiar, decapitated aspect that appertains to a police officer minus his helmet. As we entered the sergeant laid down his pen and turned to us with a benign smile.

"Good morning, Mr. Japp," said he. "What can I have the pleasure of doing for you?"

"I am sorry to say, Sergeant," replied Japp, "that I have come here on very unpleasant business," and he proceeded to give the officer a concise summary of the facts, to which our friend listened with close attention. When it was finished, the sergeant produced a sheet of blue foolscap, and, having folded a wide margin on it, dipped his pen in the ink and began his examination.

"I'd better take the doctor's statement first," said he. "The lady's name is Angelina Frood, married, living apart from husband—I shall want his address presently—last seen alive by—"

"John Strangeways, M.D.," said I, "of Maidstone-road, Rochester."

The sergeant wrote this down, and continued: "Last seen at about 8.30 P.M. on Saturday, 26th April, proceeding towards Chatham, on unknown business. Can you give me a description of her?"

I described her person, assisted by Japp, and the sergeant, having committed the particulars to writing, read them out:

"'Age 28, height 5 ft. 7 in., complexion medium, hazel eyes, abundant dark brown hair, strongly marked black eyebrows, nearly meeting over nose.'"

"No special marks that you know of?"

"No."

"Now, doctor, can you tell us how she was dressed?"

"She was wearing a snuff-brown coat and skirt," I replied, "and a straw hat of the same colour with a broad, dull green band. The hat was fixed on by two hat-pins with silver heads shaped like poppy-capsules. The coat had six buttons, small-ish, bronze buttons—about half an inch in diameter—with a Tudor rose embossed on each. Brown suede gloves with fasteners—no buttons—brown silk stockings, and brown suede shoes with small, oval bronze buckles. She had a narrow silk scarf, dull green, with three purple bands at each end—one broad band and two narrow—and knotted fringe at the ends. She wore a small circular brooch with a largish opal in the centre and a border of small pearls, of which one was missing. The missing pearl was in the position of the figure three on a clock dial. She carried a small morocco handbag with the initials A. F. stamped on it, which contained a little cardboard box, in which were six white tablets; the box was labelled with one of Dr. Partridge's labels, on which her name was written, and it was wrapped in white paper and sealed with sealing-wax. That is all I can say for certain. But she always wore a wedding-ring, and occasionally an African Zodiac ring; but some-times she carried this ring in a small purse with metal jaws and a ball fastening. I believe she always carried the purse."

As I gave this description, the sergeant wrote furiously, glancing at me from time to time with an expression of surprise, while Japp sat and stared at me open-mouthed.

"Well, doctor," said the sergeant, when he had taken down my statement and read it out, "if I find myself ailing I'm going to pop along and consult you. I reckon there isn't much that escapes your notice. With regard to that African ring now, I daresay you cart tell us what it is like."

I was, of course, able to describe it in detail, including the initials A. C. in-side, and even to give a rough sketch of some of the signs embossed on it, upon which the sergeant chuckled admiringly and wagged his head as he wrote down the description and pinned the sketch on the margin of his paper. The rest of my statement dealt with the last interview and the incidents connected with Nicholas Frood's visits to Rochester, all of which the sergeant listened to with deep interest and committed to writing.

Finally, I recounted the sinister incident—now more sinister than ever—of the murderous assault in the house near Regent's Park, whereat the sergeant looked uncommonly serious and took down the statement verbatim.

"Did you know about this, Mr. Japp?" he asked.

"I knew that something unpleasant had happened," was the reply, "but I didn't know that it was as bad as this."

"Well," said the sergeant, "it gives the present affair rather an ugly look. We shall have to make some inquiries about that gentleman."

Having squeezed me dry, he turned his attention to Japp, from whom he ex-tracted a variety of information, including the address of the banker who paid the allowance to Nicholas Frood, and that of a lady who had formerly been a theatrical colleague of Mrs. Frood's, and with whom Mr. Japp believed the latter had kept up a correspondence.

"You haven't a photograph of the missing lady, I suppose?" said the sergeant.

With evident reluctance Japp drew from his pocket an envelope and produced from it a cabinet photograph, which he looked at sadly for a few moments and then handed to me.

"I brought this photograph with me," he said, "as I knew you would want it, but I rather hope that you won't want to publish it."

"Now, why do you hope that?" the sergeant asked in a soothing and persuasive tone. "You want this lady found—or, at any rate, traced. But what better means can you suggest than publishing her portrait?"

"I suppose you are right," said Japp; "but it is a horrible thing to think of the poor girl's face looking out from posters and newspaper pages."

"It is," the sergeant agreed. "But, you see, if she is alive it is her own doing, and if she is dead it won't affect her."

While they were talking I had been looking earnestly at the beloved face, which I now felt I should never look upon again. It was an excellent likeness, showing her just as I had known her, excepting that it was free from the cloud of trouble that had saddened her expression in these latter days. As the sergeant held out his hand for it, I turned it over and read the photographer's name and address and the register number, and, having made a mental note of them, I surrendered it with a sigh.

Our business was now practically concluded. When we had each read over the statements and added our respective signatures, the sergeant attested them and, having added the date, placed the documents in his desk and rose.

"I am much obliged to you, gentlemen," said he as he escorted us to the door. "If I hear anything that will interest you I will let you know, and if I should want any further information I shall take the liberty of calling on you."

"Well," said Japp, as we turned to walk back, "the fat's in the fire now. I mean to say," he added quickly, "that we've fairly committed ourselves. I hope we haven't been too precipitate. We should catch it if she came back and found that we had raised the hue and cry and set the whole town agog."

"I am afraid there is no hope of that," said I. "At any rate, we had no choice or discretion in the matter. A suspected crime is the business of the police."

Mr. Japp agreed that this was so; and having by this time arrived at the office, we separated, he to enter his premises and I to betake myself to Chatham with no very, defined purpose, but lured thither by a vague attraction.

As I walked along the High-street, making occasional digressions into narrow alleys to explore wharves and water-side premises, I turned over the statements that had been given to the police and wondered what they conveyed to our friend, the sergeant, with his presumably extensive experience of obscure crime. To me they seemed to furnish no means whatever of starting an investigation, excepting by inquiring as to the movements of Nicholas Frood, by communicating with Angelina's late colleague or by publishing the photograph. And here I halted to write down in my notebook before I should forget them the name and address of that lady—Miss Cumbers—and of the photographers, together with the number of the photograph; for I had decided to obtain a copy of the latter for myself, and it now occurred to me that I had better get one also for Thorndyke. And this latter reflection reminded me that I had to prepare my précis of the facts for him, and that I should do well to get this done at once while the matter of the two statements was fresh in my mind. Accordingly, as I paced the deck of the Sun Pier, looking up and down the busy river, with its endless procession of barges, bawleys, tugs, and cargo boats, striving ineffectually to banish the dreadful thought that, perchance, somewhere, at this very moment there was floating on its turbid waters the corpse of my dear, lost friend: I tried to recall and write down the substance of Japp's statement, as I had heard it made and had afterwards read it. At length, finding the neighbourhood of the river too disturbing, I left the pier and took my way homewards, calling in at a stationer's on the way to provide myself with a packet of sermon paper on which to write out my summary.

When Thorndyke had given me my instructions, they had appeared to me a little pedantic. The full narrative which he asked for of all the events, without selection as to relevancy, and the account of what I knew of all the persons concerned in the case, seemed an excessive formality. But when I came to write the case out the excellence of his method became apparent in two respects. In the first place, the ordered narrative put the events in their proper sequence and exhibited their connexions; and in the second, the endeavour to state all that I knew, particularly of the persons, showed me how very little that was. Of the persons in any way concerned in the case there were but five: Angelina herself, her husband, Mrs. Gillow, Mr. Japp, and Bundy. Of the first two I knew no more than what I had observed myself and what Angelina had told me; of the last three I knew practically nothing. Not that this appeared to me of the slightest importance, but I had my instructions, and in compliance with them I determined to make such cautious inquiries as would enable me to give Thorndyke at least a few particulars of them. And this during the next few days I did; and I may as well set down here the scanty and rather trivial information that my inquiries elicited, and which I duly sent on to Thorndyke in a supplementary report.

Mrs. Gillow was the wife of a mariner who was the second mate of a sailing ship that plied to Australia, who had now been away about four months and was expected home shortly. She was a native of the locality and had known Mr. Japp for several years. She occupied the part of the house above the ground floor and kept no servant or dependent, living quite alone when her husband was at sea. She had no children. Her acquaintance with Angelina began when the latter became the tenant of the ground floor and basement; it was but a slight acquaintance, and she knew nothing of Angelina's antecedents or affairs excepting that she had left her husband.

Mr. Japp was a native of Rochester and had lived in the town all his life, having taken over his business establishment from his late partner, a Mr. Borden. He was a bachelor and was related to Angelina by marriage, his brother—now deceased—having married Angelina's aunt.

As to Bundy, he was hardly connected with the case at all, since he had seen Angelina only once or twice and had scarcely exchanged a dozen words with her. Moreover, he had but recently come to Rochester—about six weeks ago, I gathered—having answered an advertisement of Japp's for an assistant with a view to partnership; and the actual deed had not yet been executed, though the two partners were evidently quite well satisfied with one another.

That was all the information that I had to give Thorndyke; and with the exception of the London incident it amounted to nothing. Nevertheless, it was as well to have established the fact that if anyone were concerned in Angelina's disappearance, that person would have to be sought elsewhere than in Rochester.

Having sent off my summary and read over again and again the copy which I had kept, I began to realize the justice of Thorndyke's observation that the inquiry was essentially a matter for the police, who had both the experience and the necessary facilities; for whenever I tried to think of some plan for tracing my lost friend, I was brought up against the facts that I had, nothing whatever to go on and no idea how to make a start. As to Thorndyke, he had no data but those that I had given him, and I realized clearly that these were utterly insufficient to form the basis of any investigation; and I found myself looking expectantly to the police to produce some new facts that might throw at least a glimmer of light on this dreadful and baffling mystery.

I had not very long to wait. On the Friday after our call on the sergeant, I was sitting after lunch in my dining-room with a book in my hand, while my thoughts strayed back to those memorable evenings of pleasant converse with the sweet friend who, I felt, had gone from me for ever, when the door bell rang, and Mrs. Dunk presently announced:

"Sergeant Cobbledick."

"Show him in here, Mrs. Dunk," said I, laying aside my book, and rising to receive my visitor; who proved to be, as I had expected, the officer who had taken our statements. He entered with his helmet in his hand, and greeted me with a smile of concentrated benevolence.

"Sit down, Sergeant," said I, offering him an easy chair. "I hope you have some news for us."

"Yes," he replied, beaming on me. "I am glad to say we are getting on as well as we can expect. We have made quite a nice little start."

He spoke as if he had something particularly gratifying to communicate, and, having carefully placed his helmet on the table, he drew from his pocket a small paper packet, which he opened with great deliberation, extracting from it a small object, which he held out in the palm of his hand.

"There, Doctor," said he, complacently; "what do you say to that?"

I looked at the object, and my heart seemed to stand still. It was Angelina's brooch! I stared at it in speechless dismay for some moments. At length I asked, huskily:

"Where did you get it?"

"I found it," said the sergeant, gazing fondly at the little trinket, "where I hardly hoped to find it—in a pawnbroker's shop in Chatham."

"Did you discover who pawned it?" I asked.

"In a sense, yes," the sergeant replied with a bland smile.

"How do you mean—in a sense?" I inquired.

"I mean that his name was John Smith—only, of course, it wasn't; and that his address was 26, Swoffer's-alley, Chatham—only he didn't live there, because there is no such number. You see, Doctor, John Smith is the name of nearly every man who gives a false description of himself; and I went straight off to Swoffer's-alley—it was close by—and found that there wasn't any number 26."

"Then you really don't know who pawned it?"

"We won't exactly say that," he replied. "I got a fair description of the man from the pawnbroker's wife, who made out the ticket and says she could swear to the man if she saw him. He was a seafaring man, dressed in sailor's clothes—a peaked cap and pea-jacket—a shortish fellow, rather sunburnt, with a small, stubby, dark moustache and dark hair, and a mole or wart on the left side of his nose, near the tip. She asked him where he had got the brooch, and he said it had belonged to his old woman. I should say he probably picked it up."

"Why do you think so?" I asked.

"Well, if he had—er—got it in any other way, he would hardly have popped it in Chatham forty-eight hours after the—after it was lost, with the chance that the pawnbrokers had already been notified—he pawned it on Monday night."

"Then," said I, "if he picked it up, he isn't of much importance; and in any case you don't know who he is."

"Oh, but he is of a good deal of importance," said the sergeant. "I've no doubt he picked it up, but that is only a guess. He may have got it the other way. But at any rate, he had it in his possession and he will have to give an account of how he obtained it. The importance of it is this: taken with the disappearance, the finding of this brooch raises a strong suspicion that a crime has been committed, and if we could find out where it was picked up, we should have a clue to the place where the affair took place. I want that man very badly, and I'm going to have a good try to get him."

"I don't quite see how," said I. "You haven't much to go on."

"I've got his nose to go on," replied the sergeant.

"But there must be plenty of other men with moles on their noses."

"That's their lookout," he retorted. "If I come across a man who answers the description, I shall hang on to him until Mrs. Pawnbroker has had a look at him. Of course, if she says he's not the man, he'll be released."

"But she won't," said I. "If he has a mole on his nose, she will be perfectly certain that he is the man."

The sergeant smiled benignly. "There's something in that," he admitted. "Ladies are a bit cock-sure when it comes to identification. But you can generally check 'em by other evidence. And if this chap picked the brooch up, he would be pretty certain to tell us all about it when he heard where it came from. Still, we haven't got him yet."

For a while we sat, without speaking, each pursuing his own thoughts. To me, this dreadful discovery, though it did but materialize the vague fears that had been surging through my mind, had fallen like a thunderbolt. For, behind those fears, I now realized that there had lurked a hope that the mystery might presently be resolved by the return of the lost one. Now that hope had suddenly become extinct. I knew that she had gone out of my life for ever. She was dead. This poor little waif that had drifted back into our hands brought the unmistakable message of her death, with horrible suggestions of hideous and sordid tragedy. I shuddered at the thought; and in that moment, from the grief and horror that possessed my soul, there was born a passion of hatred for the wretch who had done this thing and a craving for revenge.

"There's another queer thing that has come to light," the sergeant resumed at length. "There may be nothing in it, but it's a little queer. About the husband, Nicholas Frood."

"What about him?" I asked, eagerly.

"Why, he seems to have disappeared, too. Of course, you understand, Doctor, that what I'm telling you is confidential. We are not talking about this affair outside, and we aren't telling the Press much, at present."

"Naturally," said I. "You can trust me to keep my own counsel, and yours, too."

"I'm sure I can. Well, about this man, Frood. It seems that last Friday he went away from his lodgings for a couple of days; but he hasn't come back, and nobody knows what has become of him. He was supposed to be going to Brighton, where he has some relatives from whom he gets a little assistance occasionally, but they have seen or heard nothing of him. Quaint, isn't it? You said you saw him here on the Monday."

"Yes, and I haven't seen him since, though I have kept a lookout for him. But he may have been here, all the same. It looks decidedly suspicious."

"It is queer," the sergeant agreed, "but we've no evidence that he has been in this neighbourhood."

"Have you made any other inquiries?" I asked.

"We looked up that lady, Miss Cumbers, but we got nothing out of her. She had had a letter from Mrs. Frood on the 24th—yesterday week—quite an ordinary letter, giving no hint of any intention to go away from Rochester. So there you are. The mystery seems to be concerned entirely with this neighbourhood, and I expect we shall have to solve it on the spot."

This last observation impressed me strongly. The sergeant's view of the case was the same as Thorndyke's, and expressed in almost the same words.

"Have you any theory as to what has actually happened?" I asked.

The sergeant smiled in his benignant fashion. "It isn't much use inventing theories," said he. "We've got to get the facts before we can do anything. Still, looking at the case as we find it, there are two or three things that hit us in the face. There is a strong suspicion of murder, there is no trace of the body, and there is a big tidal river close at hand. On Saturday night it was high water at half-past eleven, so there wouldn't have been much of the shore uncovered at, say, half-past nine, and there would have been plenty of water at any of the piers or causeways."

"Then you think it probable that she was murdered and her body flung into the river?"

"It is the likeliest thing, so far as we can judge. There is the river, and there is no sign of the body on shore. But, as I say, it is no use guessing. We've got people watching the river from Allington Lock to Sheerness, and that's all we can do in that line. The body is pretty certain to turn up, sooner or later. Of course, until it does, there is no real criminal case; and even when we've got the body, we may not be much nearer getting the murderer. Excepting the man Frood, there is no one who seems to have had any motive for making away with her; and if it was just a casual robbery with murder it is unlikely that we shall ever spot the man at all."

Having given expression to this rather pessimistic view, the sergeant rose, and, picking up his helmet, took his departure, after promising to let me know of any further developments.

As soon as he was gone, I wrote down the substance of what he had said, and then embodied it in a report for Thorndyke. While I was thus occupied, the afternoon post was delivered, and included a packet from the London photographer, to whom I had written, enclosing two copies of the photograph of Angelina that Mr. Japp had handed to the sergeant. Of these, I enclosed one copy in my communication to Thorndyke, on the bare chance that it might be of some assistance to him, and, having closed up the large envelope and stamped it, I went forth to drop it into the post-box.

CHAPTER IX

JETSAM

That portion of Chatham High-street which lies adjacent to the River Medway presents a feature that is characteristic of old riverside towns in the multitude of communications between the street and the shore. Some of these are undisguised entrances to wharves, some are courts or small thoroughfares lined with houses and leading to landing-stages, while others are mere passages or flights of steps, opening obscurely and inconspicuously on the street by narrow apertures, unnoticed by the ordinary wayfarer and suggesting the burrows of some kind of human water-rat.

In the days that followed the sergeant's visit to me I made the acquaintance of all of them. Now I would wander down the cobbled cartway that led to a wharf, there to cast a searching eye over the muddy fore-shore or scan the turbid water at high tide as it eddied between the barges and around the piles. Or I would dive into the mouths of the burrows, creeping down slimy steps and pursuing the tortuous passages through a world of uncleanness until I came out upon the shore, where the fresh smell of seaweed mingled with odours indescribable. I began to be an object of curiosity—and perhaps of some suspicion—to the denizens of the little, ruinous, timber houses that lined these alleys, and of frank interest to the children who played around the rubbish heaps or dabbled in the grey mud. But never did my roving eye light upon that which it sought with such dreadful expectation.

One afternoon, about a week after the sergeant's visit, when I was returning home from one of these explorations, I observed a man on my doorstep as I approached the house. His appearance instantly aroused my attention, for he was dressed in the amphibious style adopted by waterside dwellers, and he held something in his hand at which he looked from time to time. Before I reached the door it had opened and admitted him, and when I arrived I found him in the hall nervously explaining his business to Mrs. Dunk.

"Here is the doctor," said the latter; "you'd better tell him about it."

The man turned to me and held out an amazingly dirty fist. "I've got something here, sir," said he, "what belongs to you, I think." Here he unclosed his hand and exhibited a little cardboard box bearing one of Dr. Partridge's labels. It was smeared with mud and grime, but I recognized it instantly; indeed, when I took it with trembling fingers from his palm and looked at it closely, the name, "Mrs. Frood," was still decipherable under the smears of dirt.

"Where did you find this?" I asked.

"I picked it up on the strand," he replied, "about halfway betwixt the Sun Pier and the end of Ship Alley, and just below spring tide high-water mark. Is it any good?"

"Yes," I answered; "it is very important. I will get you to walk along with me to the police station."

"What for?" he demanded suspiciously. "I don't want no police stations. If it's any good, give us what you think it's worth, and have done with it."

I gave him half-a-crown to allay his suspicions, and then said: "You had better come with me to the station. I expect the police will want you to show them exactly where you found this box and help them to search the place; and I will see that you are paid for your trouble."

"But look 'ere, mister," he objected; "what's the police got to do with this 'ere box?"

I explained the position to him briefly, and then, suddenly, his face lit up. "I know," he said excitedly. "I seen the bills stuck up on the dead-'ouse door. And d'you mean to say as this 'ere box was 'ers? Cos if it was it's worth more 'n 'arf-a-crown."

"Perhaps it is," said I. "We will hear what the sergeant thinks," and with this I opened the door and went out, and my new acquaintance now followed with the greatest alacrity, taking the opportunity, as we walked along, to remind me of my promise and to offer tentative suggestions as to the scale of remuneration for his services.

Our progress along the High-street was not unnoticed. Doubtless, we appeared a somewhat ill-assorted pair, for I observed a good many persons turn to look at us curiously, and when we passed the office, on the opposite side of the road, I saw Bundy's face rise above the curtain with an expression of undissembled curiosity.

On arriving at the station, I inquired for Sergeant Cobbledick, and was fortunate enough to find him in his office. As I entered with my companion, he bestowed on the latter a quick glance of professional interest and then greeted me with a genial smile. It was hardly necessary for me to state my business, for the single quick glance of his experienced eye at my companion had furnished the diagnosis. I had only to produce the box and indicate the finder.

"This looks like a lead," said he, reaching his helmet down from a peg. "What's your name, sonny, and where do you live?"

Sonny affirmed, with apparent reluctance, that his name was Samuel Hooper and that his abode was situated in Foul Anchor Alley; and when these facts had been committed to writing by the sergeant, the latter put on his helmet and invited the said Hooper to "come along," evidently assuming that I was to form one of the party.

As we approached the office this time I saw Bundy from afar off; and by the time we were abreast of the house he was joined by Japp, who must have stood upon tiptoe to bring his eyes above the curtain. Both men watched us with intense interest, and we had barely passed the house when Bundy's head suddenly disappeared, and a few moments later its owner emerged from the doorway and hurriedly crossed the road.

"What is in the wind, Doctor?" he asked, as he came up with us. "Japp is in a rare twitter. Have they found the body?"

"No," I answered; "only the little box that was in her handbag. We are going to have a look at the place where it was found."

"To see if the bag is there, too?" said he. "It probably is, unless it has been picked up already. I think I'll come along with you, if you don't object. Then I can give Japp all the news."

I did not object, nor did the sergeant—verbally; but his expression conveyed to me that he would willingly have dispensed with Mr. Bundy's society. However, he was a suave and tactful man, and he made the best of the unwelcome addition to the party, even going so far as to offer the box for Bundy's inspection.

"It is pretty dirty," the latter observed, holding it delicately in his fingers. "Wasn't it wrapped in paper when you gave it to her, Doctor?"

"It was wrapped up in paper when I found it," said Hooper, "but I took off the paper to see what was inside, and, yer see, my 'ands wasn't very clean, a-grubbin' about in the mud." In conclusive confirmation of this statement, he exhibited them to us, and then gave them a perfunctory wipe on his trousers.

"What struck me," said Bundy, "was that it doesn't seem to have been in the water."

"It hadn't," said Hooper. "The outside paper was quite clean when I picked it up."

"It looks," observed the sergeant, "as if they had turned out the bag and thrown away what they didn't want; and then they probably threw away the bag, too. It is ten chances to one that it has been picked up, but if it hasn't it will probably be somewhere along the high-water mark. How are the tides, Hooper?"

"Just past the bottom of the nips," was the reply; and a few moments later our guide added; "It's down here," and plunged into what looked like an open door-way. We followed, one at a time, cautiously descending a flight of very filthy stone steps and stooping to avoid knocking our heads against the overhanging story of an ancient timber house. At the bottom we proceeded, still in single file, along a narrow, crooked passage between grimy walls and ruinous tarred fences until, after many twistings and turnings, we came to a flight of rough wooden steps, thickly coated with yellow mud and slimy sea-grass, which led down to the shore.

"Now," said the sergeant, turning up the bottoms or his trousers, "show us exactly where you picked the box up."

"It was just oppersight that there schooner," said our guide, taking his way along the muddy streak between the two lines of jetsam that corresponded to the springtide and neap-tide high-water marks; "betwixt her and the wharf."

We followed him, picking our way daintly, and, having inspected the spot that he indicated, squeezed in between the schooner's bilge and the piles and raked over the rubbish that the tide had deposited on the shore.

"Was you looking for anything in partickler?" Hooper asked.

"We are looking for a small leather handbag," replied the sergeant, "or anything else we can find."

"A 'andbag wouldn't 'ave been 'ere long," Hooper remarked. "Somebody would 'ave twigged it pretty quick, unless it got hidden under something big." He straightened himself up and gave a searching look up and down the shore; and then suddenly he started off with an air of definite purpose. Glancing in the direction towards which he was shaping his course, I observed, in the corner of a stage that jutted out from the quay, a heap of miscellaneous rubbish surmounted by the mortal remains of a large hamper. It looked a likely spot and we all followed, though not at his pace, being somewhat more fastidious as to where we stepped. Consequently he arrived considerably before us, and having flung away the hamper, began eagerly to grub among the underlying raffle. Just as we had come within a dozen yards of him, anxiously making the perilous passage over a stretch of peculiarly slimy mud, he stood up with a howl of triumph, and we all stopped to look at him. His arm was raised above his head, and from his hand hung by its handle a little morocco bag.

"There's no need to ask you to identify it, Doctor," said the sergeant, as he despoiled the water-rat of his prize. "It fits your description to a T."

Nevertheless, he handed it to me, drawing my attention to the initials "A. F." stamped on the leather. I turned it over gloomily, noting that it showed signs of having been in the water—though not, apparently, for any considerable time—and that none of its contents remained excepting a handkerchief tucked into an inner pocket, and returned it to him without remark.

"Now, look here, Hooper," said he, "I want you to stay down here and keep an eye on this shore until I send some of our men up, and then you can stay and help them, if you like. And remember that anything that you find—no matter what it is—you keep and hand over to me or my men; and you will be paid the full value and a reward for finding it as well. Do you understand that?"

"I do," replied Hooper. "That's a fair orfer, and you can depend on me to do the square thing. I'll stay down here until your men come."

Thereupon we left him, pursuing our way along the shore and keeping an attentive eye on all the rubbish and litter that we passed, until we came to a set of rough wooden steps by the Ship Pier.

"I had no authority to offer to pay that chap," said the sergeant, as we walked up Ship Alley, "but the superintendent has put me on to work at this case, and I'm not going to lose any chances for the sake of a few shillings. It is well to keep in with these waterside people."

"Have you published a list of things that are likely to turn up?" Bundy asked.

"We've posted up a description of the missing woman with full details of her dress and belongings," replied the sergeant. "But perhaps a list of the things that might be washed up would be useful. People are such fools. Yes, it's a good idea. I'll have a list printed of everything that might get loose and be picked up, and stick it up on the wharves and waterside premises. Then there will be nothing left to their imagination."

At the top of Ship Alley he halted, and having thanked me warmly for my prompt and timely information, turned towards Chatham Town, leaving me and Bundy to retrace our steps westward.

"That was a bit of luck," the latter remarked, "finding that bag; and he hardly deserved it. He ought to have had that piece of shore under observation from the first. But he was wise to make an acceptable offer to that bodysnatcher, Hooper. I expect he lives on the shore, watching for derelict corpses and any unconsidered trifles that the river may throw up. I see there is a reward of two pounds for the body."

"You have seen the bills, then?"

"Yes. We have got one to stick up in the office window. Rather gruesome, isn't it?"

"Horrible," I said; and for a while we walked on in silence. Presently Bundy exclaimed: "By Jove! I had nearly forgotten. I have a message for you. It is from Japp. He is taking a distinguished American archaeologist for a personally conducted tour round the town to show him the antiquities, and he thought you might like to join the party."

"That is very good of him," said I. "It sounds as if it should be rather interesting."

"It will be," said Bundy. "Japp is an enthusiast in regard to architecture and ancient buildings, and he is quite an authority on the antiquities of this town. You'd better come. The American—his name is Willard—is going to charter a photographer to come round with us and take records of all the objects of interest, and we shall be able to get copies of any photographs that we want. What do you say?"

"When does the demonstration take place?"

"The day after tomorrow. We shall do the Cathedral in the morning and the castle and the town in the afternoon. Shall I tell Japp you will join the merry throng?"

"Yes, please; and convey my very warm thanks for the invitation."

"I will," said he, halting as we arrived at the office, "unless you would like to come in and convey the joyful tidings yourself."

"No," he replied, "I won't come in now. I will get home and change my boots."

"Yes, by Jingo!" Bundy agreed, with a rueful glance at his own delicate shoes. "Mudlarking calls for a special outfit. And I clean my own shoes; but I'd rather do that than face Mrs. Dunk."

With this he retired up the steps, and I turned homeward, deciding to profit by his last remark and forestall unfavourable comment by shedding my boots on the doormat.

CHAPTER X

WHICH DEALS WITH ANCIENT
MONUMENTS AND A BLUE BOAR

On arriving home, I found awaiting me a letter from Dr. Thorndyke suggesting—in response to a general invitation that I had given him some time previously—that he should come down on Saturday to spend the weekend with me. Of course, I adopted the suggestion with very great pleasure, not a little flattered at receiving so distinguished a guest; and now I was somewhat disposed to regret my engagement to attend Mr. Japp's demonstration. However, as Thorndyke was not due until lunch time, I should have an opportunity of modifying my arrangement, if necessary.

But, as events turned out, I congratulated myself warmly on not having missed the morning visit to the Cathedral. It was a really remarkable experience; and not the least interesting part of it to me was the revelation of the inner personality of my friend, Mr. Japp. That usually dry and taciturn man of business was transfigured in the presence of the things that he really loved. He glowed with enthusiasm; he exhaled the very spirit of mediaeval romance; at every pore he exuded strange and recondite knowledge. Obedient to his behest, the ancient building told the vivid story of its venerable past, presented itself in its rude and simple beginnings; exhibited the transformations that had marked the passing centuries; peopled itself with the illustrious departed, whose heirs we were and whose resting-places we looked upon; and became to us a living thing whose birth and growth we could watch, whose vicissitudes and changing conditions we could trace until they brought us to its august old age. Under his guidance we looked down the long vista of the past, from the time when simple masons scalloped the Norman capitals within, while illustrious craftsmen fashioned the wonderful west doorway, to that last upheaval that swept away the modern shoddy and restored to the old fabric its modest comeliness.

Architectural antiquities, however, are not the especial concern of this history, though they were not without a certain influence in its unfolding. Accordingly, I shall not follow our progress—attended by the indispensable photographic recording angel—through nave and aisles, form choir to transepts, and from tower to undercroft. At the close of a delightful morning I betook myself homeward, charged with new and varied knowledge, and with a cordial invitation to my guest to join the afternoon's expedition if he were archaeologically inclined.

Apparently he was, for when, shortly after his arrival, I conveyed the invitation to him he accepted at once.

"I always take the opportunity," said he, "of getting what is practically first-hand information. Your friend, Mr. Japp, is evidently an enthusiast; he has expert technical knowledge, and he has apparently filled in his detail by personal investigation. A man like that can tell you more in an hour than guidebooks could tell you in a lifetime. We had better get a large-scale map of the town to enable us to follow the description, unless you have one."

"I haven't," said I, "but we can get one on the way to the rendezvous. You got my report, I suppose?"

"Yes," he replied, "I got it yesterday. That, in fact, was what determined me to come down. The discovery of that bag upon the shore dispels to some extent the ambiguity of our data. The finding of the brooch did not enlighten us much. It might simply have been dropped and picked up by some casual wayfarer. In fact, that is what the appearances suggested, for it is manifestly improbable that a person who had committed a crime would take the risk of pawning the product of robbery with violence in the very neighbourhood where the crime had been committed, and after an interval of time which would allow of the hue and cry having already been raised. Your sergeant is probably right in assuming that the man with the mole had nothing to do with the affair. But the finding of this bag is a different matter. It connects that disappearance with the river and it offers a strong suggestion of crime."

"Don't you think it possible that she might have fallen into the river accidentally?" I asked.

"It is possible," he admitted. "But that is where the significance of the brooch comes in. If she had fallen into the river from some wharf or pier, there does not seem to be any reason why the brooch should have become detached and fallen on land—as it apparently did. The finding of the bag where it had been thrown up by the river, and of the brooch on shore, suggests a struggle on land previous to the fall into the water. You don't happen, I suppose, to know what the bag contained?"

"I don't—excepting the packet of tablets that I gave her. When the bag was found, it was empty; at least, it contained only the handkerchief, as I mentioned in my report."

"Yes," he said reflectively. "By the way, I must compliment you on those reports. They are excellent, and with regard to this one, there are two or three rather curious circumstances. First, as to the packet of tablets. You mention that it had not been unwrapped and that, when it was found, the paper was quite clean. Therefore it had never been in the water. Therefore it had been taken out of the bag—by somebody with moderately clean hands—before the latter was dropped into the river; and it must have been thrown away on the shore above highwater mark. Incidentally, since the disappearance occurred—presumably—on the evening of the 26th of April, and the packet was found on the 7th of May, it had been lying on the shore for a full ten days. Perhaps there is nothing very remarkable in that; but the point is that Mrs. Frood was carrying the bag in her hand and she would almost certainly have dropped it if there had been any struggle. How, then, did the bag come to be in the river, and how came some of its contents to be found on the shore clean and free from any traces of submersion?"

"We can only suppose," said I, with an inward shudder—for the discussion of these hideous details made my very flesh creep—"that the murderer picked up the bag when he had thrown the body into the river, took out any articles of value, if there were any, and threw the rest on the shore."

"Yes," agreed Thorndyke, a little doubtfully, "that would seem to be what happened. And in that case, we should have to assume that the place where the packet was found was, approximately, the place where the crime was committed. For, as the packet was never immersed, it could not have been carried to that place by the tide, and one cannot think of any other agency by which it could have been moved. Its clean and unopened condition seems to exclude human agency. The question then naturally arises, Is the place where the packet was found, a place at, or near, which the tragedy could conceivably have occurred? What do you say to that?"

I considered for a few moments, recalling the intricate and obscure approach of the shore and the absence of anything in the nature of a public highway.

"I can only say," I replied at length, "that it seems perfectly inconceivable that Mrs. Frood could have been at that place, or even near it, unless she went there for some specific purpose—unless, for instance, she were lured there in some way. It is a place that is, I should say, unknown to any but the waterside people."

"We must go there and examine the place carefully," said he, "for if it is, as you say, a place to which no one could imaginably have strayed by chance, that fact has an important evidential bearing."

"Do you think it quite impossible that the package could have been carried to that place and dropped there?"

"Not impossible, of course," he replied, "but I can think of no reasonably probable way in which it could have happened, supposing the murderer to have pocketed it, and afterwards to have thrown it away. That would be a considered and deliberate act; and it is almost inconceivable that he should not have opened the packet to see what was inside, and that he should have dropped it on the dry beach when the river was close at hand. Remember that the bag was found quite near, and that it had been in the water."

"And assuming the crime to have been committed at that place, what would it prove?"

"In the first place," he replied, "it would pretty definitely exclude the theory of accidental death. Then it would suggest at least a certain amount of premeditation, since the victim would have had, as you say, to be enticed to that unlikely spot. And it would suggest that the murderer was a person acquainted with the locality."

"One of the waterside people," said I. "They are a pretty shady lot, but I don't see why any of them should want to murder her."

"It is not impossible," said he. "She was said to be shopping in Chatham, and she might have had a well-filled purse and allowed it to be seen. But that is mere speculation. The fact is that we have no data at present. We know practically nothing about Mrs. Frood. We can't say if she had any secret enemies, or if there was anyone who might have profited by her death or have had any motive for making away with her."

"We know something about her husband," said I, "and that he has disappeared in a rather mysterious fashion; and that his disappearance coincides with that of his wife."

"Yes," Thorndyke agreed, "those are significant facts. But we mustn't lose sight of the legal position. Until the body is recovered, there is no evidence of death. Until the death is proved, no charge of murder can be sustained. When the body is found it will probably furnish some evidence as to how the death occurred, if it is recovered within a reasonable time. As a matter of fact, it is rather remarkable that it has not yet been found. The death occurred—presumably—nearly a fortnight ago. Considering how very much frequented this river is, it is really rather unaccountable that the body has not come to light. But I suppose it is time that we started for the rendezvous."

I looked at my watch and decided that it was, and we accordingly set forth in the direction of the office, which was the appointed meeting-place, calling at a stationer's to provide ourselves each with a map. We chose the six inch town plan, which contained the whole urban area, including the winding reaches of the river, folding them so as to show at an opening the peninsula on which the city of Rochester is built.

"A curious loop of the river, this," said Thorndyke, scanning the map as we went along. "Rather like that of the Thames at the Isle of Dogs. You notice that there are quite a number of creeks on the low shore at both sides. Those will be places to watch. A floating body has rather a tendency to get carried into shallow creeks and to stay there. But I have no doubt the longshoremen are keeping an eye on them as a reward has been offered. Perhaps we might be able to go down and have a look at the shore when we have finished our perambulation of the town."

"I don't see why not," I replied, though, to tell the truth, I was not very keen on this particular exploration. To Thorndyke this quest was just an investigation to be pursued with passionless care and method. To me it was a tragedy that would colour my whole life. To him, Angelina was but a missing woman whose disappearance had to be explained by patient inquiry. To me she was a beloved friend whose loss would leave me with a life-long sorrow. Of course, he was not aware of this; he had no suspicion of the shuddering horror that his calm, impersonal examination of the evidential details produced in me. Nor did I intend that he should. It was my duty and my privilege to give him what assistance I could, and keep my emotions to myself.

"You will bear in mind," said he, as we approached the office, "that my connexion with the case of Mrs. Frood is not to be referred to. I am simply a friend staying with you for a day or two."

"I won't forget," said I, "though I don't quite see why it should matter."

"It probably doesn't matter at all," he replied. "But one never knows. Facts which might readily be spoken of before a presumably disinterested person might be withheld from one who was known to be collecting evidence for professional purposes. At any rate, I make it a rule to keep out of sight as far as possible."

These observations brought us to the office, where we found our three friends together with a young man, who was apparently acting as deputy during the absence of the partners, and the photographer. I presented Thorndyke to my friends, and when the introduction had been made Mr. Japp picked up his hat, and turned to the deputy.

"You know where to find me, Stevens," he said, "if I should be really wanted—really, you understand. But I don't particularly want to be found. Shall we start now? I propose to begin at the bridge, follow the Highstreet as far as Eastgate House, visit Restoration House, trace the city wall on the southwest side, and look over the castle. By that time we shall be ready for tea. After tea we can trace the north-east part of the wall and the gates that opened through it, and that will finish our tour of inspection."

Hereupon the procession started, Mr. Japp and his guest leading, Thorndyke, Bundy, and I following, and the photographer bringing up the rear.

"Let me see," said Bundy, looking up at Thorndyke with a sort of pert shyness, "weren't you down here a week or two ago?"

"Yes," replied Thorndyke; "and I think I had the honour of being inspected by you while I was reading your proclamation respecting a certain lost key."

"You had," said Bundy; "in fact, I may say that you raised false hopes in my partner and me. We thought you were going to find it."

"What, for ten shillings!" exclaimed Thorndyke.

"We would have raised the fee if you had made a firm offer," said Bundy, removing his monocle to polish it with his handkerchief. "It was a valuable key. Belonged to a gate that encloses part of the city wall."

"Indeed!" said Thorndyke. "I don't wonder you were anxious about it considering what numbers of dishonest persons there are about. Ha! Here is the bridge. Let us hear what Mr. Japp has to say about it."

Mr. Japp's observations were concise. Having cast a venomous glance at the unlovely structure, he turned his back on it and remarked acidly: "That is the new bridge. It is, as you see, composed of iron girders. It is not an antiquity, and I hope it never will be. Let us forget it and go on to the Guildhall." He strode forward doggedly and Bundy turned to us with a grin.

"Poor old Japp," said he, "he does hate that bridge. He has an engraving of the old stone one in his rooms, and I've seen him stand in front of it and groan. And really you can't wonder. It is an awful come-down. Just think what the town must have looked like from across the river when that stone bridge was standing."

Here we halted opposite the Guildhall, and when we had read the inscription, admired the magnificent ship weathercock—said to be a model of the Rodney—and listened to Japp's observations on the architectural features of the building, the photographer was instructed to operate on its exterior while we entered to explore the Justice Room and examine the portraits. From the Guildhall we passed on to the Corn Exchange, the quaint and handsome overhanging clock of which had evidently captured Mr. Willard's fancy.

"That clock," said he, "is a stroke of genius. It gives a character to the whole street. But what in creation induced your City Fathers to allow that charming little building to be turned into a picture theatre?"

Japp shook his head and groaned. "You may well ask that," said he, glaring viciously at the inane posters and the doorway, decorated in the film taste. "If good Sir Cloudesley Shovel, who gave it to the town, could rise from his grave and look at it, now he'd—bah! The crying need of this age is some means of protecting historic buildings from town councils. To these men an ancient building is just old-fashioned—out-of-date; a thing to be pulled down and replaced by something smart and up-to-date in the corrugated iron line." He snorted fiercely, and as the photographer dismounted his camera, he turned and led the way up the street. I lingered to help the photographer with his repacking, and meanwhile Thorndyke and Bundy walked on together, chatting amicably and suggesting to my fancy an amiable mastiff accompanied by a particularly well-groomed fox terrier.

"Do you usually give your patients a weekend holiday?" Bundy was inquiring as I overtook them.

"I haven't any patients," replied Thorndyke. "My medical practice is conducted mostly in the Law Courts."

"Good gracious!" exclaimed Bundy. "Do you mean that you live by resuscitating moribund jurymen and fattening up murderers for execution, and that sort of thing?"

"Not at all," replied Thorndyke. "Nothing so harmless. I am what is known as a Medical Expert. I give opinions on medical questions that affect legal issues."

"Then you are really a sort of lawyer?"

"Yes. A medico-legal hybrid; a sort of centaur or merman, with a doctor's head and a lawyer's tail."

"Well," said Bundy, "there are some queer professions; I once knew a chap in the furniture trade who described himself as a 'worm-eater'—drilled worm-holes in faked antiques, you know."

"And what," asked Thorndyke, "might be the analogy that you are suggesting? You don't propose to associate me with the diet of worms, I hope."

"Certainly not," said Bundy, "though I suppose your practice is sometimes connected with exhumations. But I was thinking that you must know quite a lot about crime."

"A good deal of my practice is concerned with criminal cases," Thorndyke admitted.

"Then you will be rather interested in our local mystery. Has the doctor told you about it?"

"You mean the mystery of the disappearing lady? But of what interest should it be to me? I was not acquainted with her."

"I meant a professional interest. But I suppose you are not taking a 'bus-man's holiday': don't want to be bothered with mysteries that don't concern you. Still, I should like to hear your expert opinion on the case."

"You mistake my functions," said Thorndyke. "A common witness testifies to facts known to himself. An expert witness interprets facts presented to him by others. Present me your facts, and I will try to give you an interpretation of them."

"But there are no facts. That is what constitutes the mystery."

"Then there is nothing to interpret. It is a case for the police, and not for the scientific expert."

Here our conversation was interrupted by our arrival at the House of the Six Poor Travellers, and by a learned disquisition by Japp on the connotation of the word Proctor—which, it appeared, was sometimes used in the Middle Ages in the sense of a cadger or swindler. Thence we proceeded to Eastgate House, where Japp mounted his hobby and discoursed impressively on the subject of ceilings, taking as his text a specimen modelled *in situ*, and bearing the date 1590.

"The fellow who put up that ceiling," said he, "took his time about it, no doubt. But his work has lasted three hundred and fifty years. That is the best way to save time. Your modern plasterer will have his ceiling up in a jiffy; and it will be down in a jiffy, and to do all over again. And never worth looking at at all."

Mr. Willard nodded. "It is very true," said he. "What is striking me in looking at all this old work is the great economy of time that is effected by taking pains and using good material, to say nothing of the beauty of the things created."

"If he goes on talking like that," whispered Bundy, "Japp'll kiss him. We must get them out of this."

Mercifully—if such a catastrophe was imminent—the ceiling discourse brought our inspection here to an end. From Eastgate House we went back to the Maidstone-road, and when we had inspected Restoration House, began to trace out the site of the city wall, which Thorndyke carefully marked on his map, to Japp's intense gratification. This perambulation brought us to the castle—which was dealt with rather summarily, as Mr. Willard had already examined it—and we then returned to the office for tea, which Bundy prepared and served with great success in his own sitting-room, while Japp dotted in with red ink on Thorndyke's map the entire city wall, including the part which we had yet to trace; and ridiculously small the ancient city looked when thus marked out on the modern town.

After tea we retraced our steps to the site of the East Gate, and, having inspected a large fragment of the wall at the end of an alley, traced its line across the Highstreet, and then proceeded down Free School-lane to the fine angle-bastion at the northern corner of the lane. Thence we followed the scanty indications as far as the site of the North Gate, and thereafter through a confused and rather unlovely neighbourhood until, on the edge of the marshes, we struck into a narrow lane, enclosed by a dilapidated tarred fence, a short distance along which we came to a closed gate, which I recognized as the one through which I had passed with Bundy on the day when we were made acquainted with the tragic history of Bill the Bargee. As Japp unlocked the gate and admitted us to the space of waste land, Bundy remarked to Thorndyke: "That is the gate that the missing key belonged to. You see there is no harm done so far. The wall is still there."

"Yes," said Thorndyke, "and not much improved in appearance by your builders' attentions. Those patches suggest the first attempts of an untalented dental student at conservation."

"They are rather a disfigurement," said Japp. "But the men had to have a job found for them, and that is the result. Perhaps they won't show so much in the photograph."

While the photographer was setting up his camera and making the exposure, Japp explained the relation of this piece of wall to the North Gate and the Gate that faced the bridge, and marked its position on Thorndyke's map.

"And that," he continued, "concludes our perambulation. The photographer is chartered by Mr. Willard, but I understand that we are at liberty to secure copies of the photographs, if we want them. Is that not so, Mr. Willard?"

"Surely," was the cordial reply; "only I stipulate that they shall be a gift from me, and I shall ask a favour in return. If there is a plate left, I should like to have a commemorative group taken, so that when I recall this pleasant day, I can also recall the pleasant society in which I spent it."

We all acknowledged the kindly compliment with a bow, and as the photographer announced that he had a spare plate, we grouped ourselves against a portion of undisfigured wall, removed our hats, and took up easy and graceful postures on either side of Mr. Willard. When the exposure had been made, and the photographer proceeded to pack up his apparatus, Thorndyke tendered his very hearty thanks to Mr. Japp and his friend for their hospitality.

"It has been a great privilege," said he, "to be allowed to share in the products of so much study and research, and I assure you it is far from being unappreciated. Whenever I revisit Rochester—which I hope to do before long—I shall think of you gratefully, and of your very kind and generous friend, Mr. Willard."

Our two hosts made suitable acknowledgments; and while these compliments were passing, I turned to Bundy.

"Can we get down to the shore from here?" I asked. "Thorndyke was saying that he would like to have a look at the river. If it is accessible from here we might take it on the way home."

"It isn't difficult to get at," replied Bundy. "If he wants to get a typical view of the river with the below-bridge traffic, by far the best place is Blue Boar Pier. It isn't very far, and it is on your way home—more or less. I'll show you the way there if you like. Japp is dining with Willard, so he won't want me."

I accepted the offer gladly, and as the exchange of compliments seemed to be completed and our party was moving towards the gate, I tendered my thanks for the day's entertainment and bade my hosts farewell, explaining that we were going riverwards. Accordingly we parted at the gate, Japp and Willard turning towards the town, while Thorndyke, Bundy, and I retraced our steps towards the marshes.

At the bottom of the lane Bundy paused to explain the topography. "That path," said he, "leads to Gas House road and the marshes by the North Shore. But there isn't much to see there. If we take this other track we shall strike Blue Boar-lane, which will take us to the pier. From there we can get a view of the whole bend of the river right across to Chatham."

Thorndyke followed the description closely with the aid of his map, marking off our present position with a pencil. Then we struck into a rough cart-track, with the wide stretch of the marshes on our left, and, following this, we presently came out into the lower part of Blue Boar-lane and turned our faces towards the river. We had not gone far when I observed a man approaching whose appearance seemed to be familiar. Bundy also observed him, for he exclaimed: "Why, that is old Cobbledick! Out of uniform, too. Very irregular. I shall have to remonstrate with him. I wonder what he has been up to. Prowling about the river bank in search of clues, I expect. And he'll suspect us of being on the same errand."

Bundy's surmise appeared to be correct, for as the sergeant drew nearer and recognized us, his face took on an expression of shrewd inquiry. But I noticed with some surprise that his curiosity seemed to be principally concerned with Thorndyke, at whom he gazed with something more than common attention. Under the circumstances I should have passed him with a friendly greeting, but he stopped, and, having wished me "Good evening," said: "Could I have a few words with you, Doctor?" upon which I halted, and Thorndyke and Bundy walked on slowly. The sergeant looked after them, and, turning his back to them, drew from his pocket with a mysterious air a small dirty brown bundle, which he handed to me.

"I wanted you just to have a look at that," he said.

I opened out the bundle, though I had already tentatively recognized it. But when it was unrolled it was unmistakable. It was poor Angelina's scarf.

"I thought there couldn't be any doubt about it," the sergeant said cheerfully when I had announced the identification. "Your description was so clear and exact. Well, this gives us a pretty fair kick-off. You can see that it has been in the water—some time, too. So we know where to look for the body. The mysterious thing is, though, that we've still got to look for it. It ought to have come up on the shore days ago. And it hasn't. There isn't a longshoreman for miles up and down that isn't on the lookout for it. You can see them prowling along the seawalls and searching the creeks in their boats. I can't think how they can have missed it. The thing is getting serious."

"Serious?" I repeated.

"Well," he explained, "there's no need for me to point out to a medical gentleman like you that bodies don't last for ever, especially in mild weather such as we've been having, and in a river where the shore swarms with rats and shore-crabs. Every day that passes is making the identification more difficult."

The horrible suggestions that emerged from his explanation gave me a sensation of physical sickness. I fidgeted uneasily, but still I managed to rejoin huskily: "There's the clothing, you know."

"So there is," he agreed; "and very good means of identification in an ordinary case—accidental drowning, for instance. But this is a criminal case. I don't want to have to depend on the clothing."

"Was the scarf found floating?" I asked, a little anxious to change the subject to one less gruesome.

"No," he replied. "It was on the shore by the small creek just below Blue Boar Pier, under an empty fish-trunk. One of the Customs men from the watch-house found it. He noticed the trunk lying out on the shore as he was walking along and went out to see if there was anything in it. Then, when he found it was empty, he turned it over, and there was the scarf. He recognized it at once—there's a list of the articles stuck up on the watch-house—and kept it to bring to me. But it happened that I came down here—as I do every day—just after he'd found it. But I mustn't keep you here talking, though I'm glad I met you and got your confirmation about this scarf."

He smiled benignly and raised his hat, whereupon I wished him "Good evening" and went on my way with a sigh of relief. He was a pleasant, genial man, but his matter-of-fact way of looking at this tragedy that had eaten so deeply into my peace of mind, was to me positively harrowing. But, of course, he did not understand my position in the case.

"Well," said Bundy, when I hurried up, "what's the news? Old Cobbledick was looking mighty mysterious. And wasn't he interested in us? Why he's gazing after us still. Has he had a bite? Because if he hasn't, I have. Some beastly mosquito."

"Don't rub it," said Thorndyke, as Bundy clapped his hand to his cheek. "Leave it alone. We'll put a spot of ammonia or iodine on it presently."

"Very well," replied Bundy, with a grimace expressive of resignation. "I am in the hands of the Faculty. What sort of fish was it that Isaak Walton Cobbledick had hooked? Or is it a secret?"

"I don't think there is any secrecy about it," said I. "One of the Customs men has found Mrs. Frood's scarf," and I repeated what the sergeant had told me as to the circumstances.

"It is a gruesome affair," said Bundy, "this search for these ghastly relics. Look at those ghouls down on the shore there. I suppose that is the fish-trunk."

As he spoke, we came out on the shore to the right of the pier and halted to survey the rather unlovely prospect. Outside the stunted sea-wall a level stretch of grey-green grass extended to the spring high-water mark, beyond which a smooth sheet of mud—now dry and covered with multitudinous cracks—spread out to the slimy domain of the ordinary tides. At the edge of the dry mud lay a derelict fish-trunk around which a group of bare-legged boys had gathered—and all along the shore, on the faded grass, on the dry mud and wading in the soft slime, the human water-rats were to be seen, turning over drift-rubbish, prying under stranded boats or grubbing in the soft mud. Hard by, on the grass near the sea-wall, an old ship's long-boat had been hauled up above tide-marks to a permanent berth and turned into a habitation by the erection in it of a small house. A short ladder gave access to it from without and the resident had laid down a little causeway of flat stones leading to the wall.

"Mr. Noah seems to be at home," observed Bundy, as we approached the little amphibious residence to inspect it. He pointed to a thin wisp of smoke that issued from the iron chimney; and, almost as he spoke, the door opened and an old man came out into the open stern-sheets of the boat with a steaming tin pannikin in his hand. His appearance fitted his residence to a nicety; for whereas the latter appeared to have been constructed chiefly from driftwood and wreckage, his costume suggested a collection of assorted marine salvage, with a leaning towards oil-skin.

"Mr. Noah" cast a malevolent glance at the searchers; then, having fortified himself with a pull at the pannikin, he turned a filmy blue eye on us.

"Good evening," said Thorndyke. "There seems to be a lot of business-doing here," and he indicated the fish-trunk and the eager searchers.

The old man grunted contemptuously. "Parcel of fules," said he, "a-busyin' theirselves with what don't concern 'em, and lookin' in the wrong place at that."

"Still," said Bundy, "they have found something here."

"Yes," the old man admitted, "they have. And that's why they ain't goin' to find anything more." He refreshed himself with a drink of—presumably—tea, and continued: "But the things is a-beginning to come up. It's about time she come up. But she won't come up here."

"Where do you suppose she will come up?" asked Bundy.

The old man regarded him with a cunning leer. "Never you mind where she'll come up," said he. "It ain't no consarn o' yourn."

"But how do you know where she'll come up?" Bundy persisted.

"I knows," the old scarecrow replied conclusively, "becos I do. Becos I gets my livin' along-shore, and it's my business for to know."

Having made this pronouncement, Mr. Noah looked inquiringly into the pannikin, emptied it at a draught, and, turning abruptly, retired into the ark, shutting the door after him with a care suited to its evident physical infirmity.

"I wonder if he really does know," said Bundy, as we walked away past the Customs watch-house.

"We can fairly take it that he doesn't," said Thorndyke, "seeing that the matter is beyond human calculation. But I have no doubt that he knows the places where bodies and other floating objects are most commonly washed ashore, and we may assume that he is proposing to devote his probably extensive leisure to the exploration of those places. It wouldn't be amiss to put the sergeant in communication with him."

"Probably the sergeant knows him," said I, "but I will mention the matter the next time I see him."

At the top of Blue Boar-lane Bundy halted and held out his hand to Thorndyke. "This is the parting of the ways," said he.

"Oh, no, it isn't," replied Thorndyke. "You've got to have your mosquito-bite treated. Never neglect an insect-bite, especially on the face."

"As a matter of fact," said I, "you have got to come and have dinner with us. We can't let you break up the party in this way."

"It's very nice of you to ask me," he began, hesitatingly, a little shy, as I guessed, of intruding on me and my visitor; but I cut him short, and, hooking my arm through his, led him off, an obviously willing captive. And if his presence hindered me from discussing with Thorndyke the problem that had occasioned his visit, that was of no consequence, since we should have the following day to ourselves; and he certainly contributed not a little to the cheerfulness of the proceedings. Indeed, I seemed to find in his high spirits something a little pathetic; a suggestion that the company or two live men—one of them a man of outstanding intellect—was an unusual treat, and that his life with old Japp and the predatory females might be a trifle dull. He took to Thorndyke amazingly, treating him with a sort of respectful cheekiness, like a schoolboy dining with a favourite head-master; while Thorndyke, fully appreciative of his irresponsible gaiety, developed a quiet humour and playfulness which rather took me by surprise. The solemn farce of the diagnosis and treatment of the mosquito bite was an instance; when Thorndyke, having seated the patient in the surgery chair and invested him with a large towel, covered the table with an assortment of preposterous instruments and bottles of reagents, and proceeded gravely to examine the bite through a lens until Bundy was as nervous as a cat, and then to apply the remedy with meticulous precision on the point of a fine sable brush.

It was a pleasant evening, pervaded by a sense of frivolous gaiety that was felt gratefully by the two elder revellers and was even viewed indulgently by Mrs. Dunk. As to Bundy, his high spirits flowed unceasingly—but, I may add, with faultless good manners—and when, at length, he took his departure, he shook our hands with a warmth which, again, I found slightly pathetic.

"I *have* had a jolly evening!" he exclaimed, looking at me with a queer sort of wistfulness. "It has been a red-letter day," and with this he turned abruptly and walked away.

We watched him from the threshold, bustling jauntily along the pavement; and as I looked at him, there came unbidden to my mind the recollection of that other figure that I had watched from this same threshold, walking away in the fading light—walking into the fog that was to swallow her up and hide her from my sight for ever.

From these gloomy reflections I was recalled by Thorndyke's voice.

"A nice youngster, that, Strangeways. Gay and sprightly, but not in the least shallow. I often think that there was a great deal of wisdom in that observation of Spencer's, that happy people are the greatest benefactors to mankind. Your friend,

Bundy, has helped me to renew my youth; and who could have done one a greater service?"

CHAPTER XI

THE MAN WITH THE MOLE

When I had seen my guest off by the last train on Saturday night, I walked homeward slowly, cogitating on the results of his visit. It seemed to me that they were very insignificant. In the morning we had explored the piece of shore on which the bag and the box of tablets had been found, making our way to it by the narrow and intricate alleys which seemed to be the only approach; and we had reached the same conclusion. It was an impossible place.

"If we assume," said Thorndyke, "as we must, on the apparent probabilities, that the tragedy occurred here, we must assume that there are some significant circumstances that are unknown to us. Mrs. Frood could not have strayed here by chance. We can think of no business that could have brought her here; and since she was neither a child nor a fool, she could not have been enticed into such an obviously sinister locality without some plausible pretext. There is evidently something more than meets the eye."

"Something, you mean, connected with her past life and the people she knew?"

"Exactly. I am having careful inquiries made on the subject in likely quarters, including the various theatrical photographers. They form quite a promising' source of information, as they are not only able to give addresses but they can furnish us with photographs of members of the companies who would have been colleagues, and, at least, acquaintances."

"If you come across any photographs of Mrs. Frood," I said, "I should like to see them."

"You shall," he replied. "I shall certainly collect all I can get, on the chance that they may help us with the identification of the body; which may possibly present some difficulty."

Here I was reminded of Cobbledick's observations, and, distasteful as they were, I repeated them to Thorndyke.

"The sergeant is quite right," said he. "This is apparently a criminal case, involving a charge of wilful murder. To sustain that charge, the prosecution will have to produce incontestable evidence as to the identity of the deceased. Clothing alone would not be sufficient to secure a conviction. The body would have to be identified. And the sergeant's anxiety is quite justified. Have you had any experiences of bodies recovered from the water?"

"Yes," I replied; "and I don't like to think of them." I shuddered as I spoke, for his question had recalled to my memory the incidents of a professional visit to Poplar Mortuary. There rose before my eyes the picture of a long black, box with a small glass window in the lid, and of a thing that appeared at that window; a huge, bloated, green and purple thing, with groups or radiating wrinkles, and in the middle a button-like object that looked like the tip of a nose. It was a frightful picture; and yet I knew that when the river that we stood by should give up its dead—

I put the thought away with a shiver and asked faintly: "About the man Frood. Don't you think that his disappearance throws some light on the mystery?"

"It doesn't throw much light," replied Thorndyke, "because nothing is known about it. Obviously the coincidence in time of the disappearance, added to the known character of the man and his relations with his wife, make him an object of deep suspicion. His whereabouts will have to be traced and his time accounted for. But I have ascertained that the police know nothing about him, and my own inquiries have come to nothing, so far. He seems to have disappeared without leaving a trace. But I shall persevere. Your object—and mine—is to clear up the mystery, and if a crime has been committed, to bring the criminal to justice."

So that was how the matter stood; and it did not appear to me that much progress had been made towards the elucidation of the mystery. As to the perpetrator of that crime, he remained a totally unknown quantity, unless the deed could be fixed on the missing man, Frood. And so matters remained for some days. Then an event occurred which seemed to promise some illumination of the darkness; a promise that it failed to fulfil.

It was about a week after Thorndyke's visit. I had gone out after lunch to post off to him the set of photographs which had been delivered to me by the photographer with my own set. I went into the post-office to register the package, and here I found Bundy in the act of sending off a parcel. When we had transacted our business we strolled out together, and he asked: "What are you going to do now, Doctor?"

"I was going to walk down to Blue Boar Pier," said I, "to see if anything further has been discovered."

"Should I be in the way if I walked there with you?" he asked. "I've got nothing to do at the moment. But perhaps you would rather go alone. You've had a good deal of my society lately."

"Not more than I wanted, Bundy," I answered. "You are my only chum here, and you are not unappreciated, I can assure you."

"It's nice of you to say that," he rejoined, with some emotion. "I've sometimes felt that I was rather thrusting my friendship on you."

"Then don't ever feel it again," said I. "It has been a bit of luck for me to find a man here whom I could like and chum in with."

He murmured a few words of thanks, and we walked on for a while without speaking. Presently, as we turned into the lane by the Blue Boar Inn, he said, a little hesitatingly. "Don't you think, Doc, that it is rather a mistake to let your mind run so much on this dreadful affair? It seems to be always in your thoughts. And it isn't good for you to think so much about it. I've noticed you quite a lot, and you haven't been the same since—since it happened. You have looked worried and depressed."

"I haven't felt the same," said I. "It has been a great grief to me."

"But," he urged, "don't you think you should try to forget it? After all, she was little more than an acquaintance."

"She was a great deal more than that, Bundy," said I. "While she was alive, I would not admit even to myself that my feeling towards her was anything more than ordinary friendship. But it was; and now that she is gone, there can be no harm in recognizing the fact, or even in confessing it to you, as we are friends."

"Do you mean, Doc," he said in a low voice, "that you were in love with her?"

"That is what it comes to, I suppose," I answered. "She was the only woman I had ever really cared for."

"And did she know it?" he asked.

"Of course she didn't," I replied indignantly. "She was a lady and a woman of honour. Of course she never dreamed that I cared for her, or she would never have let me visit her."

For a few moments he walked at my side in silence. Then he slipped his arm through mine, and pressing it gently with his hand, said softly and very earnestly: "I'm awfully sorry, Doc. It is frightfully hard luck for you, though it couldn't have been much better even if—but it's no use talking of that. I *am* sorry, old chap. But still, you know, you ought to try to put it away. *She* wouldn't have wished you to make yourself unhappy about her."

"I know," said I. "But I feel that the office belongs to me, who cared most for her, to see that the mystery of her death is cleared up and that whoever wronged her is brought to justice."

He made no reply to this but walked at my side with his arm linked in mine, meditating with an air of unwonted gravity.

When we reached the head of the pier the place was deserted excepting for one man; a sea-faring person, apparently, who was standing with his back to us, studying intently the bills that were stuck on the wall of the lookout. As we were passing, my eye caught the word "Wanted" on a new bill, and pausing to read it over the man's shoulder, I found that it was a description of the unknown man—"with a mole on the left side of his nose"—who had pawned the opal brooch. Bundy read it, too, and as we walked away he remarked: "They are rather late in putting out those bills. I should think that gentleman will have left the locality long ago, unless he was a local person," an opinion with which I was disposed to agree.

After a glance round the shore and at "the Ark"—which was closed but of which the chimney emitted a cheerful smoke suggestive of culinary activities on the part of "Mr. Noah "—we sauntered up past the head of the creek, along the rough path by the foundry, and out upon the upper shore.

"Well, I'm hanged!" exclaimed Bundy, glancing back at the watch-house, "that chap is still reading that bill. He must be a mighty slow reader, or he must find it more thrilling than I did. Perhaps he knows somebody with a mole on his nose."

I looked back at the motionless figure; and at that moment another figure appeared and advanced, as we had done, to look over the reader's shoulder.

"Why, that looks like old Cobbledick—come to admire his own literary productions. There's vanity for you. Hallo! What's up now?"

As Bundy spoke, the reader had turned to move away and had come face to face with the sergeant. For a moment both men had stood stock still; then there was a sudden, confused movement on both sides, with the final result that the sergeant fell, or was knocked, down and that the stranger raced off, apparently in our direction. He disappeared at once, being hidden from us by the foundry buildings, and we advanced towards the end of the fenced lane by which we had come, to intercept him, waiting by the edge of a trench or dry ditch.

"Here he comes," said Bundy, a trifle nervously, as rapid footfalls became audible in the narrow, crooked lane. Suddenly the man appeared, running furiously, and as he caught sight of us, he whipped out a large knife, and, flourishing it with a menacing air, charged straight at us. I watched an opportunity to trip him up; but as he approached Bundy pulled me back with such energy that he and I staggered on the brink of the ditch, capsized, and rolled together to the bottom. By the time we had managed to scramble up, the man had disappeared into the wilderness of sheds, scrap-heaps, derelict boilers, and stray railway-waggons that filled the area of land between the foundry and the coal-wharves and jetties.

"Come on, Bundy," said I, as my companion stood tenderly rubbing various projecting portions of his person; "we mustn't lose sight of him."

But Bundy showed no enthusiasm; and at this moment a rapid crescendo of heavy footfalls was followed by the emergence of the sergeant, purple-faced and panting, from the end of the lane.

"Which way did he go?" gasped Cobbledick.

I indicated the wilderness, briefly explaining how the fugitive had escaped us, whereupon the sergeant started forward at a lumbering trot and we followed. But it was an unfavourable hunting-ground, for the bulky litter—the heaps of coal-dust, the wagons, the cranes, the piles of condemned machinery, mingled with clumps of bushes—gave the fugitive every opportunity to disappear. And, in fact, he had disappeared without leaving a trace. Presently we came out on a wharf beside which a schooner was berthed; a trim-looking little craft with a white underbody and black top-sides, bearing a single big yard on her fore-mast and the name *Anna* on her counter. She was all ready for sea and was apparently waiting for high water, for her deck was all clear and a man on it was engaged in placidly coiling a rope on the battened hatch while another watched him from the door of the deckhouse. On this peaceful scene the sergeant burst suddenly and hailing the rope-coiler demanded:

"Have you seen a man run past here?"

The mariner dropped the rope, and looking up drowsily, repeated: "Have I seen a mahn?"

"Yes, a sea-faring man with a mole on his nose."

The mariner brightened up perceptibly. "Please?" said he.

"A sailor-man with a mole on his nose."

"Ach!" exclaimed the mariner. "Vos it tied on?"

"Tied on!" the sergeant snorted impatiently. "Of course it wasn't. It grew there."

Here the second mariner apparently asked some question, for our friend turned to him and replied: "*Ja. Maulwurf*," on which I heard Bundy snigger softly.

"No, no," I interposed; "not that sort of mole. A kind of wart, you know. *Das Mal.*"

On this the second mariner fell out of the deckhouse door, and the pair burst into yells of laughter, rolling about the deck in agonies of mirth, wiping their eyes, muttering *Maulwurf, Maulwurf,* and screeching like demented hyenas.

"Well," Cobbledick demanded impatiently, "have you seen him?"

The mariner shook his head. "No," he replied, shakily. "I have not any mahn seen."

"Well, why couldn't you say so at first" the sergeant growled.

"I vos zo zubbraised," the mariner explained, glancing at his shipmate; and the pair burst out into fresh howls of laughter.

The sergant turned away with a sort of benevolent contempt and ran his eye despairingly over the wilderness. "I suppose we had better search this place," said he, "though he is pretty certain to have got away."

At his suggestion we separated and examined the possible hiding-places systematically, but, of course, with no result. Once only I had a momentary hope that we had not lost our quarry, when the sergeant suddenly stooped and began cautiously to stalk an abandoned boiler surrounded by a clump of bushes; but when the grinning countenance of Bundy appeared at the opposite end and that reprobate crept out stealthily and proceeded to stalk the sergeant, the last hope faded.

"I certainly thought I saw someone moving in those bushes," said Cobbledick, with a disappointed air.

"So did Mr. Bundy," said I "You must have seen one another."

The sergeant glanced suspiciously at our colleague, but made no remark; and we continued our rather perfunctory search. At length we gave it up and slowly returned to the neighbourhood of the pier. By this time the tide had turned, and a few loiterers were standing about watching the procession of barges moving downstream on the ebb. Among them was a grave-looking, sandy-haired man who leaned against the watch-house, smoking reflectively as he surveyed the river. To this philosopher Cobbledick addressed himself, explaining, as he was in plain clothes:

"Good afternoon. I am a police officer and I am looking for a man who is described on that bill." Here he indicated the poster.

The philosopher turned a pale grey, and somewhat suspicious eye on him, and having removed his pipe, expectorated thoughtfully but made no comment on the statement.

"A sea-faring man," continued the sergeant, "with a mole on the left side of his nose." He looked enquiringly at the philosopher, who replied impassively:

"Nhm—nhm."

"Do you happen to have seen a man answering that description?"

"Nhm—nhm," was the slightly ambiguous reply.

"You *have* seen him?" the sergeant asked, eagerly.

"Aye."

"Do you know if he belongs to any of the craft that trade here?"

"Nhm—nhm."

"Do you happen to know which particular vessel he belongs to?"

"Aye," was the answer, accompanied by a grave nod.

"Can you tell me," the sergeant asked patiently, "which vessel that is, and where she is at present?"

Our friend replaced his pipe and took a long draw at it, gazing meditatively at a schooner which was moving swiftly down the river under the power of an auxiliary motor, and setting her sails as she went. I had noticed her already, and observed that she had a white underbody and black top-sides, and that she carried a single long yard on her fore-mast. At length our friend removed his pipe, expectorated, and nodded gravely at the schooner.

"Yon," said he, and replaced his pipe, as a precaution, I supposed, against unnecessary loquacity.

Cobbledick gazed wistfully at the receding schooner. "Pity," said he. "I should have liked to have a look at that fellow."

"You could get the schooner held up at Sheerness, couldn't you?" I asked.

"Yes; I could send a 'phone message to Garrison Point Fort. But, you see, she's a foreigner. Might make trouble. And he is probably not the man we want. After all, it's only a matter of a mole."

"Maulwurf," murmured Bundy.

"Yes," said the sergeant, with a faint grin; "those beggars were laughing at us. Well, it can't be helped."

We stood for a moment or two watching the schooner set one sail after another. Presently Bundy observed:

"Methinks, Sergeant, that Mr. Noah is trying to attract your attention."

We glanced towards the Ark, the tenant of which was seated in the stern-sheets, scrubbing a length of rusty chain. As he caught the sergeant's eye, he beckoned mysteriously, whereupon we descended the bank, and, picking our way across the muddy grass by his little causeway of stepping-stones, approached the foot of the short ladder.

"Well, Israel," said the sergeant, resting his hands on the gunwale of the old boat as he made a rapid survey of the interior, "giving the family plate a bit of a polish, eh?"

"Plate!" exclaimed the old man, holding up the chain, which, as I now saw, had a number of double hooks linked to it, "this ain't plate. 'Tis what we calls a creeper."

"A creeper," repeated the sergeant, looking at it with renewed interest. "Ha, yes, hm. A creeper, hey? Well, Israel, what's a-doing? Have you got something to show us?"

The old man laid down the creeper and the scrubbing-brush—which had a strong suggestion of salvage in its appearance—and moved towards the door of the Ark. "Come along inside," said he.

Cobbledick mounted the ladder and motioned me to follow, which I did, while Bundy discretely sauntered away and sat down on the bank. On entering, I observed that the Ark followed closely the constructional traditions. Like its classical prototype, it was "pitched with pitch, within and without," and was furnished with a single small window, let into the door and hermetically sealed.

Seeing that our host looked at me with some disfavour, the tactful sergeant hastened to make us known to one another.

"This is Dr. Strangeways, Israel. He was Mrs. Frood's doctor, and he knows all about this affair. This, Doctor, is Mr. Israel Bangs, the eminent long-shoreman, a sort of hereditary Grand Duke of the Rochester foreshore."

I bowed ceremoniously, and the Grand Duke acknowledged the introduction with a sour grin. Then, lifting the greasy lid of a locker, he dived into it and came to the surface, as it were, with a small shoe in his hand.

"What do you say to that?" he demanded, holding the shoe under the sergeant's nose. The sergeant said nothing, but looked at me; and I, suddenly conscious of the familiar sickening sensation, could do no more than nod in reply. Soiled, muddy and sodden as it was, the poor little relic instantly and vividly recalled the occasion when I had last seen it, then all trim and smart, peeping coyly beneath the hem of the neat brown skirt.

"Where did you find it, Israel?" asked Cobbledick.

"Ah," said Bangs, with a sly leer, "that's tellin', that is. Never you mind where I found it. There's the shoe."

"Don't be a fool, Israel," said the sergeant.' "What use do you suppose the shoe is to me if I don't know where you found it? I've got to put it in evidence, you know."

"You can put it where you like, so long as you pays for it," the old rascal replied, doggedly. "The findin' of it's my business."

There ensued a lengthy wrangle, but the sergeant, though patient and polite, was firm. Eventually Israel gave way.

"Well," he said, "if you undertakes not to let on to Sam Hooper or any of his lot, I'll tell you. I found it on the mud, side of the long crik betwixt Blue Boar Head and Gas-'us Point."

The sergeant made a note of the locality, and, after having sworn not to divulge the secret to Sam Hooper or any other of the shore-rat fraternity, and having ascertained that Israel had no further information to dispose of, rose to depart; and, I noticed that, as we passed out towards the ladder, he seemed to bestow a glance of friendly recognition on the creeper.

"Well," said Bundy, when we rejoined him, "what had Mr. Noah to say? I hope you remembered me kindly to my old friends, Shem, Ham, and Japhet."

"He has found one of Mrs. Frood's shoes," answered the sergeant, producing it from his pocket and offering it for inspection. Bundy glanced at it indifferently, and then remarked: "It seems to answer the description, but, for my part, I don't quite see the use of all this searching and prying. It only proves what we all know. There's no doubt that she fell into the river. The question is, how did she get there? It is not likely that it was an accident, and, if it wasn't, it must have been a crime. What we want to know is, who is the criminal?"

Cobbledick pocketed the shoe with an impatient gesture. "That's the way they always talk," said he. "They will always begin at the wrong end. The question, 'Who is the murderer?' does not arise until it is certain that there has been a murder; and it can't be certain that there has been a murder until it is certain that the missing person is dead. And that certainty can hardly be established until the body is found. But, in the meantime, these articles are evidence enough to justify us in making other inquiries, and they may give us a hint where to look for the body. They do, in fact. They suggest that the body is probably not very far away, and more likely to be upstream than down."

"I don't see how they do," said Bundy.

"I do," retorted the sergeant, "and that's enough for me."

Bundy, with his customary discretion, took this as closing the discussion, and further—as I guessed—surmising that the sergeant might wish to have a few words with me alone, took his leave of us when we reached the vicinity of the office.

"That is not a bad idea of old Israel's," said Cobbledick, when Bundy had gone. "The creeper, I mean."

"What about it?" I asked.

"You know what a creeper is used for, I suppose," said he. "In the old days, the revenue boats used to trail them along over the bottom in shallow water where they suspected that the smugglers had sunk their tubs. You see they couldn't always get a chance to land the stuff. Then they used to fill the spirits into a lot of little ankers or tubs, lash them together into a sort of raft and sink the raft close in-shore, on a dark night, in a marked place where their pals could go some other night and fish them up. Well the revenue cutters knew most of those places and used to go there and drift over them trailing creepers. Of course, if there were any tubs there, the creepers hooked on to the lashings and up they came."

"But what do you suppose is Israel's idea?" I asked. "Why, as the body ought to have come up long before this, and it hasn't, he thinks it has been sunk. It might have been taken up the river in a boat, and sunk in mid-stream with a weight of some sort. Or it might have got caught by a lost anchor or on some old moorings. That would account for its not coming up and for these oddments getting detached and drifting ashore. So old Israel is going to get to work with a creeper. I expect he spends his nights creeping over the likely spots, and that is what makes him so deuced secret about the place where he found that shoe. He reckons that the body is somewhere thereabouts."

I made no comment on this rather horrible communication. Of course, it was necessary that the body should be searched for, since its discovery was the indispensable condition of the search for the murderer. But I did not want to hear more of the dreadful details than was absolutely unavoidable.

When we reached the Guildhall, I halted and was about to take leave of the sergeant when he said, somewhat hesitatingly:

"Do you remember, Doctor, when you met me last Saturday, you had a gentleman with you?"

"I remember," said I.

"Now, I wonder if you would think I was taking a liberty if I were to ask what that gentleman's name was. I had an idea that I knew his face."

"Of course it wouldn't be a liberty," I replied. "His name is Thorndyke; Dr. John Thorndyke."

"Ah!" exclaimed Cobbledick, "I thought I couldn't be mistaken. It isn't the sort of face that one would forget. I once heard him give evidence at the Old Bailey. Wonderful evidence it was, too. Since then I've read reports of his investigations from time to time. He's a marvellous man. The way he has of raking up evidence from nowhere is perfectly astonishing. Did you happen to talk to him about this case at all?"

"Well, you see, Sergeant," I answered, rather evasively, "he had come down here for the weekend as my guest—"

"Exactly, exactly," Cobbledick interrupted, unconsciously helping me to avoid answering his question, "he came down for a rest and a change, and wouldn't want to be bothered with professional matters. Still, you know, I think he would be interested in this case. It is quite in his own line. It is a queer case; a very queer case in some respects."

"In what respects?" I asked.

It was Cobbledick's turn to be evasive. He had apparently said more than he had intended, and now drew in his horns perceptibly.

"Why," he replied, "when you come to think of—of the—er—the character of the lady, for instance. Why should anyone want to do her any harm? And then there is the mystery as to how it happened, and the place, and—in fact, there are a number of things that are difficult to understand. But I mustn't keep you standing here. If you should happen to see Dr. Thorndyke again, it might be as well to tell him about the case. It would be sure to interest him; and if he should, by any chance, want to know anything that you are not in a position to tell him, why, you know where I am to be found. I shouldn't want to make any secrets with him. And he might spot something that we haven't noticed."

I promised to follow the sergeant's advice, and, having bid him adieu, turned back, and walked slowly homeward. As I went I reflected profoundly on my conversation with Cobbledick; from which, as it seemed to me, two conclusions emerged. First, there were elements in this mystery that were unknown to me. I had supposed that the essence of the mystery was the mere absence of data. But it now appeared from the sergeant's utterances, and still more from his evasions, that he saw farther into the affair than I did; either because he had more facts, or because, by reason of his greater experience, the facts meant more to him than they did to me. The second conclusion was that he was in some way in difficulties; that he was conscious of an inability to interpret satisfactorily the facts that were known to him. His evident eagerness to get into touch with Thorndyke made this pretty clear; and the two conclusions together suggested a further question. How much did Thorndyke know? Did he know all that the sergeant knew? Did he perchance know more? From the scanty data with which I had supplied him, might he possibly have drawn some illuminating inferences that had carried his understanding of the case beyond either mine or Cobbledick's? It was quite possible. Thorndyke's great reputation rested upon his extraordinary power of inference and constructive reasoning from apparently unilluminating facts. The facts in this case seemed unilluminating enough. But they might not be so to him. And again I recalled how both he and the sergeant seemed to look to the finding of the body as probably furnishing the solution of the mystery.

CHAPTER XII

THE PRINTS OF A VANISHED HAND

Mr. Bundy's opinion that no particular significance attached to the finding of further relics of the missing woman was one that I was myself disposed to adopt. The disappearance of poor Angelina was an undeniable fact, and there seemed to be no doubt that her body had fallen, or been cast, into the river. On these facts, the recovery of further articles belonging to her, and presumably detached from the body, shed no additional light. From the body itself, whenever it should be surrendered by the river, one hoped that something fresh might be learned. But all that anyone could say was that Angelina Frood had disappeared, that her disappearance was almost certainly connected with a crime, and that the agents of that crime and their motives for committing it were alike an impenetrable mystery, a mystery that the finding of further detached articles tended in no way to solve.

I shall, therefore, pass somewhat lightly over the incidents of the succeeding discoveries, notwithstanding the keen interest in them displayed by Sergeant Cobbledick and even by Thorndyke. On Monday, the 25th of May, the second shoe was found (to Israel Bangs' unspeakable indignation) by Samuel Hooper of Foul Anchor Alley, who discovered it shortly after high-water, lying on the gridiron close to Gas-house Point, and brought it in triumph to the police station.

After this, there followed a long interval, occupied by a feverish contest between Israel Bangs and Samuel Hooper. But the luck fell to the experienced Israel. On Saturday, the 20th of June, that investigator, having grounded his boat below a wharf between Gas-house Point and the bridge, discovered a silver-headed hat-pin lying on the shore between two of the piles of the wharf. Its identity was unmistakable. The silver poppy-head that crowned the pin was no trade production that might have had thousands of indistinguishable fellows. It was an individual work wrought by an artist in metal, and excepting its fellow, there was probably not another like it in the world.

The discovery of this object roused a positive frenzy of search. The stretch of muddy shore between Gas-house Point and the bridge literally swarmed with human shore-rats, male and female, adult and juvenile. Every day, and all the day, excepting at high-water, Israel Bangs hovered in his oozy little basket of a boat on the extreme edge of the mud, scanning every inch of slime, and glowering fiercely at the poachers ashore who were raking over his preserves. But nothing came of it. Day after day passed. The black and odorous mud was churned up by countless feet; the pebbles were sorted out severally by innumerable filthy hands; every derelict pot, pan, box, or meat-tin was picked up again and again, and explored to its inmost recesses. But in vain. Not a single relic of any kind was brought to light by' all those searchings and grubbings in the mud. Presently the searchers began to grow discouraged. Some of them gave up the search; others migrated to the shore beyond the bridge, and were to be seen wading in the mud below the Esplanade, the cricket-ground, or the boat-building yards. So the month of June ran out, and the third month began. And still there was no sign of the body.

Meanwhile I watched the two professional investigators, and noted a certain similarity in their outlook and methods. Both were keenly interested in the discoveries; and both, I observed, personally examined the localities of the finds. The sergeant conducted me to each spot in turn, making appropriate, but not very illuminating, comments; and I perceived that he was keeping a careful account of time and place. So, too, with Thorndyke, who had now taken to coming down regularly each weekend. He visited each spot where anything had been found, marking it carefully on his map, together with a reference number, and inquiring minutely as to the character of the object, its condition, and the state of the tide and the hour of the day when it was discovered; all of which particulars he entered in his notebook under the appropriate reference number.

Both of my friends, too, expressed increasing surprise and uneasiness at the non-appearance of the body. The sergeant was really worried, and he expressed his sentiments in a tone of complaint as if he felt that he was not being fairly treated.

"It's getting very serious, Doctor," he protested.

"Nearly three months gone—three summer months, mind you—and not a sign of it. I don't like the look of things at all. This case means a lot to me. It's my chance. It's a detective-inspector's job, and if I bring it off it'll be a big feather in my cap. I want to get a conviction, and so far I haven't got the material for a coroner's verdict. I've half a mind to do a bit of creeping myself."

Thorndyke's observations on the case were much to the same effect. Discussing it one Saturday afternoon at the beginning of July, when I had met him at Strood Station and was walking with him into Rochester, he said:

"My feeling is that the crux of this case is going to be the question of identity—if the body ever comes to light. Of course, if it doesn't, there is no case: it is simply an unexplained disappearance. But if the body is found and is unrecognizable excepting by clothing and other extrinsic evidence, it will be hard to get a conviction even if the unrecognizable corpse should give some clue to the circumstances of death."

"I suppose," said I, "the police are searching for Nicholas Frood."

"I doubt it," he replied. "They are not likely to be wasting efforts to find a murderer when there is no evidence that a murder has been committed. What could they do if they did find him? The woman was not in his custody or even living with him. And his previous conduct is not relevant in the absence of evidence of his wife's death."

"You said you were making some inquiries yourself."

"So I am. And I am not without hopes of picking up his tracks. But that is a secondary matter. What we have to settle beyond the shadow of a doubt is the question, 'What has become of Angelina Frood? Is she dead' And, if she is, what was the cause and what were the circumstances of her death?' The evidence in our possession points to the conclusion that she is dead, and that she met her death by foul means. That is the belief that the known facts produce. But we have got to turn that belief into certainty. Then it will be time to inquire as to the identity of the criminal."

"Do you suppose the body would be unrecognizable now?"

"I feel no doubt that it would be quite unrecognizable by ordinary means if it has been in the water all this time. But it would still be identifiable in the scientific sense, if we could only obtain the necessary data. It could, for instance, be tested by the Bertillon measurements, if we had them; and it would probably yield fingerprints, clear enough to recognize, long after the disappearance of all facial character or bodily traits."

"Would it really?" I exclaimed.

"Certainly," he replied. "Even if the whole outer skin of the hand had come off bodily, like a glove, as it commonly does in long-submerged bodies, that glove-like cast would yield fairly clear fingerprints if property treated—with dilute formalin, for instance. And then the fingers from which the outer skin had become detached would still yield recognizable fingerprints, if similarly treated; for you must remember that the papillary ridges which form the fingerprint pattern, are in the true skin. The outer skin is merely moulded on them. But, unfortunately, the question is one of merely academic interest to us as we have no original fingerprints of Mrs. Frood's by which to test the body. The only method of scientific identification that seems to be available is that of anthropometric measurements, as employed by Bertillon."

"But," I objected, "the Bertillon system is based on the existence of a record of the measurements of the person to be identified. We have no record of the measurements of Mrs. Frood."

"True," he agreed. "But you may remember that Dr. George Bertillon was accustomed to apply his system, not only to suspected persons who had been arrested, but also to stray garments, hat, gloves, shoes, and so forth, that came into the possession of the police. But it is clear that, if such garments can be compared with a table of recorded measurements, they can be used as standards of comparison to determine the identity of a dead body. Of course, the measurements would have to be taken, both of the garments and of the body, by someone having an expert knowledge of anthropometrical methods."

"Of course," I agreed. "But it seems a sound method. I must mention it to Cobbledick. He has the undoubted shoes, and I have no doubt that he could get a supply of worn garments from Mrs. Gillow."

"Yes," said Thorndyke. "And, speaking of Mrs. Gillow reminds me of another point that I have been intending to inquire into. You mentioned to me that Mrs. Gillow told you, at the time of the disappearance, that she had been expecting a tragedy of some kind. She must have had some grounds for that expectation."

"She said it was nothing but a vague, general impression."

"Still, there must have been something that gave her that impression. Don't you think it would be well to question her a little more closely?"

"Perhaps it might," said I, not very enthusiastically. "We are close to the house now. We can call in and see her, if you like."

"I think we ought to leave no stone unturned," said he; and a minute or two later, when we arrived opposite the office, he remarked, looking across attentively at the two houses: "I don't see our friend Bundy's face at the window."

"No," I replied, "he is playing tennis somewhere up at the Vines. But here is Mrs. Gillow, herself, all dressed up and evidently going out visiting."

The landlady had appeared at the door just as we were crossing the road. Perceiving that we were bearing down on her, she paused, holding the door ajar. I ran up the steps, and having wished her "good afternoon" asked if she had time to answer one or two questions.

"Certainly," she replied, "though I mustn't stay long because I have promised to go to tea with my sister at Frinsbury. I usually go there on a Saturday. Perhaps we had better go into poor Mrs. Frood's room."

She opened the door of the sitting-room, and we all went in and sat down.

"I have been talking over this mysterious affair, Mrs. Gillow," said I, "with my friend, Dr. Thorndyke, who is a lawyer, and he suggested that you might be able to throw some light on it. You remember that you had had some forebodings of some sort of trouble or disaster."

"I had," she replied, dismally, "but that was only because she always seemed so worried and depressed, poor dear. And, of course, I knew about that good-for-nothing husband of hers. That was all. Sergeant Cobbledick asked me the same question, but I had nothing to tell him."

"Did the sergeant examine the rooms?" asked Thorndyke.

"Yes, he looked over the place, and he opened her little davenport—it isn't locked—and read through one or two letters that he found there, but he didn't take them away. All he took with him was a few torn-up letters that he found in the waste-paper basket."

"If those other letters are still in the davenport," said Thorndyke, "I think it would be well for us to look through them carefully, if you don't mind, Mrs. Gillow."

"I don't see that there could be any harm in it," she replied. "I've never touched anything in her rooms, myself, since she went away. I thought it better not to. I haven't even washed up her tea-things. There they are, just as she left them, poor lamb. But if you are going to look through those letters, I will ask you to excuse me, or I shall keep my sister waiting for tea."

"Certainly, Mrs. Gillow," said I. "Don't let us detain you. And, by the way," I added, as I walked with her to the door, "it would be as well not to say anything to anybody about my having come here with my friend."

"Very well, sir," she replied. "I think you are right. The least said, the soonest mended," and with this profound generalization she went out and I shut the street door after her.

* * * *

When I returned to the sitting-room, I found Thorndyke engaged in a minute examination of the tea-things, and in particular of the spoon. I proceeded at once to the davenport, and, finding it unlocked, lifted the desk-lid and peered into the interior. It contained a supply of papers and envelopes, neatly stacked, and one or two letters, which I took out. They all appeared to be from the same person—the Miss Cumbers, of whom I had heard—and a rapid glance at the contents showed that they were of no use as a source of information. I passed them to Thorndyke—who had laid down the spoon and was now looking inquisitively about the room—who scanned them rapidly and returned them to me.

"There is nothing in them," said he. "Possibly the contents of the waste-paper basket were more illuminating. But I suspect not, as the sergeant appears to be as much in the dark as we are. Shall we have a look at the bedroom before we go?"

I saw no particular reason for doing so, but, assuming that he knew best, I made no objection. Going out into the hall, we entered the deserted bedroom, the door of which was locked, though the key had not been removed. At the threshold Thorndyke paused and stood for nearly half a minute looking about the room in the same queer, inquisitive way that I had noticed in the other room, as if he were trying to fix a mental picture of it. Meanwhile, full of the Bertillon system, I had walked across to the wardrobe to see what garments were available for measurement. I had my hand on the knob of the door when my glance fell on two objects on the dressing-table; an empty tumbler and a small water-bottle, half-full. There was nothing very remarkable about these objects, taken by themselves, but, even from where I stood, I could see that both bore a number of finger-marks which stood out conspicuously on the plain glass.

"By Jove!" I exclaimed. "Here is the very thing that you were speaking of. Do you see what it is?"

Apparently he had, for he had already taken his gloves out of his pocket and was putting them on.

"Don't touch them, Strangeways," said he, as I was approaching to inspect them more closely. "If these are Mrs. Frood's fingerprints they may be invaluable. We mustn't confuse them by adding our own."

"Whose else could they be?" I asked.

"They might be Sergeant Cobbledick's," he replied. "The sergeant has been in here." He drew a chair up to the table, and, taking a lens from his pocket, began systematically to examine the markings.

"They are a remarkably fine set," he remarked, "and a complete set—the whole ten digits. Whoever made them held the bottle in the right hand and the tumbler in the left. And I don't think they are the sergeant's. They are too small and too clear and delicate."

"No," I agreed, "and the probabilities are against their being his. There is no reason why he should have wanted to take a drink of water during the few minutes that he spent here. It would have been different if it had been a beer bottle. But it would have been quite natural for Mrs. Frood to drink a glass of water while she was dressing or before she started out."

"Yes," said he. "Those are the obvious probabilities. But we must turn them into certainties if we can. Probabilities are not good data to work from. But the question is now, what are we to do? I have a small camera with me, but it would not be very convenient to take the photographs here, and it would occupy a good deal of time. On the other hand, these things would be difficult to pack without smearing the fingerprints. We want a couple of small boxes."

"Perhaps," said I, "we may find something that will do if we take a look round."

"Yes," he agreed, "we must explore the place. Meanwhile, I think I will develop up these prints for our immediate information, as we have to try to find some others to verify them."

He went back to the sitting-room, where he had put down the two cases that he always brought with him: a small suitcase that contained his toilet necessaries and a similar-sized case covered with green canvas which had been rather a mystery to me. I had never seen it open, and had occasionally speculated on the nature of its contents. My curiosity was now to be satisfied, for, when he returned with it in his hand he explained: "This is what I call my research-case. It contains the materials and appliances for nearly every kind of medico-legal investigation, and I hardly ever travel without it."

He placed it on a chair and opened it, when I saw that it formed a complete portable laboratory, containing, among other things a diminutive microscope, a little folding camera, and an insufflator, or powder-spray. The latter he now took from its compartment, and, lifting the tumbler with his gloved hand, stood it on a corner of the mantelpiece and blew over it with the insufflator a cloud of impalpably fine white powder, which settled evenly on the surface of the glass. He then tapped the tumbler gently once or twice with a lead pencil, when most of the powder coating either jarred off or crept down the surface. Finally, he blew at it lightly, which removed the rest of the powder, leaving the fingerprints standing out on the clear glass as if they had been painted on with Chinese white.

While he was operating in the same manner on the water-bottle—having first emptied it into the ewer—I examined the tumbler with the aid of his lens. The markings were amazingly clear and distinct. Through the lens I could see, not only the whole of the curious, complicated ridge-pattern, but even the rows of little round spots that marked the orifices of the sweat glands. For the first time, I realized what a perfect means of identification these remarkable imprints furnished.

"Now," said Thorndyke, when he had finished with the bottle, "the two questions are, where shall we look for confirmatory fingerprints, and where are we to get the boxes that we want for packing these things? You said that Mrs. Frood had a kitchen."

"Yes. But won't you try the furniture here; the wardrobe door, for instance. The dark, polished mahogany ought to give good prints."

"An excellent suggestion, Strangeways," said he. "We might even find the sergeant's fingerprints, as he has probably had the wardrobe open."

He sprayed the three doors of the wardrobe, and when he had tapped them and blown away the surplus powder, there appeared near the edge of each a number of finger-marks, mostly rather indistinct, and none of them nearly so clear as those on the glass.

"This is very satisfactory," said Thorndyke. "They are poor prints, but you can see quite plainly that there are two pairs of hands, one pair much larger than the other; and the prints of the larger hands are evidently not the same pattern as those on the glass, whereas those of the smaller ones are quite recognizable as the same, in spite of their indistinctness. As the large ones are almost certainly Cobbledick's, the small ones are pretty certainly Mrs. Frood's. But we mustn't take anything for granted. Let us go down to the kitchen. We shall have a better chance there."

The door of the basement staircase was still unlocked, as Mrs. Gillow had described it. I threw it open, and we descended together, I carrying the insufflator and he bearing the tumbler and bottle in his gloved hands. When he had put the two articles down on the kitchen table, he proceeded to powder first the kitchen door and then the side-door that gave on to the passage between the two houses. Both of them were painted a dark green and both yielded obvious finger-marks, and though these were mere oval smudges, devoid of any trace of pattern, their size and their groupings showed clearly enough that they appertained to a small hand. But we got more conclusive confirmation from a small aluminium frying-pan that had been left on the gas stove; for, on powdering the handle, Thorndyke brought into view a remarkably clear thumbprint, which was obviously identical with that on the water-bottle.

"I think," said he, "that settles the question. If Mrs. Gillow has not touched anything in these premises—as she assures us that she has not—then we can safely assume that these are Mrs. Frood's fingerprints."

"Are you going to annex the frying-pan to produce in evidence?" I asked.

"No," he replied. "This verification is for our own information: to secure us against the chance of producing Cobbledick's fingerprints to identify the body. I propose, for the present, to say nothing to anyone as to our possessing this knowledge. When the time comes we can tell what we know. Until then we shall keep our own counsel."

Once more I found myself dimly surprised at my friend's apparently unnecessary secrecy, but, assuming that he knew best, I made no comment, but watched with somewhat puzzled curiosity his further proceedings. His interest in the place was extraordinary. In a queer, catlike fashion he prowled about the premises, examining the most trivial objects with almost ludicrous attention. He went carefully through the cooking appliances and the glass and china; he peered into cupboards, particularly into a large, deep cupboard in which spare crockery was stored, and which was, oddly enough, provided with a Yale lock; he sorted out the meagre contents of the refuse-bin, and incidentally salved from it a couple of cardboard boxes that had originally contained groceries, and he explored the, now somewhat unsavoury, larder.

"I suppose," he said reflectively, "the dustman must have used the side door. Do you happen to know?"

"I don't," said I, inwardly wondering what the deuce the dustman had to do with the case. "I understand that the door of the passage was not used."

"But she couldn't have had the dust-bin carried up the stairs and out at the front door," he objected.

"I should think not," said I. "Perhaps we could judge better if we had a look at the passage."

He adopted the suggestion and we opened the side-door—which had a Yale night-latch—and went out into the covered passage that was common to the two houses. The door that opened on to the street was bolted on the inside, but the bolts were in good working order, as we ascertained by drawing them gently; so this gave no evidence one way or the other. Then Thorndyke carefully examined the hard gravel floor of the passage, apparently searching for dropped fragments, or the dustman's footprints; but though there were traces suggesting that the side-doors had been used, there were no perceptible tracks leading to the street or in any way specifically suggestive of dustmen.

"Japp seems fond of Yale locks," observed Thorndyke, indicating the second side-door, which was also fitted with one. "I wonder where he keeps his dust-bin."

"Would it be worth while to ask him?" said I, more and more mystified by this extraordinary investigation.

"No," he replied, very definitely. "A question often gives more information than it elicits."

"It might easily do that in my case," I remarked with a grin; upon which he laughed softly and led the way back into the house. There I gathered up the two boxes and the insufflator and made my way up to the bedroom, he following with the tumbler and the water-bottle. Then came the critical business of packing these two precious objects in the boxes in such a way as to protect the fingerprints from contact with the sides; which was accomplished very neatly with the aid of a number of balls of plasticine from the inexhaustible research-case.

"This is a little disappointing," said Thorndyke, looking at the hair-brush and comb as he took off his gloves. "I had hoped to collect a useful sample of hair. But her excessive tidiness defeats us. There seems to be only one or two short hairs and one full length. However, we may as well have them. They won't be of much use for comparison with the naked eye, but even a single hair can be used as a colour control under the microscope."

He combed the brush until the last hair was extracted from it, and then drew the little collection from the comb and arranged it on a sheet of paper. There were six short hairs, from two to four inches long, and one long hair, which seemed to have been broken off, as it had no bulb.

"Many ladies keep a combing-bag," he remarked, as; he bestowed the collection in a seed-envelope from the: research-case; "but I gather from your description that Mrs. Frood's hair was luxuriant enough to render that economy unnecessary. At any rate, there doesn't seem to be such a bag. And now I think we have finished, and we haven't done so badly."

"We have certainly got an excellent set of fingerprints," said I. "But it seems rather doubtful whether there will ever be an opportunity of using them; and if there isn't, we shan't be much more forward for our exploration. Of course, there is the hair."

"Yes," said Thorndyke, "there is the hair. That may be quite valuable. And perhaps there are some other matters—but time will show."

With this somewhat cryptic conclusion he proceeded with great care to pack the two boxes in his suitcase, wedging them with his pyjamas so that they should not get shaken in transit.

As we walked home I reflected on Thorndyke's last remark. It seemed to contain a suggestion that the mystery of Angelina's death was not so complete to him as it was to me. For my own part, I could see no glimmer of light in any direction. She seemed to have vanished without leaving a trace excepting those few derelict objects which had been washed ashore and which told us nothing. But was it possible that those objects bore some significance that I had overlooked? That they were charged with some message that I had failed to decipher? I recalled a certain reticence on the part of Cobbledick which had made me suspect him of concealing from me some knowledge that he held or some inferences that he had drawn; and now there was this cryptic remark of Thorndyke's, offering the same suggestion. Might it possibly be that the profound obscurity was only in my own mind, the product of my inexperience, and that to these skilled investigators the problem presented a more intelligible aspect? It might easily be. I determined cautiously to approach the question.

"You seemed," said I, "to imply, just now, that there are certain data for forming hypotheses as to the solution of this mystery that envelops the disappearance of Mrs. Frood. But I am not aware of any such data. Are you?"

"Your question, Strangeways," he replied, "turns on the meaning of the word 'aware.' If two men, one literate and the other illiterate, look at a page of a printed book, both may be said to be aware of it; that is to say that in both it produces a retinal image which makes them conscious of it as a visible object having certain optical properties. In the case of the illiterate man the perception of the optical properties is the total effect. But the literate man has something in his consciousness already, and this something combines, as it were, with the optical perception, and makes him aware of certain secondary properties of the printed characters. To both, the page yields a visual impression; but to one only does it yield what we may call a psychical impression. Are they both aware of the page?"

"I appreciate your point," said I, with a sour smile, "and I seem to be aware of a rather skilful evasion of my question."

He smiled in his turn and rejoined: "Your question was a little indirect. Shall we have it in a more direct form?"

"What I wanted to know," said I, "though I suppose I have no right to ask, is whether there appears to you to be any prospect whatever of finding any solution of the mystery of Mrs. Frood's death."

"The answer to that question," he replied, "is furnished by my own proceedings. I am not a communicative man, as you may have noticed, but I will say this much: that I have taken, and am taking, a good deal of trouble with this case, and am prepared to take more, and that I do not usually waste my efforts on problems that appear to be unsolvable. I am not disposed to say more than that, excepting to refer you again to the instance of the printed page and to remind you that whatever I know I have either learned from you or from the observation, in your company, of objects equally visible to both of us."

This reply, if not very illuminating, at least answered my question, as it conveyed to me that I was not likely to get much more information out of my secretive friend. Nevertheless, I asked: "About the man Frood: you were saying that you had some hopes of running him to earth."

"Yes, I have made a start. I have ascertained that he did apparently set out for Brighton the day before Mrs. Frood's disappearance, but he never arrived there. That is all I know at present. He was seen getting into the Brighton train, but he did not appear at the Brighton barrier—my informant had the curiosity to watch all the passengers go through—and he never made the visit which was the ostensible object of his journey. So he must have got out at an intermediate station. It may he difficult to trace him, but I am not without hope of succeeding eventually. Obviously, his whereabouts on the fatal day is a matter that has to be settled. At present he is the obvious suspect; but if an alibi should be proved in his case, a search would have to be initiated in some other direction."

This conversation brought us to my house in time to relieve Mrs. Dunk's anxieties on the subject of dinner; and as the daylight was already gone, the photographic operations were postponed until the following morning. Indeed, Thorndyke had thought of taking the objects to his chambers, where a more efficient outfit was available, but, on reflection, he decided to take the photographs in my presence so that I could, if necessary, attest their genuineness on oath. Accordingly, on the following morning, we very carefully extracted the tumbler and the bottle from their respective boxes and set them up, with a black coat of mine for a background, at the end of a table. Then Thorndyke produced his small folding camera—which pulled out to a surprising length—and, having fitted it with a short-focus objective, made the exposures, and developed the plates in a dark cupboard by the light of a little red lamp from the research case. When the plates were dry we inspected them through a lens, and found them microscopically sharp. Finally, at Thorndyke's suggestion, I scratched my initials with a needle in the corner of each plate.

"Well," I said, when he had finished, "you have got the evidence that you wanted, and in a very complete form. It remains to be seen now whether you will ever get an opportunity to use it."

"Don't be pessimistic, Strangeways," said he. "We have had exceptional luck in getting this splendid series of fingerprints. Let us hope that Fortune will not desert us after making us these gifts."

"What is to be done with the originals?" I asked.

"Shall I put them back where we found them?"

"I think not," he replied. "If you have a safe or a secure lock-up cupboard, where they could be put away, out of sight, and from whence they could be produced if necessary, I will ask you to take charge of them."

There was a cupboard with a good lock in the old bureau that I had found in my bedroom, and to this I conveyed the precious objects and locked them in. And so ended—at least, for the present—the episode of our raid on poor Angelina's abode.

CHAPTER XIII

THE DISCOVERY IN BLACK BOY-LANE

On a fine, sunny afternoon, about ten days after our raid on Angelina's rooms (it was Tuesday, the 14th of July, to be exact), I was sitting in my dining-room, from which the traces of lunch had just been removed, idly glancing over the paper, and considering the advisability of taking a walk, when I heard the doorbell ring. There was a short interval; then the door was opened, and the sounds of strife and wrangling that followed this phenomenon informed me that the visitor was Mr. Bundy, between whom and Mrs. Dunk there existed a state of chronic warfare. Presently the dining-room door opened—in time for me to catch a concluding growl of defiance from Mrs. Dunk—and that lady announced gruffly: "Mr. Bundy."

My visitor tripped in smilingly, "all teeth and monocle," as his inveterate enemy had once expressed it, holding a Panama hat, which had temporarily superseded the velour.

"Well, John," said he, "coming out to play?" He had lately taken to calling me John; in fact, a very close and pleasant intimacy had sprung up between us. It dated from the occasion when I had confided to him my unfortunate passion for poor Angelina. That confidence he had evidently taken as a great compliment, and the matter of it had struck a sympathetic chord in his kindly nature. From that moment there had been a sensible change in his manner towards me. Beneath his habitual flippancy there was an undertone of gentleness and sympathy, and even of affection. Nor had I been unresponsive. Like Thorndyke, I found in his sunny temperament, his invariable cheerfulness and high spirits, a communicable quality that took effect on my own state of mind. And then I had early recognized that, in spite of his apparent giddiness, Bundy was a man of excellent intelligence and considerable strength of character. So the friendship had ripened naturally enough.

I rose from my chair and, dropping the paper, stretched myself. "You are an idle young dog," said I. "Why aren't you at work?"

"Nothing doing at the office except some specifications. Japp is doing them. Come out and have a roll round."

"Well, Jimmy," said I. "Your name is Jimmy, isn't it?"

"No, it is not," he replied with dignity. "I am called Peter—like the Bishop of Rumtifoo, and, by a curious coincidence, for the very same reason."

"Let me see," said I, falling instantly into the trap, "what was that reason?"

"Why, you see," he replied impressively, "the Bishop was called Peter because that was his name."

"Look here, young fellow my lad," said I, "you'll get yourself into trouble if you come up here pulling your elder's legs."

"It was only a gentle tweak, old chap," said he. "Besides, you aren't so bloom-ing senile, after all. You are only cutting your first crop of whiskers. Are you com-ing out? I saw old Cobble dick just now, turning down Blue Boar Lane and looking as miserable as a wet cat."

"What was he looking miserable about?"

"The slump in relics, I expect. He is making no head way with his investiga-tion. I fancy he had reckoned on getting an inspectorship out of this case, whereas, if he doesn't reach some sort of conclusion, he is likely to get his rapples knucked, as old Miss Barman would say. I suspect he was on his way to the Ark to confer with Mr. Noah. What do you say to a stroll in the direction of Mount Ararat?"

It was a cunning suggestion on the part of Bundy, for it drew me instantly. Repulsive as old Israel's activities were to me, the presence of those fingerprints, securely locked up in my bureau, had created in me a fresh anxiety to see the first stage of the investigation completed so that the search for the murderer could be commenced in earnest. Not that my presence would help the sergeant, but that I was eager to hear the tidings of any new discovery.

Bundy's inference had been quite correct. We arrived at the head of the Blue Boar pier just in time to see the sergeant slowly descending the ladder, watched gloomily by Israel Bangs. As the former reached terra firma he turned round and then observed us.

"Any news, Sergeant?" I asked, as he approached across the grass.

He shook his head discontentedly. "No," he replied, "not a sign; not a vestige. It's a most mysterious affair. The things seemed to be coming up quite regularly until that hatpin was found. Then everything came to an end. Not a trace of any-thing for nigh upon a month. And what, in the name of Fortune, can have become of the body? That's what I can't make out. If this goes on much longer, there won't be any body: and then we shall be done. The case will have to be dropped."

He took off his hat (he was in plain clothes as usual) and wiped his forehead, looking blankly first at me and then at Bundy. The latter also took off his hat and whisked out his handkerchief, bringing with it a little telescope which fell to the ground and was immediately picked up by the sergeant. "Neat little glass, this," he remarked, dusting it with his handkerchief. "It's lucky it fell on the turf." He took off the cap, and pulling out the tubes, peered vaguely through it up and down the river. Presently he handed it to me. "Look at those craft down below the dock-yard," said he.

I took the little instrument from him and pointed it at the group of small, cutter-rigged vessels that he had indicated, of which the telescope, small as it was, gave a brilliantly sharp picture.

"What are they?" I asked. "Oyster dredgers?"

"No," he replied. "They are bawleys with their shrimp-trawls down. But there are plenty of oyster dredgers in the lower river and out in the estuary, and what beats me is why none of them ever brings up anything in the trawls or dredges—anything in our line, I mean."

"What did you expect them to bring up?" Bundy asked.

"Well, there are the things that have washed ashore, and there are the other things that haven't washed ashore yet. And then there is the body."

"Mr. Noah would have something to say if they brought that up," said Bundy. "By the way, what had he got to say when you called on him?"

"Old Bangs? Why he is getting a bit shirty. Wants me to pay him for all the time he has lost on creeping and searching. Of course, I can't do that, I didn't employ him."

"Did he find the hat-pin that you spoke of?" Bundy asked.

"Yes; and he has been grubbing round the place where he found it ever since, as if he thought hat-pins grew there."

"Still," said Bundy, "it is not so unreasonable. A hatpin couldn't have floated ashore. If the hat came off, the two hat-pins must have fallen out at pretty much the same time and place."

"Yes," the sergeant agreed, reflectively, "that seems to be common sense; and, if it is, the other hat-pin ought to be lying somewhere close by. I must go and have a look there myself." He again reflected for a few moments and then asked: "Would you like to see the place where Israel found the pin?"

As I had seen the place already and had shown it to Thorndyke, I left Bundy to answer.

"Why not?" he assented, rather, I suspected, to humour the sergeant than because he felt any particular interest in the place. Thereupon Cobbledick, whose enthusiasm appeared to have been revived by Bundy's remark, led the way briskly towards the wilderness by the coal-wharves, through that desolate region and along a cart-track that skirted the marshes until we came out into a sort of lesser wilderness to the west of Gas-House Road. Here the sergeant slipped through a large hole in a corrugated iron fence which gave access to a wharf littered with the unpresentable debris resulting from the activities of a firm of ship-knackers. Advancing to the edge of the wharf, Cobbledick stood for a while looking down wistfully at the expanse of unspeakable mud that the receding tide had uncovered.

"I suppose it is too dirty to go down," he said in a regretful tone.

Bundy's assent to this proposition was most emphatic and unqualified, and the sergeant had to content himself with a bird's-eye view. But he made a very thorough inspection, walking along the edge of the wharf, scrutinizing its base, pile by pile, and giving separate attention to each pot, tin, or scrap of driftwood on the slimy surface. He even borrowed Bundy's telescope to enable him to examine the more distant parts of the mud, until the owner of the instrument was reduced to the necessity of standing behind him, for politeness' sake, to get a comfortable yawn.

"Well," said Cobbledick, at long last, handing back the telescope, "I suppose we must give it up. But it's disappointing."

"I don't quite see why," said Bundy. "You have found enough to prove that the body is in the river, and no number of further relics would prove any more."

"No, there's some truth in that," Cobbledick agreed. "But I don't like the way that everything seems to have come to a stop." He crawled dejectedly through the hole in the fence and walked on for a minute or two without speaking. Presently he halted and looked about him. "I suppose Black Boy-lane will be our best way," he remarked.

"Which is Black Boy-lane?" I asked.

"It is the lane we came down after we left Japp and Willard that day," Bundy explained.

"I remember," said I, "but I didn't know it had a name."

"It was named after a little inn that used to stand somewhere near the top; but it was pulled down years ago. Here's the lane."

We entered the little, tortuous alley that wound between the high, tarred fences, and as it was too narrow for us to walk abreast, Bundy dropped behind. A little way up the lane I noticed an old hat lying on the high grass at the foot of the fence. Bundy apparently noticed it, too, for just after we had passed it I heard the sound of a kick, and the hat flew over my shoulder. At the same moment, and impelled by the same kick, a small object, which I at first thought to be a pebble, hopped swiftly along the ground in front of us, then rolled a little way, and finally came to rest, when I saw that it was a button. I should probably have passed it without further notice, having no use for stray buttons. But the more thrifty sergeant stooped and picked it up; and the instant that he looked at it he stopped dead.

"My God! Doctor," he exclaimed, holding it out towards me. "Look at this!"

I took it from him, though I had recognized it at a glance. It was a small bronze button with a Tudor Rose embossed on it.

"This is a most amazing thing," said Cobbledick.

"There can't be any doubt as to what it is."

"Not the slightest," I agreed. "It is certainly one of the buttons from Mrs. Frood's coat. The question is, how on earth did it get here?"

"Yes," said the sergeant, "that is the question; and a very difficult question, too."

"Aren't you taking rather a lot for granted?" suggested Bundy, to whom I had passed the little object for inspection. "It doesn't do to jump at conclusions too much. Mrs. Frood isn't likely to have had her buttons made to order. She must have bought them somewhere. She might even have bought them in Rochester. In any case, there must be thousands of others like them."

"I suppose there must be," I admitted, "though I have never seen any buttons like them."

"Neither have I," said Cobbledick, "and I am going to stick to the obvious probabilities. The missing woman wore buttons like this, and I shall assume that this is one of her buttons unless someone can prove that it isn't."

"But how do you account for one of her buttons being here?" Bundy objected.

"I don't account for it," retorted Cobbledick. "It's a regular puzzle. Of course, someone—a child, for instance—might have picked it up on the shore and dropped it here. But that is a mere guess, and not a very likely one. The obvious thing to do is to search this lane thoroughly and see if there are any other traces; and that is what I am going to do now. But don't let me detain you two gentlemen if you had rather not stay."

"I shall certainly stay and help you, Sergeant," said I; and Bundy, assuming the virtue of enthusiasm, if he had it not, elected also to stay and join in the search.

"We had better go back to the bottom of the lane," said Cobbledick, "and go through the grass at the foot of the fence from end to end. I will take the right hand side and you take the left."

We retraced our steps to the bottom of the lane and began a systematic search, turning over the grass and weeds and exposing the earth inch by inch. It was a slow process and would have appeared a singular proceeding had any wayfarer passed through and observed us, but fortunately it was an unfrequented place, and no one came to spy upon us. We had traversed nearly half the lane when Bundy stood up and stretched himself. "I don't know what your back is made of, John," said he. "Mine feels as if it was made of broken bottles. How much more have we got to do?"

"We haven't done half yet," I replied, also standing up and rubbing my lumbar region; and at this moment the sergeant, who was a few yards ahead, hailed us with a triumphant shout. We both turned quickly and beheld him standing with one arm raised aloft and the hand grasping a silver-topped hat-pin.

"What do you say to that, Mr. Bundy?" he demanded as we hurried forward to examine the new "find." 'Shall we be jumping at conclusions if we say that this hat-pin is Mrs. Frood's?"

"No," Bundy admitted after a glance at the silver poppy-head. "This seems quite distinctive, and, of course, it confirms the button. But I don't understand it in the least. How can they have come here?"

"We won't go into that," said the sergeant, in a tone of suppressed excitement that showed me pretty clearly that he had already gone into it. "They are here. And now the question arises, what became of the hat? It couldn't have dropped off down at the wharf, or this hat-pin wouldn't be here; but it must have fallen off when both hat-pins were gone. Now what can have become of it?"

"It might have been picked up and taken possession of by some woman," I suggested. "It was a good hat, and if the body was brought here soon after the crime, as it must have been, it wouldn't have been much damaged. But why trouble about the hat? Appearances suggest that the body was either brought up or taken down this lane. That is the new and astonishing fact that needs explaining."

"We don't want to do any explaining now," said Cobbledick. "We are here to collect facts. If we can find out what became of the hat, that may help us when we come to consider the explanations."

"Well, it obviously isn't here," said I.

"No," he agreed, "and it wouldn't have been left here. A murderer mightn't have noticed the button, or even the hat-pin, on a dark, foggy night. But he'd have noticed the hat; and he wouldn't have left it where it must have been seen, and probably led to inquiries. He might have taken it with him, or he might have got rid of it. I should say he would have got rid of it. What is on the other side of these fences?"

We all hitched ourselves up the respective fences far enough to look over. On the one side was a space of bare, gravelly ground with thin patches of grass and numerous heaps of cinder; on the other was an area of old waste land thickly covered with thistles, ragwort, and other weeds. The sergeant elected to begin with the latter, as the less frequented and therefore more probably undisturbed. Setting his foot on the buttress of a post, he went over the fence with surprising agility, considering his figure, and was lost to view; but we could hear him raking about among the herbage close to the fence, and from time to time I stood on the buttress and was able to witness his proceedings. First he went to the bottom of the lane and from that point returned by the fence, searching eagerly among the high weeds. I saw him thus proceed, apparently to the top of the lane in the neighbourhood of the remains of the city wall. Thence he came back, but now at a greater distance from the fence, and as he was still eagerly peering and probing amongst the weeds, it was evident that he had had no success. Suddenly, when he was but a few yards away, he uttered an exclamation and ran forward. Then I saw him stoop, and the next moment he fairly ran towards me holding the unmistakable brown straw hat with the dull green ribbon.

"That tells us what we wanted to know," he said breathlessly, handing the hat to me as he climbed over the fence; "at least, I think it does. I'll tell you what I mean—but not now," he added in a lower tone, though not unheard by Bundy, as I inferred later.

"I suppose we need hardly go on with the search any further?" I suggested, having had enough of groping amongst the grass.

"Well, no," he replied. "I shall go over it again later on, but we've got enough to think about for the present. By the way, Mr. Bundy, I've found something belonging to you. Isn't this your property?"

He produced from his pocket a largish key, to which was attached a wooden label legibly inscribed "Japp and Bundy, High-street, Rochester."

"By Jove!" exclaimed Bundy, "it is Japp's precious key! Where on earth did you find it, Sergeant?"

"Right up at the top," was the reply. "Close to the old wall."

"Now, I wonder how the deuce it got there," said Bundy. "Some fool must have thrown it over the fence from pure mischief. However, here it is. You know there was a reward of ten shillings for finding it, Sergeant. I had better settle up at once. You needn't make any difficulties about it," he added, as the sergeant seemed disposed to decline the payment. "It won't come out of my pocket. It is the firm's business."

On this understanding Cobbledick pocketed the proffered note and we walked on up the lane, the sergeant slightly embarrassed, as we approached the town, by the palpably unconcealable hat. Very little was said by any of us, for these new discoveries, with the amazing inferences that they suggested, gave us all abundant material for thought. The sergeant walked with eyes bent on the ground, evidently cogitating profoundly; my mind surged with new speculations and hypotheses, while Bundy, if not similarly preoccupied, refrained from breaking in on our meditations.

When, at length, by devious ways, we reached the Highstreet in the neighbourhood of the Corn Exchange, we halted, and the sergeant looked at me as if framing a question. Bundy glanced up at the quaint old clock, and remarked:

"It is about time I got back to the office. Mustn't leave poor old Japp to do all the work, though he never grumbles. So I will leave you here."

I realized that this was only a polite excuse to enable the sergeant to have a few words with me alone, and I accepted it as such.

"Good-bye, then," said I, "if you must be off, and in case I don't see you before, I shall expect you to dinner on Saturday if you've got the evening free. Dr. Thorndyke is coming down for the weekend, and I know you enjoy ragging him."

"He is pretty difficult to get a rise out of, all the same," said Bundy, brightening up perceptibly at the invitation. "But I shall turn up with very great pleasure." He bestowed a mock ceremonious salute on me and the sergeant, and, turning away, bustled off in the direction of the office. As soon as he was out of earshot Cobbledick opened the subject of the new discoveries.

"This is an extraordinary development of our case, Doctor," said he. "I didn't want to discuss it before Mr. Bundy, though he is really quite a discreet gentleman, and pretty much on the spot, too. But he isn't a party to the case, and it is better not to talk too freely. You see the points that these fresh finds raise?"

"I see that they put a new complexion on the affair, but to me they only make the mystery deeper and more incomprehensible."

"In a way they do," Cobbledick agreed, "but, on the other hand, they put the case on a more satisfactory footing. For instance, we understand now why the body has never come to light. It was never in the river at all. Then as to the perpetrator; he was a local man—or, at least, there was a local man in it; a man who knew the town and the waterside neighbourhood thoroughly. No stranger would have found Black Boy-lane. Very few Rochester people know it."

"But," I asked, "what does the finding of these things suggest to you?"

"Well," he replied, "it suggests several questions. Let me just put these things away in my office, and then we can talk the matter over." He went into his office, and shortly returned relieved—very much relieved—of the conspicuous hat. We turned towards the bridge, and he resumed: "The first question and the most important one is, which way was the body travelling? It is obvious that it was carried through Black Boy-lane. But in which direction? Towards the town or towards the river? When you think of the circumstances; when you recall that it was a foggy night when she disappeared; it seems at first more probable that the crime might have been committed in, or near, the lane, and the body carried down to the river. But when you consider all the facts, that doesn't seem possible. There is that box of tablets, picked up dry and clean on Chatham Hard. That seems to fix the locality where the crime occurred."

"And there is the brooch," said I.

"I don't attach much importance to that," he replied. "It might have been picked up anywhere. But the box of tablets couldn't have got from Black Boy-lane to Chatham except by the river, and it hadn't been in the river. But the hat seems to me to settle the question. You see, one hat-pin was found on the shore and the other in the lane near the hat. Now, one hat-pin might have dropped out and left the hat still fixed on the head. But when the hat came off, the pins must have come off with it. The hat came off near the top of the lane. If both the pins had been in it they would both have come out there.

"But one pin was found on the shore; therefore when the body was at the shore the hat must have been still on the head, though it had probably got loosened by all the dragging about in the boat and in landing the body. You agree to that, Doctor?"

"Yes, it seems undeniable," I answered.

"Very well," said he. "Then the body was being carried up the lane. The next question is: was it being carried by one person or by more than one? Well, I think you will agree with me, Doctor, that it could hardly have been done by one man. It is quite a considerable distance from the shore to the top of the lane. She was a goodsized woman, and a dead body is a mighty awkward thing to carry at the best of times. I should say there must have been at least two men."

"It certainly does seem probable," I admitted.

"I think so," said he. "Then we come to another question. Was it really a dead body? Or might the woman have been merely insensible?"

"Good God, Sergeant!" I exclaimed. "You don't think it possible that it could have been a case of forcible abduction, and that Mrs. Frood is still alive?"

"I wouldn't say it was impossible," he replied, "but I certainly don't think it is the case. You see, nearly three months have passed and there is no sign of her. But in modern England you can't hide a full-grown, able-bodied woman who has got all her wits about her. No, Doctor, I am afraid we must take the view that the woman who was carried up Black Boy-lane was a dead woman. All I want to point out is that the other view is a bare possibility, and that we mustn't forget it."

"But," I urged, "don't you think that the fact that she was being carried to-wards the town strongly suggests that she was alive? Why on earth should a murderer bring a body, at great risk of discovery, from the river, where it could easily have been disposed of, up into the town? It seems incredible."

"It does," he agreed. "It's a regular facer. But, on the other hand, suppose she was alive. What could they have done with her? How could they have kept her out of sight all this time? And why should they have done it?"

"As to the motive," said I, "that is incomprehensible in any case. But what do you suppose actually happened?"

"My theory of it is," he replied, "that two men, at least, did the job. Both may have been local waterside men, or there may have been a stranger with a water-rat in his pay. I imagine the crime was committed at Chatham, somewhere near the Sun Pier, and that the body was put in a boat and brought up here. It was a densely foggy night, you remember, so there would have been no great difficulty; and there wouldn't be many people about. The part of it that beats me is what they meant to do with the body. They seem to have brought it deliberately from Chatham right up into Rochester Town; and they have got rid of it somehow. They must have had some place ready to stow it in, but what that place can have been, I can't form the ghost of a guess. It's a fair knock-out."

"You don't suppose old Israel Bangs knows anything about it?" I suggested.

The sergeant shook his head. "I've no reason to suppose he does," he replied. "And it is a bad plan to make guesses and name names."

We walked up and down the Esplanade for nearly an hour, discussing various possibilities; but we could make nothing of the incredible thing that seemed to have happened in spite of its incredibility. At last we gave it up and returned to the Guildhall, where, as we parted, he said a little hesitatingly: "I heard you tell Mr. Bundy that Dr. Thorndyke was coming down for the weekend. It wouldn't be amiss if you were to put the facts of the case before him. It's quite in his line, and I think he would be interested to hear about it; and he might see something that I have missed. But, of course, it must be in strict confidence."

I promised to try to find an opportunity to get Thorndyke's opinion on the case, and with this we separated, the sergeant retiring to his office and I making my way homeward to prepare a report for dispatch by the last post.

CHAPTER XIV

SERGEANT COBBLEDICK IS ENLIGHTENED

The custom which had grown upon my part of meeting Thorndyke at the station on the occasion of his visits was duly honoured on the present occasion, for the surprising discoveries in Black Boy-lane, which I had described in my report to him, made me eager to hear his comments. Unfortunately, on this occasion, he had come down by an unusually late train, and the opportunity for discussion was limited to the time occupied by the short walk from Rochester Station to my house. For it was close upon dinner time, and I rather expected to find Bundy awaiting us.

"Your report was quite a thrilling document," he remarked, as we came out of the station approach. "These new discoveries seem to launch us on a fresh phase of the investigation."

"Do they seem to you to offer any intelligible suggestions?" I asked.

"There is no lack of suggestions," he replied. "To a person of ordinary powers of imagination, a number of hypotheses must present themselves. But, of course, the first thing to consider is not what might have happened, but what did happen, and what we can safely infer from those happenings. We can apparently take it as proved that the body was carried through the lane; and everything goes to show that it was carried from the river towards the town. The first clear inference is that we can completely exclude accident, pure and simple. The body—living or dead—may be assumed to have been carried by some person or persons. We can dismiss the idea that the woman walked up the lane. But if someone carried the body, someone is definitely implicated. The affair comes unquestionably into the category of crime."

"That doesn't carry us very far," I said, with a sense of disappointment.

"It carries us a stage farther than our previous data did, for it excludes accident, which they did not. Then it suggests not only premeditation, but arrangement. If the body was brought up from the river, there must have been some place known to, and probably prepared by, those who brought it, in which it could be deposited; and that place must have been more secure than the river from which it was brought. But the river, itself, was a very secure hiding-place, especially if the body had been sunk with weights. Now, this is all very remarkable. If you consider the extraordinary procedure; the seizure of the victim at Chatham; the conveyance of the body from thence to this considerable distance; the landing of it at the wharf; the conveyance of it by an apparently selected route—at enormous risk of discovery, in spite of the fog to an appointed destination: I say, Strangeways, that if you consider this astounding procedure, you cannot fail to be convinced that there was some definite purpose behind it."

"Yes," I agreed, "that seems to be so. But what could the purpose be? It appears perfectly incomprehensible. It only makes the mystery more unsolvable than ever."

"Not at all," he rejoined. "There is nothing so hopeless to investigate as the perfectly obvious and commonplace. As soon as an apparently incomprehensible motive appears, we are within sight of a solution. There may be innumerable explanations of a common-place action; but an outrageously unreasonable action; pursued with definite and considered purpose, can admit of but one or two. The action, with its underlying purpose, must be adjusted to some unusual conditions. We have only to consider to what conditions it could be adjusted, and which, if any, of those conditions actually exist, and the explanation of the apparently incomprehensible action comes into view. But here we are at our destination, and there is our friend, Bundy, standing on the doorstep. By the way, I have brought one or two photographs of Mrs. Frood for you to look at."

We arrived in time to intervene and put an end to a preliminary skirmish between the irrepressible Bundy and Mrs. Dunk, and when greetings had been exchanged, Thorndyke went up to his room to wash and deposit his luggage.

"Well, John," said Bundy, when he had hung up his hat, "it is very pleasant to see my old friend after this long separation. Very good of him, too, to invite an insignificant outsider like me to meet his distinguished colleague. You are a benefactor to me, John."

"Don't talk nonsense, Peterkin," said I. "You know we are always glad to see you. I invite you for my own pleasure and Thorndyke's, not for yours."

Bundy gave my arm a grateful squeeze. "Good old John," said he. "Nothing like doing it handsomely. But here is the great man himself," he added, as Thorndyke entered the dining-room, carrying a cardboard box, "with instruments of magic. He's going to do a conjuring trick."

Thorndyke opened the box and delicately picked out four photographs, all mounted and all of cabinet size, which he stood up in a row on the mantelpiece. Two of them were from the same negative, one being printed in red carbon, the other in sepia. The remaining two were ordinary silver prints of the conventional trade type.

Bundy looked at the collection with not unnatural surprise.

"Where did these, things come from?" he asked.

"They came from London," replied Thorndyke, "where things of this kind grow. Strangeways asked me to get him some samples. How do you like them? My own preference is for the carbons, and of the two I think I like the red chalk print the better."

I ran my eye along the row and found myself in strong agreement with Thorndyke. It was not only that the carbon prints had the advantage of the finer medium. The treatment was altogether more artistic, and the likeness seemed better, in spite of a rather over-strong top-lighting.

"Yes," I said, "the carbons are infinitely superior to the silver prints, and of the two I think the red is the better because it emphasises the shadows less."

"Is the likeness as good as in the silver prints?" Thorndyke asked.

"Better, I think. The expression is more natural and spontaneous. What do you say, Peter?"

As I spoke I looked at him, not for the first time, for I had already been struck by the intense concentration with which he had been examining the two carbons. And it was not only concentration. There was a curious expression of surprise, as if something in the appearance of the portraits puzzled him.

He looked up with a perplexed frown. "As to the likeness," said he, "I don't know that I am a particularly good judge. I only saw her once or twice. But, as far as I remember, it seems to be quite a good likeness, and there can be no question as to the superiority, in an artistic sense, of the carbons. And I agree with you that the shadows are less harsh in the red than in the sepia. Who is the photographer?"

He picked up the red print and, turning it over, looked at the back. Then, finding that the back of the card was blank, he picked up the sepia print and inspected it in the same way, but with the same result. There was no photographer's name either on the back or front.

"I have an impression," said Thorndyke, "that the carbons were done by a City photographer. But my man will know. He got them for me."

Bundy set the two photographs back in their places, still, as it seemed to me, with the air of a man who is trying vainly to remember something. But, at this moment, Mrs. Dunk entered with the soup tureen, and we forthwith took our places at the table.

We had finished our soup, and I was proceeding to effect the dismemberment of an enormous sole, when Bundy, having fortified himself with a sip of Chablis, cast a malignant glance at Thorndyke.

"I have got some bad news for you, Doctor," said he.

"Which doctor are you addressing?" Thorndyke asked. "There's only one now," replied Bundy. "T'other one has been degraded to the rank of John."

"That happens to be my rank, too," observed Thorndyke.

"Oh, but I couldn't think of taking such a liberty," Bundy protested, "though it is very gracious and condescending of you to suggest it. No, your rank and tine will continue to be that of doctor."

"And what is your bad news?"

"It is a case of a lost opportunity," said Bundy. "'Of all the sad words of tongue or pen,' and so on. It might have been ten shillings. But it never will now. Cobbledick has got your ten bob."

"Do you mean that Cobbledick has found the missing key?"

"Even so, alackaday! The chance is gone for ever."

"Where did he find it?" Thorndyke asked.

"Ah!" exclaimed Bundy. "There it is again. The tragedy of it! He wasn't looking for it at all. He just fell over it in a field where he was searching for relics of Mrs. Frood."

"Your description," said Thorndyke "is deficient in geographical exactitude. Could you bring your ideas of locality to a somewhat sharper focus? There are probably several fields in the neighbourhood of Rochester."

"So there are," said Bundy. "Quite a lot. But this particular field lies on the right, or starboard, side of a small thoroughfare called Black Boy-lane."

"Let me see," said Thorndyke. "Isn't that the lane that we went down after leaving our friends on the day of the Great Perambulation?"

"Yes," replied Bundy, looking at him in astonishment, "but how did you know its name?" (He was, of course, not aware of my report to Thorndyke describing the discoveries and the place.)

"That," said Thorndyke "is an irrelevant question. Now when you say 'the right-hand side'—"

"I mean the right-hand side looking towards the town, of course. As a matter of fact, Cobbledick found the key among the thistles near to the fence, and quite close to the outside of the city wall."

"How do you suppose it got there?" Thorndyke asked.

"I've no idea. Someone must have taken it out of the gate and thrown it over the fence. That is obvious. But who could have done it I can't imagine. Of course, you suspect Cobbledick, but that is only jealousy."

The exchange of schoolboy repartee continued without a sensible pause on either side. But yet I seemed to detect in Thorndyke's manner a certain reflectiveness underlying the levity of his verbal conflict with Bundy; a reflectiveness that seemed to have had its origin in the "news" that the latter had communicated. Of course, I had said nothing, in my report, about the finding of the key. Why *should* I? Those reports referred exclusively to matters connected with the disappearance of poor Angelina. The loss and the recovery of the key were items of mere local gossip with which Thorndyke could have no concern excepting in connexion with Bundy's facetious fiction. And yet it had seemed to me that Thorndyke showed quite a serious interest in the announcement. However, he made no further reference to the matter, and the conversation drifted to other topics.

It was almost inevitable that, sooner or later, some reference should be made to the discoveries in the lane. It was Bundy, of course, who introduced the subject; and I was amazed by the adroit way in which Thorndyke conveyed the impression of complete ignorance, without making any statement, and the patient manner in which he listened to the account of the adventure, and even elicited amplified details by judicious questions. But he eluded all Bundy's efforts to extract an opinion on the significance of the discoveries.

"But," the latter protested, "you said that if I would give you the facts, you would give me the explanation."

"The explanation is obvious," said Thorndyke. "If you found these objects in the lane, they must have been dropped there."

"Well, of course they must," said Bundy. "That is quite obvious."

"Exactly," agreed Thorndyke. "That is what I am pointing out."

"But why was the body being carried up the lane? And where was it being carried to?"

"Ah," protested Thorndyke, "but now you are going beyond your facts. You haven't proved that there was any body there at all."

"But there must have been, or the things couldn't have dropped off it."

"But you haven't proved that they did drop off it. They may have, or they may not. That is a question of fact; and as I impressed on you on a previous occasion, evidence as to fact is the function of the common witness. The expert witness explains the significance of facts furnished by others. I have explained the facts that you have produced, and now you ask me to explain something that isn't a fact at all. But that is not my function. I am an expert."

"I see," said Bundy; "and now I understand why judges are so down on expert witnesses. It is my belief that they are a parcel of impostors. Wasn't Captain Bunsby an expert witness? Or was he only an oracle?"

"It is a distinction without a difference," replied Thorndyke. "Captain Bunsby is the classical instance of oracular safety. It was impossible to dispute the correctness of his pronouncements."

"Principally," said I, "because no one could make head or tail of them."

"But that was the subtlety of the method," said Thorndyke. "A statement cannot be contested until it is understood. From which it follows that if you would deliver a judgment that cannot be disputed, you must take proper precautions against the risk of being understood."

Bundy adjusted his eyeglass and fixed on Thorndyke a glare of counterfeit defiance. "I am going to take an early opportunity of seeing you in the witness-box," said he. "It will be the treat of my life."

"I must try to give you that treat," replied Thorndyke. "I am sure you will be highly entertained, but I don't think you will be able to dispute my evidence."

"I don't suppose I shall," Bundy retorted with a grin, "if it is of the same brand as the sample that I have heard."

Here the arrival of Mrs. Dunk with the coffee ushered in a truce between the disputants, and when I had filled the cups Thorndyke changed the subject by recalling the incidents of our perambulation with Japp and Mr. Willard; and Bundy, apparently considering that enough chaff had been cut for one evening, entered into a discussion on the conditions of life in mediaeval Rochester with a zest and earnestness that came as a refreshing change, after so much frivolity. So the evening passed pleasantly away until ten o'clock, when Bundy rose to depart.

"Shall we see him home, Thorndyke?" said I. "We can do with a walk after our pow-wow."

"Somebody ought to see him home," said Thorndyke. "He looks comparatively sober now, but wait till he gets out into the air." (Bundy's almost ascetic abstemiousness in respect of wine, I should explain, had become a mild joke between us.) "But I think I won't join the bacchanalian procession. I have a letter to write, and I can get it done and posted by the time you come back."

As we walked towards the office arm-in-arm—Bundy keeping up the fiction of a slight unsteadiness of gait—my guest once more expressed enjoyment of our little festivals.

"I suppose," said he, "Dr. Thorndyke is really quite a big bug in his way."

"Yes," I replied; "he is in the very front rank; in fact, I should say that he is the greatest living authority on his subject."

"Yes," said Bundy, thoughtfully, "one feels that he is a great man, although he is so friendly and so perfectly free from side. I hope I don't cheek him too much."

"He doesn't seem to resent it," I answered, "and he certainly doesn't object to your society. He expressly said, when he wrote last, that he hoped to see something of you."

"That was awfully nice of him," Bundy said with very evident gratification; and he added, after a pause: "Lord! John, what a windfall it was for me when you came down with that letter from old Turcival. It has made life a different thing for me."

"I am glad to hear it, Peter," said I; "but you haven't got all the benefit. It was a bit of luck for me to strike a live bishop in my new habitat, and a Rumtifoozlish one at that. But here we are at the episcopal palace. Shall I assist your lordship up the steps?"

We carried out the farce to its foolish end, staggering together up the steps, at the top of which I propped him securely against the door and rang the bell, with the comfortable certainty that there was no one in the house to disturb.

"Good night, John, old chap," he said cordially, as I retired.

"Good night, Peter, my child," I responded; and so took my way homeward to my other guest.

I arrived at my house in time to meet Thorndyke returning from the adjacent pillar-box, and we went in together.

"Well," said he, "I suppose we had better turn in, according to what is, I believe, the custom of this household, and turn out betimes in the morning, for a visit, perhaps, to Black Boy-lane."

"Yes," I replied, "we may as well turn in now. You are not going to leave these photographs there, are you?"

"They are your photographs," he replied; "that is, if you care to have them. I brought them down for you."

I thanked him very warmly for the gift, and gathered up the portraits carefully, replacing them, for the present, in their box. Then we turned out the lights and made our way up to our respective bedrooms.

At breakfast on the following morning Thorndyke opened the subject of our investigation by cross-examining me on the matter of my report, and the more detailed account that Bundy had given.

"What does Sergeant Cobbledick think of the new developments?" he asked, when I had given him all the detail that I could.

"In a way he is encouraged. He is glad to get something more definite to work on. But for the present he seems to be high and dry. He gave me quite a learned exposition of the possibilities of the case, but he had to admit when he had finished that he was still in the dark so far as any final conclusion was concerned. He even suggested that I should put the facts before you—he recognized you when we met him on the road near Blue Boar Pier—and ask if you could make any suggestion."

"Can you recall the sergeant's exposition of the case?"

"I think so. It made rather an impression on me at the time," and here I repeated, as well as I could remember them, the various inferences that Cobbledick had drawn from the presence in the lane of the things that we had found. Thorndyke listened with deep attention, nodding his head approvingly as each point was made.

"A very admirable analysis, Strangeways," he said when I had finished. "It does the sergeant great credit. So far as it goes, it is an excellent interpretation of the facts that are in his possession. There are, perhaps, one or two points that he has overlooked."

"If there are," said I, "it would be a great kindness to draw his attention to them. He is naturally anxious to get on with the case, and he has taken endless trouble over it."

"I shall be very glad to give him a hint or two," said Thorndyke. "After breakfast I should like to go over the ground with you, and then we might go along to the station and see if he is in his office."

I agreed to this program, and as soon as we had finished our breakfast we went forth, making our way by Free School-lane and The Common to the marshes west of Gas House-road. From there we entered Black Boy-lane at the lower end, and slowly followed its windings, Thorndyke looking about him attentively, and occasionally peering over the fences, which his stature enabled him to do without climbing. At the top of the lane, where it opened into a paved thoroughfare, we observed no less a personage than Sergeant Cobbledick, standing on the pavement and looking at the few adjacent houses with an expression of profound speculation. His speculative attitude changed suddenly to one of eager interest when he saw us; and on my presenting him to Thorndyke, he stood stiffly at "attention" and raised his hat with an air that I can only describe as reverent.

"Dr. Strangeways was telling me, just now," said Thorndyke, "of your very interesting observations on these new developments. He also said that you would like to talk the matter over with me."

"I should, indeed, sir," the sergeant said, earnestly; "and if I might suggest it, my office will be very quiet, being Sunday, and I could show you the things that have been found, if you would like to see them."

"As to the things that have been found," said Thorndyke, "I am prepared to take them as read. They have been properly identified. But we could certainly talk more conveniently in your office."

In a few minutes we turned into a narrow street which brought us to the side of the Guildhall, and the sergeant, having shown us into his office and given some instructions to a constable, entered and locked the door.

"Now, Sergeant," said Thorndyke, "tell us what your difficulty is."

"I've got several difficulties, Sir," replied Cobbledick. "In the first place, here is a body being carried up the lane. You agree with me, Sir, that it was going up and not down?"

"Yes; your reasons seem quite conclusive."

"Well, then, Sir, the next question is, was this a dead body, or was the woman drugged or insensible? The fact that she was being taken from the river towards the town suggests that she was alive and being taken to some house where she could be hidden; but, of course, a dead body might be taken to a house to be destroyed by burning or to be dismembered or even buried, say under the cellar. I must say my own feeling is that it was a dead body."

"The reasons you gave Dr. Strangeways for thinking so seem to be quite sound. Let us proceed on the assumption that it was a dead body."

"Well, Sir," said Cobble dick, gloomily, "there you are. That's all. We have got a body brought up from the river. We can trace it up to near the top of the lane. But there we lose it. It seems to have vanished into smoke. It was being taken up into the town; but where? There's nothing to show. We come out into the paved streets, and, of course, there isn't a trace. We seem to have come to the end of our clues; and I am very much afraid that we shan't get any more."

"There," said Thorndyke, "I am inclined to agree with you, Sergeant. You won't get any more clues for the simple reason that you have got them all."

"Got them all!" exclaimed Cobbledick, staring in amazement at Thorndyke.

"Yes," was the calm reply; "at least, that is how it appears to me. Your business now is not to search for more clues but to extract the meaning from the facts that you possess. Come, now, Sergeant," he continued, "let us take a bird's-eye view of the case, as it were, reconstructing the investigation in a sort of synopsis. I will read the entries from my notebook:

"On Saturday, the 26th of April, Mrs. Frood disappeared. On the 1st of May the brooch was found at the pawn-brokers. On the 7th of May the box of tablets and the bag were found on the shore at Chatham, apparently fixing the place of the crime. On the 9th of May the scarf was found at Blue Boar Head. On the 15th of May a shoe was found in the creek between Blue Boar Head and Gas House Point. On the 25th of May the second shoe was found on the gridiron near Gas House Point. On the 20th of June a hat-pin was found on the shore a little west of the last spot; always creeping steadily up the river, you notice."

"Yes," said Cobbledick, "I noticed that, and I'm hanged if I can account for it in any way,"

"Never mind," said Thorndyke. "Just note the fact. Then on the 14th of July four articles were found; near the bottom of the lane a button; near the middle of the lane a hat-pin, and, abreast of it in the field, the hat, itself. Finally, at the top of the lane, in the field, you found the missing key."

"I don't see what the key has got to do with it," said the sergeant. "It don't seem to me to be in the picture."

"Doesn't it?" said Thorndyke. "Just consider a moment, Sergeant. But perhaps you have forgotten the date on which the key disappeared?"

"I don't know that I ever noticed when it was lost."

"It wasn't lost," said Thorndyke. "It was taken away—probably out of the gate—and afterwards thrown over the fence. But I daresay Dr. Strangeways can give you the date."

I reflected for a few moments. "Let me see," said I. "It was a good while ago, and I remember that it was a Saturday, because the men who were filling the holes in the city wall had knocked off at noon for a weekend. Now when was it? I went to the wine merchant's that day, and—." I paused with a sudden shock of recollection. "Why!" I exclaimed. "It was *the* Saturday; the day Mrs. Frood disappeared!"

Cobbledick seemed to stiffen in his chair as he suddenly turned a startled look at Thorndyke.

"Yes," agreed the latter; "the key disappeared during the morning of the 26th of April and Mrs. Frood disappeared on the evening of the same day. That is a coincidence in time. And if you consider what gate it was that this key unlocked; that it gave entrance—and also excluded entrance—to an isolated, enclosed area of waste land in which excavations and fillings-in are actually taking place; I think you will agree that there is matter for investigation."

As Thorndyke was speaking Cobbledick's eyes opened wider and wider, and his mouth exhibited a like change.

"Good Lord, Sir!" he exclaimed at length, "you mean to say—"

"No, I don't," Thorndyke interrupted with a smile. "I am merely drawing your attention to certain facts which seem to have escaped it. You said that there was no hint of a place to which the body could have been conveyed. I point out a hint which you have overlooked. That is all."

"It is a pretty broad hint, too," said Cobbledick, "and I am going to lose no time in acting on it. Do you happen to know, Doctor, who employed the workmen?"

"I gathered that Japp and Bundy had the contract to repair the wall. At any rate, they were supervising the work, and they will be able to tell you where to find the foreman. Probably they have a complete record of the progress of the work. You know Mr. Japp's address on Boley Hill, I suppose, and Mr. Bundy lives over the office."

"I'll call on him at once," said Cobbledick, "and see if he can give me the particulars, and I'll get him to lend me the key. I suppose you two gentlemen wouldn't care to come and have a look at the place with me?"

"I don't see why not," said Thorndyke. "But I particularly wish not to appear in connexion with the case, so I will ask you to say nothing to anyone of your having spoken to me about it, and, of course, we go to the place alone."

"Certainly," the sergeant agreed emphatically. "We don't want any outsiders with us. Then if you will wait for me here I will get back as quickly as I can. I hope Mr. Bundy is at home."

He snatched up his hat and darted out of the office, full of hope and high spirits. Thorndyke's suggestion had rejuvenated him.

"It seems to me," I said, when he had gone, "a rather remarkable thing that you should have remembered all the circumstances of the loss of this key."

"It isn't really remarkable at all," he replied. "I heard of it after the woman had disappeared. But as soon as she had disappeared, the loss of this particular key at this particular time became a fact of possible evidential importance. It was a fact that had to be noted and remembered. The connexion of the tragedy with the river seemed to exclude it for a time; but the discoveries in the lane at once revived its importance. The fundamental rule, Strangeways, of all criminal investigation is to note everything, relevant or irrelevant, and forget nothing."

"It is an excellent rule," said I, "but it must be a mighty difficult one to carry out," and for a while we sat, each immersed in his own reflections.

The sergeant returned in an incredibly short space of time, and he burst into the office with a beaming face, flourishing the key. "I found him at home," said he, "and I've got all the necessary particulars, so we can take a preliminary look round." He held the door open, and when we had passed out, he led the way down the little street at a pace that would have done credit to a sporting lamp-lighter. A very few minutes brought us to the gate, and when he had opened it and locked it behind us, he stood looking round the weed-grown enclosure as if doubtful where to begin.

"Which patch in the wall is the one they were working at when the key disappeared?" Thorndyke asked.

"The last but one to the left," was the reply.

"Then we had better have a look at that, first," said Thorndyke. "It was a ready-made excavation."

We advanced towards the ragged patch in the wall, and as we drew near I looked at it with a tumult of emotions that swamped mere anxiety and expectation.

I could see what Thorndyke thought, and that perception amounted almost to conviction. Meanwhile, my colleague and the sergeant stepped close up to the patch and minutely examined the rough and slovenly joints of the stonework.

"There is no trace of its having been opened," said Thorndyke. "But there wouldn't be. I think we had better scrape up the earth at the foot of the wall. Something might easily have been dropped and trodden in in the darkness." He looked towards the shed, in which a couple of empty lime barrels still remained, and, perceiving there a decrepit shovel, he went and fetched it. Returning with it, he proceeded to turn up the surface of the ground at the foot of the wall, depositing each shovelful of earth on a bare spot, and spreading it out carefully. For some time there was no result, but he continued methodically, working from one end of the patch towards the other. Suddenly Cobbledick uttered an exclamation and stooped over a freshly deposited shovelful.

"By the Lord!" he ejaculated, "it is a true bill! You were quite right, sir." He stood up, holding out between his finger and thumb a small bronze button bearing an embossed Tudor Rose. Thorndyke glanced at me as I took the button from the sergeant and examined it.

"Yes," I said, "it is unquestionably one of her buttons."

"Then," said he, "we have got our answer. The solution of the mystery is contained in that patch of new rubble."

The sergeant's delight and gratitude were quite pathetic. Again and again he reiterated his thanks, regardless of Thorndyke's disclaimers and commendations of the officer's own skilful and patient investigation.

"All the same," said Cobbledick, as he locked the gate and pocketed the key, "we haven't solved the whole problem. We may say that we have found the body; but the problem of the crime and the criminal remains. I suppose, sir, you don't see any glimmer of light in that direction?"

"A glimmer, perhaps," replied Thorndyke, "but it may turn out to be but a mirage. Let us see the body. It may have a clearer message for us than we expect."

Beyond this rather cryptic suggestion he refused to commit himself; nor, when we had parted from the sergeant, could I get anything more definite out of him.

"It is useless to speculate," he said, by way of closing the subject. "We think that we know what is inside that wall. We may be right, but we may possibly be wrong. A few hours will settle our doubts. If the body is there, it may tell us all that we want to know."

This last observation left me more puzzled than ever.

The condition of the body might, and probably would, reveal the cause of death and the nature of the crime; but it was difficult to see how it could point out the identity of the murderer. However, the subject was closed for the time being, and Thorndyke resolutely refused to reopen it until the fresh data were available.

CHAPTER XV

THE END OF THE TRAIL

Shortly after breakfast on the following morning Sergeant Cobbledick made his appearance at my house. I found him in the consulting-room, walking about on tiptoe with his hat balanced in his hands, and evidently in a state of extreme nervous tension.

"I have got everything in train, Doctor," said he, declining a seat. "I dug up the foreman yesterday evening and he dug up one of his mates to give him a hand, if necessary; and I have the authority to open the wall. So we are all ready to begin. The two men have gone down to the place with their tools, and Mr. Bundy has gone with them to let them in. He didn't much want to go, but I thought it best that either he or Mr. Japp should be present. It is their wall, so to speak. I suppose you are coming to see the job done."

"Is there any need for me to be there?" I asked. Cobbledick looked at me in surprise. He had evidently assumed that I should be eager to see what happened. "Well," he replied, "you are the principal witness to the identity of the remains. You saw her last, you know. What is your objection, Doctor?"

I was not in a position to answer this question. I could not tell him what this last and most horrible search meant to me; and apart from my personal feelings in regard to poor Angelina, there was no objection at all, but, on the contrary, every reason why I should be present.

"It isn't a very pleasant affair," I replied, "seeing that I knew the lady rather well. However, if you think I had better be there, I will come down with you."

"I certainly think your presence would be a help," said he. "We don't know what may turn up, and you know more about her than anybody else."

Accordingly, I walked down with him, and when he had admitted me with his key—Bundy had presumably used the duplicate—he closed the gate and locked it from within. The actual operations had not yet commenced, but the foreman and his mate were standing by the wall, conversing affably with Bundy, who looked nervous and uncomfortable, evidently relishing his position no more than I did mine.

"This is a gruesome affair, John, isn't it?" he said in a low voice. "I don't see why old Cobbledick wanted to drag us into it. It will be an awful moment when they uncover her, if she is really there. I'm frightfully sorry for you, old chap."

"I should have had to see the body in any case," said I; "and this is less horrible than the river."

Here my attention was attracted by the foreman, who had just drawn a long, horizontal chalk line across the patch of new rubble, a little below the middle.

"That's about the place where we left off that Saturday, so far as I remember," he said. "We had built up the outer case, and we filled in the hollow with loose bricks and stones, but we didn't put any mortar to them until Monday morning. Then we mixed up a lot of mortar, quite thin, so that it would run, and poured it on top of the loose stuff."

"Rum way of building a wall isn't it?" observed Cobbledick.

The foreman grinned. "It ain't what you'd call the highest class of masonry," he admitted. "But what can you expect to do with a gang of corner-boys who've never done a job of real work in their lives?"

"No, that's true," said the Sergeant. "But you made a soft job for the grave-diggers, didn't you? Why they'd only got to pick out the loose stuff and then dump it back on top when they'd put the body in. Then you came along on Monday morning and finished the job for them with one or two bucketsful of liquid mortar. How long would it have taken to pick out that loose stuff?"

"Lord bless yer," was the answer, "one man who meant business could have picked the whole lot out by hand in an hour; and he could have chucked it back in less. As you say, Sergeant, it was a soft job."

While they had been talking, the foreman's familiar demon had been making a tentative attack on the outer casing with a great, chisel-ended steel bar and a mason's hammer. The foreman now came to his aid with a sledge hammer, the first stroke of which caused the shoddy masonry to crack in all directions like pie-crust. Then the fractured pieces of the outer shell were prised off, revealing the "loose stuff" within. And uncommonly loose it was; so loose that the unjoined bricks and stones, with their adherent gouts of mortar, came away at the lightest touch of the great crowbar.

As soon as a breach had been made at the top of the patch, the labourer climbed up and began flinging out the separated bricks and stones. Then he attacked a fresh course of the outer shell with a pick, and so exposed a fresh layer of the loose filling.

"There'll be a fresh job for the unemployed to build this up again," the sergeant observed with a sardonic smile.

"Ah," replied the foreman, "there generally is a fresh job when you take on a crowd of casuals. Wonderful provident men are casuals. Don't they take no thought for the morrow! What O!"

At this moment the labourer stood upright on his perch and laid down his pick. "Well, I'm blowed!" he exclaimed. "This is a rum go, this is."

"What's a rum go?" demanded the foreman.

"Why, here's a whole bed of dry quick-lime," was the reply.

"Ha!" exclaimed the sergeant, knitting his brows anxiously.

The foreman scrambled up, and after a brief inspection confirmed the man's statement. "Quick-lime it is, sure enough. Just hand me up that shovel, Sergeant."

"Be careful," Cobbledick admonished, as he passed the shovel up. "Don't forget what there probably is underneath."

The foreman took the shovel and began very cautiously to scrape away the surface, flinging the scrapings of lime out on to the ground, where they were eagerly scrutinized by the sergeant, while the labourer picked out the larger lumps and cast them down. Thus the work went on for about a quarter of an hour, without any result beyond the accumulation on the ground below of a small heap of lime. At length I noticed the foreman pause and look attentively at the lime that he had just scraped up in his shovel.

"Here's something that I don't fancy any of our men put in," he said, picking the object out and handing it down to the Sergeant. The latter took it from him and held it out for me to see. It was another of Angelina's coat buttons.

In the course of the next few minutes two more buttons came to light, and almost immediately afterwards I saw the labourer stoop suddenly and stare down at the lime with an expression that made my flesh creep, as he pointed something out to the foreman.

"Ah!" the latter exclaimed. "Here she is! But, my word! There ain't much left of her. Look at this, Sergeant."

Very gingerly, and with an air of shuddering distaste, he picked something out of the lime and held it up; and even at that distance I could see that it was a human ulna. Cobbledick took it from him with the same distasteful and almost fearful manner, and held it towards me for inspection. I glanced at it and looked away. "Yes," I said. "It is a human arm bone."

On this, Cobbledick beckoned for the labourer to come down, and, taking out his official notebook, wrote something in pencil and tore out the leaf.

"Take this down to the station and give it to Sergeant Brown. He will tell you what else to do." He gave the paper to the man, and having let him out of the gate, came back and climbed up to the exposed surface of the excavation, where I saw him draw on a pair of gloves and then stoop and begin to pick over the lime.

"This is a horrid business, isn't it?" said Bundy. "Why the deuce couldn't Cobbledick carry on by himself? I don't see that it is our affair. Do you think we need stay?"

"I don't see why you need. You have finished your part of the business. You have seen the wall opened. I am afraid I must stay a little longer, as Cobbledick may want me to identify some of the other objects that may be found. But I shan't stay very long. There is really no question of the identity of the body, and there is no doubt now that the body is there. Detailed identification is a matter for the coroner."

As we were speaking, we walked slowly away from the wall among the mounds of rubbish, now beginning to be hidden under a dense growth of nettles, ragwort and thistles. It was a desolate, neglected place, sordid of aspect and contrasting unpleasantly in its modern squalor with the dignified decay of the ancient wall. We had reached the further fence and were just turning about, when the sergeant hailed me with a note of excitement in his voice. I hurried across and found him standing up with his eyes fixed on something that lay in the palm of his gloved hand.

"This seems to be the ring that you described to me, Doctor," said he. "Will you just take a look at it?"

He reached down and I received in my hand the little trinket of deep-toned, yellow gold that I remembered so well. I turned it over in my palm, and as I looked on its mystical signs, its crude, barbaric workmanship and the initials "A. C." scratched inside, the scene in that dimly lighted room—years ago, it seemed to me now—rose before me like a vision. I saw the gracious figure in the red glow of the lamp and heard the voice that was never again to sound in my ears, telling the story of the little bauble, and for a few moments, the dreadful present faded into the irredeemable past.

"There isn't any doubt about it, is there, Doctor?" the sergeant asked anxiously.

"None, whatever," I replied. "It is unquestionably Mrs. Frood's ring."

"That's a mercy," said Cobbledick; "because we shall want every atom of identification that we can get. The body isn't going to help us much. This lime has done its work to a finish. There's nothing left, so far as I can see, but the skeleton and the bits of metal belonging to the clothing. Would you like to come up and have a look, Doctor? There isn't much to see yet, but I have uncovered some of the bones."

"I don't think I will come up, Sergeant, thank you," said I. "When you have finished, I shall have to look over what has been found, as I shall have to give evidence at the inquest. And I think I need hardly stay any longer. There is no doubt now about the identity, so far as we are concerned, at any rate."

"No," he agreed. "There is no doubt in my mind, so I need not keep you any longer if you want to be off. But, before you go, there is one little matter that I should like to speak to you about." He climbed down to the ground, and, walking away with me a little distance, continued:

"You see, Doctor, some medical man will have to examine the remains, so as to give evidence before the coroner. If it is impossible to identify them as the remains of Mrs. Frood, it will have to be given in evidence that they are the remains of a person who might have been Mrs. Frood; that they are the remains of a woman of about her size and age, I mean. Of course, the choice of the medical witness doesn't rest with the police, but if you would care to take on the job, our recommendation would have weight with the coroner. You see, you are the most suitable person to make the examination, as you actually knew her."

I shook my head emphatically. "For that very reason, Sergeant, I couldn't possibly undertake the duty. Even doctors have feelings, you know. Just imagine how you would feel, yourself, pawing over the bones of a woman who had once been your friend."

Cobbledick looked disappointed. "Yes," he admitted, "I suppose there is something in what you say. But I didn't think doctors troubled about such things very much; and you have got such an eye for detail—and such a memory. However, if you'd rather not, there is an end of the matter."

He climbed back regretfully to the opening in the wall, and I rejoined Bundy. "I have finished here now," said I. "That was a ring of hers that Cobbledick had found. Are you staying any longer?"

"Not if you are going away," he replied. "I am not wanted now, and I can't stick this charnel-house atmosphere; it is getting on my nerves. Let us clear out."

We walked towards the entrance with a feeling of relief at escaping from the gruesome place, and had arrived within a few yards of it when there came a loud knocking at the gate, at which Bundy started visibly.

"Good Lord!" he exclaimed, "it's like Macbeth. Here, take my key and let the beggars in, whoever they are."

I unlocked the gate and threw it open, when I saw, standing in the lane, two men, bearing on their shoulders a rough, unpainted coffin, and accompanied by the labourer, who carried a large sieve. I stood aside to let them pass in, and when they had entered, Bundy and I walked out, shutting and locking the gate after us. We made our way up the lane in silence, for there was little to say but much to think about; indeed, I would sooner have been alone, but the gruesome atmosphere of the place we had come from seemed to have affected Bundy's spirits so much that I thought it only kind to ask him to come back to lunch with me; an invitation that he accepted with avidity.

During lunch we discussed the tragic discovery, and Bundy, now that he had escaped from physical contact with the relics of mortality, showed his usual shrewd common sense.

"Well;" he said, "the mystery of poor Angelina Frood is solved at last—at least, so far as it is ever likely to be."

"I hope not," I replied, "for the essential point of the mystery is not solved at all. It has only just been completely propounded. We now know beyond a doubt that she was murdered, and that the murder was a deliberate crime, planned in advance. What we want to know—at least, what I want to know, and shall never rest until I do know—is, who committed this diabolical crime?"

"I am afraid you never will know, John," said he. "There doesn't seem to be the faintest clue."

"What do you mean?" I demanded. "You seem to have forgotten Nicholas Frood."

Bundy shook his head. "You are deluding yourself, John. Nicholas seems, from your account of him, to be quite capable of having murdered his wife. But is there anything to connect him with the crime? If there is, you have never told me of it. And the law demands positive evidence. You can't charge a man with murder because he seems a likely person and you don't know of anybody else. What have you got against him in connexion with this present affair?"

"Well, for instance, I know that he was prowling about this town, and that he was trying to find out where she lived."

"But why not?" demanded Bundy. "She was a runaway wife, and he was her husband."

"Then I happen to have noticed that he carried a sheath-knife."

"But do you know that she was killed with a sheath-knife?"

"No, I don't," I answered savagely. "But I say again that I shall never rest until the price of her death has been paid. There must be some clue. The murder could not have been committed without a motive, and it must be possible to discover what that motive was. Somebody must have stood to benefit in some way by her death; and I am going to find that person, or those persons, if I give up the rest of my life to the search."

"I am sorry to hear you say that, John," he said as he rose to depart. "It sounds as if you were prepared to spend the rest of your life chasing a will-o'-the-wisp. But we are premature. The inquest may bring to light some new evidence that will put the police on the murderer's track. You must remember that they have been engaged in tracing the body up to now. When the inquest has been held and the facts are known they will be able to begin the search for the murderers. And I wish them and you good luck."

I was rather glad when he was gone, for his dispassionate estimate of the difficulties of the case only served to confirm my own secret hopelessness. For I could not deny that these wretches seemed to have covered up their tracks completely. In the three months that had passed no whisper of any suspicious circumstance had been heard.

From the moment when poor Angelina had faded from my sight into the fog to that of her dreadful reappearance in the old wall, no human eye seemed to have seen her. And now that she had come back, what had she to tell us of the events of that awful night? The very body, on which Thorndyke had relied for evidence, at least, of the manner of the crime, had dwindled to a mere skeleton such as might have been exhumed from some ancient tomb. The cunning of the murderer had outwitted even Thorndyke.

The thought of my friend reminded me that I had to report to him the results of the opening of the wall; results very different from what he had anticipated when he had given the sergeant the too-fruitful hint. I accordingly wrote out a detailed report, so far as my information went; but I held it back until the last post in case anything further should come to my knowledge. And it was just as well that I did; for about eight o'clock, Cobbledick called to give me the latest tidings.

"Well, Doctor," he said, with a smile of concentrated benevolence, "I have got everything in going order. I have seen the coroner and made out a list of witnesses. You are one of them, of course; in fact, you are the star witness. You were the last person to see her alive, and you were present at the exhumation. Dr. Baines—he's rather a scientific gentleman—is to make the post-mortem examination, and tell us the cause of death, if he can. He won't have much to go on. The lime has eaten up everything—it would, naturally, after three months—but the bones look quite uninjured, so far as I could judge."

"When does the inquest open?" I asked.

"The day after tomorrow. I've got your summons with me, and I may as well give it to you now."

I looked at the little blue paper and put it in my pocketbook. "Do you think the coroner will get through the case in one day?" I asked.

"No, I am sure he won't," replied Cobbledick. "It is an important case, and there will be a lot of witnesses. There will be the evidence as to the building of the wall; then the opening of it and the description of what we found in it; then the identification of the remains—that is you, principally; and then there will be all the other evidence, the pawnbroker, Israel Bangs, Hooper, and the others. And then, of course, there will be the question as to the guilty parties. That is the most important of all."

"I didn't know you had any evidence on that subject," said I.

"I haven't much," he replied. "From the time when she disappeared nobody saw her alive or dead, and, of course, nothing has ever been heard of any occurrence that might indicate a crime. All we have to go on—and it is mighty little—is the fact that she was hiding from her husband, and that he was trying to find her. Also that he had made one attempt on her life. That is where your evidence will come in, and that of the matron at the 'Poor Travellers.' I've had a talk with her."

"Do you know anything of Frood's movements about the time of the disappearance?"

"Practically nothing, excepting that he went away from his lodgings the day before. You see, we were not in a position to start tracing possible criminals. We had no real evidence of any crime. We knew that the woman had disappeared, and she appeared to have got into the river. But there was nothing to show how. It looked suspicious, but it wasn't a case. So long as no body was forthcoming there was no evidence of death, and nobody could have been charged. Even if we had found the body in the river, unless there had been distinct traces of violence, it would have been merely a case of 'found dead,' or 'found drowned.' But now the affair is on a different footing entirely. The body has been discovered under conditions which furnish prima facie evidence of murder, whatever the cause of death may turn out to have been. There is sure to be a verdict of wilful murder—not that the police are dependent on the coroner's verdict. So now we can get a move on and look for the murderer."

"What chance do you think there is of finding him?" I asked.

"Well," said Cobbledick with a benevolent smile, "we mustn't be too cocksure. But, leaving the husband out of the question and taking the broad facts, it doesn't look so unpromising. This wasn't a casual crime—fortunately. There's nothing so hopeless as a casual crime, done for mere petty robbery. But this crime was thought out. The place of burial was selected in advance. The key of the place was obtained, so that the murderer could not only get in but could lock himself—or more probably themselves—in and work secure from chance disturbance. And the time seems to have been selected; a weekend, with two whole nights to do the job in. All this points to very definite premeditation; and that points to a very definite motive. The person who planned this crime had something considerable to gain by Mrs. Frood's death; it may have been profit or it may have been the satisfaction of revenge.

"Well, that is a pretty good start. When we know what property she had, who comes into it at her death, if any of it is missing, and if so, what has become of it; we can judge concerning the first case. And if we find that she had any enemies besides her husband; anyone whom she had injured or who owed her a grudge; then we can judge of the second case.

"Then there is another set of facts. This murderer couldn't have been a complete stranger to the place. He knew about the wall and what was going on there. He knew the river and he possessed, or had command of, a boat. He knew the waterside premises and he knew his way—or had someone to show him the way—across the marshes and up Black Boy-lane. One, at least, of the persons concerned in this affair was a local man who knew the place well. So you see, Doctor, we have got something to go on, after all."

I listened to the sergeant's exposition with deep interest and no little revival of my drooping hopes. It was a most able summary of the case, and I felt that I should have liked Thorndyke to hear it; in fact, I determined to embody it in the amplification of my report. With the facts thus fully and lucidly collated, it did really seem as though the perpetrator of this foul crime must inevitably fall into our hands. Having refreshed the sergeant with a couple of glasses of port, I shook his hand warmly and wished him the best of success in the investigation that he was conducting with so much ability.

When he had gone I wrote a full account of our interview to add to my previous report, and expressed the hope that Thorndyke would be able to be present at the inquest, when I myself should "be and appear" at the appointed place to give evidence on the day after the morrow.

CHAPTER XVI

THE INQUIRY AND A SURPRISE

On the morning of the inquest I started from my house well in advance of time, and in a distinctly uncomfortable frame of mind. Perhaps it was that the formal inquiry brought home to me with extra vividness the certainty that my beloved friend was gone from me for ever, and that she had died in circumstances of tragedy and horror. Not that I had ever had any doubt, but now the realization was more intense. Again, I should have to give evidence. I should have to reconstitute for the information of strangers scenes and events that had for me a certain sacred intimacy. And then, above all, I should have to view—and that not cursorily—the decayed remains of the woman who had been so much to me. That would be naturally expected from a medical man and no one would guess at what it would cost me to bring myself to this last dreadful meeting.

Walking down the High-street thus wrapped in gloomy reflections, it was with mixed feelings that I observed Bundy advancing slowly towards me, having evidently awaited my arrival. In some respects I would sooner have been alone, and yet his kindly, sympathetic companionship was not altogether unwelcome.

"Good morning, John," said he. "I hope I am not *de trop*. It is a melancholy errand for you, poor old chap, and I can't do much to make it less so, but I thought we might walk down together. You know how sorry I am for you, John."

"Yes, I know and appreciate, and I am always glad to see you, Peter. But why are you going there! Have you had a summons?"

"No, I have no information to give. But I am interested in the case, of course, so I am going to attend as a spectator. So is Japp, though he is really a legitimately interested party. In fact, I am rather surprised they didn't summon him as a witness."

"So am I. He really knows more about the poor girl than I do. But, of course, he knows nothing of the circumstances of her death."

By this time we had arrived at the Guildhall, and here we encountered Sergeant Cobbledick, who was evidently on the lookout for me.

"I am glad you came early, Doctor," said he. "I want you just to pop round to the mortuary. You know the way. There's a tray by the side of the coffin with all her belongings on it. I'll get you to take a careful look at them, so that you can tell the jury that they are really her things. And you had better run your eye over the remains. You might be able to spot something of importance. At any rate, they will expect you to have viewed the body, as you are the principal witness to its identity. I've told the constable on duty to let you in. And, of course, you can go in, too, Mr. Bundy, if you want to."

"I don't think I do, thank you," replied Bundy. But he walked round with me to the mortuary, where the constable unlocked the door as he saw us approaching. I mentioned my name to the officer, but he knew me by sight, and now held the door open and followed me in, while Bundy halted at the threshold, and stood, rather pale and awe-stricken, looking in at the long table and its gruesome burden.

The tray of which Cobbledick had spoken was covered with a white table-cloth, and on this the various objects were arranged symmetrically like the exhibits in a museum. At the top was the hat, flanked on either side by a silver-headed hat-pin. The carefully smoothed scarf was spread across horizontally, the six coat-buttons were arranged in a straight vertical line, and the two shoes were placed at the bottom centre. At one side was the handbag, and at the other, to balance it, the handkerchief with its neatly embroidered initials; and on this were placed the Zodiac ring, the wedding ring, the box of tablets, and the brooch. On the lateral spaces the various other objects were arranged with the same meticulous care for symmetrical effect: a neat row of hair pins, a row of hooks and eyes, one or two rows of buttons from the dress and under garments, the little metal jaws of the purse, two rows of coins, silver and bronze, a pair of glove-fasteners with scorched fragments of leather adhering, a little pearl handled knife, a number of metal clasps and fastenings and other small metallic objects derived from the various garments, and a few fragments of textiles, scorched as if by fire; a couple of brown shreds, apparently from the stockings, a cindery fragment of the brown coat, and a few charred and brittle tatters of linen.

I looked over the pitiful collection while the constable stood near the door and probably watched me. There was something unspeakably pathetic in the spectacle of these poor fragments of wreckage, thus laid out, and seeming, in the almost grotesque symmetry of their disposal, to make a mute appeal for remembrance and justice. This was all that was left of her; this and what was in the coffin.

So moved was I by the fight of these relics, thus assembled and presented in a sort of tragic synopsis, that it was some time before I could summon the resolution to look upon her very self, or at least upon such vestiges of her as had survived the touch of "decay's effacing fingers." But the time was passing, and it had to be. At last I turned to the coffin, and, lifting the unfastened lid, looked in.

It could have been no different from what I had expected; but yet the shock of its appearance seemed to strike me a palpable blow. Someone had arranged the bones in their anatomical order; and there the skeleton lay on the bottom of the coffin, dry, dusty, whitened with the powder of lime, such a relic as might have been brought to light by the spade of some excavator in an ancient barrow or prehistoric tomb. And yet this thing was she—Angelina! That grisly skull had once been clothed by her rich, abundant hair! That grinning range of long white teeth had once sustained the sweet, pensive mouth that I remembered so well. It was incredible. It was horrible. And yet it was true.

For some moments I stood as if petrified, holding up the coffin lid and gazing at the fearful shape in a trance of horror. And then suddenly I felt, as it were, a clutching at my throat and the vision faded into a blur as my eyes filled. Hastily I clapped down the coffin lid and strode towards the door with the tears streaming down my face.

Vaguely I was aware of Bundy taking my arm and pressing it to his side, of his voice as he murmured shakily, "Poor old John!" Passively I allowed him to lead me to a quiet corner above a flight of steps leading down to the river, where I halted to wipe my eyes, faintly surprised to note that he was wiping his eyes too; and that his face was pale and troubled. But if I was surprised, I was grateful, too; and never had my heart inclined more affectionately towards him than in this moment of trial that had been lightened by his unobtrusive sympathy and perfect understanding.

We stayed for a few minutes, looking down on the river and talking of the dead woman and the sad and troubled life from which this hideous crime had snatched her; then, as the appointed time approached, we made our way to the room in which the inquiry was to be held. As we entered, a pleasant-looking, shrewd-faced man, who looked like a barrister and who had been standing by a constable, approached and accosted me.

"Dr. Strangeways? My name is Anstey. I do most of the court work in connexion with Thorndyke's cases, and I am representing him here today. He had hoped to come down, himself, but he had to go into the country on some important business, so I have to come to keep the nest warm—to watch the proceedings and make a summary of the evidence. You mentioned to him that the case would take more than one day."

"Yes," I answered, "that is what I understand. Will Dr. Thorndyke be here tomorrow?"

"Yes; he has arranged definitely to attend tomorrow. And I think he expects by then to have some information of importance to communicate."

"Indeed!" I said eagerly. "Do you happen to know the nature of it?"

Anstey laughed. "My dear Doctor," said he, "you have met Thorndyke, and you must know by now that he is about as communicative as a Whitstable native. No one ever knows what cards he holds."

"Yes," I agreed, "he is extraordinarily secretive. Unnecessarily so, it has seemed to me."

Anstey shook his head. "He is perfectly right, Doctor. He knows his own peculiar job to a finish. He is, in a way, like some highly-specialized animal, such as the three-toed sloth, for instance, which seems an abnormal sort of beast until you see it doing, with unapproachable perfection, the thing that nature intended it to do. Thorndyke is a case of perfect adaptation to a special environment."

"Still," I objected, "I don't see the use of such extreme secrecy."

"You would if you followed his cases. A secret move is a move against which the other player—if there is one—can make no provision or defence or countermove. Thorndyke plays with a wooden face and without speaking. No one knows what his next move will be. But when it comes, he puts down his piece and says 'check'; and you'll find it is mate."

"But," I still objected, "you are talking of an adversary and of counter-moves. Is there any adversary in this case?"

"Well, isn't there?" said he. "There has been a crime committed. Someone has committed it; and that someone is not advertising his identity. But you can take it that he has been keeping a watchful eye on his pursuers, ready, if necessary, to give them a lead in the wrong direction. But it is time for us to take our places. I see the jury have come back from viewing the body."

We took our places at the long table, one side of which was allocated to the jury and the other to witnesses in waiting, the police officers, the press-men, and other persons interested in the case. A few minutes later, the coroner opened the proceedings by giving a very brief statement of the circumstances which had occasioned the inquiry, and then proceeded to call the witnesses.

The first witness was Sergeant Cobbledick, whose evidence took the form of a statement covering the whole history of the case, beginning with Mr. Japp's notification of the disappearance of Mrs. Frood and ending with the opening of the wall and the discovery of the remains. The latter part of the evidence was given in minute detail and included a complete list of the objects found with the remains.

"Does any juryman wish to ask the witness any questions?" the Coroner inquired when the lengthy statement was concluded. He looked from one to the other, and when nobody answered he called the next witness. This was Dr. Baines, a somewhat dry-looking gentleman, who gave his evidence clearly, concisely, and with due scientific caution.

"You have examined the remains which form the subject of this inquiry?" the coroner asked.

"Yes. I have examined the skeleton which is now lying in the mortuary. It is that of a rather strongly-built woman, five feet seven inches in height, and about thirty years of age."

"Were you able to form any opinion as to the cause of death?"

"No; there were no signs of any injury nor of disease."

"Are we to understand," asked one of the jurymen, "that you consider deceased to have died a natural death?"

"I have no means of forming any opinion on the subject."

"But if she died from violence, wouldn't there be some signs of it?"

"That would depend on the nature of the violence."

"Supposing she had been shot with a revolver."

"In that case there might be a fracture of one or more bones, but there might be no fracture at all. Of course, there would be a bullet."

"Did you find a bullet?"

"No. I did not see the bones until they had been brought to the mortuary."

"There has been no mention of a bullet having been found," the coroner interposed, "and you heard Sergeant Cobbledick say that the lime had all been sifted through a fine sieve. We must take it that there was no bullet. But," he continued, addressing the witness, "the conditions that you found would not exclude violence, I presume?"

"Not at all. Only violence that would cause injury to the bones."

"What kinds of violence would be unaccompanied by injury to the bones?"

"Drowning, hanging, strangling, suffocation, stabbing; and, of course, poisoning usually leaves no traces on the bones."

"Can you give us no suggestion as to the cause of death?"

"None whatever," was the firm reply.

"You have heard the description of the missing woman, Mrs. Frood. Do these remains correspond with that description?"

"They are the remains of a woman of similar stature and age to Mrs. Frood, so far as I can judge. I can't say more than that. The description of Mrs. Frood was only approximate; and the estimate of the stature, and especially the age, of a skeleton can only be approximate."

This being all that could be got out of the witness, who was concerned only with the skeleton, and naturally refused to budge from that position, the coroner glanced at his list and then called my name. I rose and took my place at the top corner of the table, when I was duly sworn, and gave my name and description.

"You heard Sergeant Cobbledick's description of the articles which have been found, and which are now lying in the mortuary?" the coroner began.

I replied "Yes," and he continued: "Have you examined those articles, and, if so, can you tell us anything about them?"

"I have examined the articles in the mortuary, and I recognized them as things I know to have been the property of Mrs. Angelina Frood."

Here I described the articles in detail, and stated when and where I had seen them in her possession.

"You have inspected the remains of deceased in the mortuary. Can you identify them as the remains of any particular person?"

"No. They are quite unrecognizable."

"Have you any doubt as to whose remains they are?" asked the juryman who had spoken before.

"That question, Mr. Pilley," said the coroner "is not quite in order. The witness has said that he was not able to identify the remains. Inferences as to the identity of deceased, drawn from the evidence, are for the jury. We must not ask witnesses to interpret the evidence. When did you last see Mrs. Frood alive, Doctor?"

"On the 26th of April," I replied; and here I described that last interview, recalling our conversation almost verbatim. When I came to her expressions of uneasiness and foreboding, the attention of the listeners became more and more intense, and it was evident that they were deeply impressed. Particularly attentive was the foreman of the jury, a keen-faced, alert-looking man, who kept his eyes riveted on me, and, when I had finished this part of my evidence, asked: "So far as you know, Doctor, had Mrs. Frood any enemies? Was there anyone whom she had reason to be afraid of?"

This was a rather awkward question. It is one thing to entertain a suspicion privately, but quite another thing to give public expression to it. Besides, I was giving sworn evidence as to facts actually within my knowledge.

"I can't say, positively," I replied after some hesitation, "that I know of any enemy or anyone whom she had reason to fear."

The coroner saw the difficulty, and interposed with a discreet question.

"What do you know of her domestic affairs, of her relations with her husband, for instance?"

This put the matter on the basis of fact, and I was able to state what I knew of her unhappy married life in Rochester and previously in London; and further questions elicited my personal observations as to the character and personality of her husband. My meeting with him at Dartford Station, the incidents in the Poor Travellers' rest-house, the meeting with him on the bridge; all were given in full detail and devoured eagerly by the jury. And from their questions and their demeanour it became clear to me that they were in full cry after Nicholas Frood.

The conclusion of my evidence brought us to the luncheon hour. I had, of course, to take Mr. Anstey back to lunch with me, and a certain wistfulness in Bundy's face made me feel that I ought to ask him, too. I accordingly presented them to one another and issued the invitation.

"I am delighted to meet you, Mr. Bundy," Anstey said heartily. "I have heard of you from my friend Thorndyke, who regards you with respectful admiration."

"Does he?" said Bundy, blushing with pleasure, but looking somewhat surprised. "I can't imagine why. But are you an expert, too?"

"Bless you, no," laughed Anstey. "I am a mere lawyer, and, on this occasion, what is known technically as a devil—technically, you understand. I am watching this case for Thorndyke."

"But I didn't know that Dr. Thorndyke was interested in the case," said Bundy, in evident perplexity.

"He is interested in everything of a criminal and horrid nature," replied Anstey. "He never lets a really juicy crime mystery pass without getting all the details, if possible. You see, they are his stock in trade."

"But he never would discuss this case—not seriously," objected Bundy.

"Probably not," said Anstey. "Perhaps there wasn't much to discuss. But wait till the case is finished. Then he will tell you all about it."

"I see," said Bundy. "He is one of those prophets who predict after the event."

"And the proper time, too," retorted Anstey. "It is no use being premature."

The conversation proceeded on this plane of playful repartee until we arrived at my house, where Mrs. Dunk, having bestowed a wooden glance of curiosity at Anstey and a glare of defiance at Bundy, handed me a telegram addressed to R. Anstey, K.C., care of Dr. Strangeways. I passed it to Anstey, who opened it and glanced through it.

"What shall I say in answer?" he asked, placing it in my hand.

I read the message and was not a little puzzled by it.

"Ask Strangeways come back with you tonight. Very urgent. Reply time and place."

"What do you suppose he wants me for?" I asked.

"I never suppose in regard to Thorndyke," he replied.

"But if he says it is urgent, it is urgent. Can you come up with me?"

"Yes, if it is necessary."

"It is. Then I'll say yes. And you had better arrange to stay the night—there is a spare bedroom at his chambers—and come down with him in the morning. Can you manage that?"

"Yes," I replied; "and you can say that we shall be at Charing Cross by seven-fifteen."

I could see that this transaction was as surprising to Bundy as it was to me. But, of course, he asked no questions, nor could I have answered them if he had. Moreover, there was not much time for discussion as we had to be back in the court room by two o'clock, and what talk there was consisted mainly of humorous comments by Anstey on the witnesses and the jury.

Having sent off the telegram on our way down, we took our places once more, and the proceedings were resumed punctually by the calling of the foreman of the repairing gang; who deposed to the date on which the particular patch of rubble was commenced and finished and its condition when the men knocked off work on Saturday, the 26th of April. He also mentioned the loss of the key, but could give no particulars. The cross-examination elicited the facts that he had communicated to Cobbledick and me as to the state of the loose filling.

"How many men," the coroner asked, "would it have taken to bury the body in the way in which it was buried; and how long?"

"One man could have done it easily in one night, if he could have got the body there. The stuff in the wall was all loose, and it was small stuff, easy to handle. No building had to be done. It was just a matter of shovelling the lime in and then chucking the loose stuff in on top. And the lime was handy to get at in the shed, and one of the barrels was open."

"Can you say certainly when the body was buried?"

"It must have been buried on the night of the 26th of April or on the 27th, because on Monday morning, the 28th, we ran the mortar in, and by that evening we had got the patch finished."

The next witness was the labourer, Thomas Evans, who had lost the key. His account of the affair was as follows:

"On the morning of Saturday, the 26th of April, the foreman gave me the key, because he had to go to the office. I took the key and opened the gate, and I left the key in the lock for him to take when he came. Then I forgot all about it, and I suppose he did, too, because he didn't say anything about it until we had knocked off work and were going out. Then he asks me where the key was, and I said it was in the gate. Then he went and looked but it wasn't there. So we searched about a bit in the grounds and out in the lane; but we couldn't see nothing of it nowhere."

"When you let yourself in, did you leave the gate open or shut it?"

"I shut the gate, but, of course, it was unlocked. The key was outside."

"So that anyone passing up the lane could have taken it out without your noticing?"

"Yes. We was working the other side of the grounds, so we shouldn't have heard anything if anybody had took it."

That completed the evidence as to the key, and when Evans was dismissed the matron of the Poor Travellers was called. As she took her place, a general straightening of backs and air of expectancy on the part of the jury suggested that her evidence was looked forward to with more than common interest. And so it turned out to be. Her admirably clear and vivid presentment of the man, Nicholas Frood; his quarrelsome, emotional temperament, his shabby condition, his abnormal appearance, the evidences of his addiction to drink and drugs, his apparently destitute state, and, above all, the formidable sheath-knife that he wore under his coat; were listened to with breathless attention, and followed by a fusilade of eager, and often highly improper, questions. But the coroner was a wise and tactful man, and he unobtrusively intervened to prevent any irregularities; as, for instance, "It is not permissible," he observed, blandly, "to ask a witness if a certain individual seemed to be a likely person to commit a crime. And a coroner's court is not a criminal court. It is not our function to establish any person's guilt, but to ascertain how deceased met with her death. If the evidence shows that she was murdered, we shall say so in our verdict. If the evidence points clearly to a particular person as the murderer, we shall name that person in the verdict. But we are not primarily investigating a crime; we are investigating a death. The criminal investigation is for the police."

This reminder cooled the ardour of the criminal investigators somewhat, but there were signs of a fresh outbreak when Mrs. Gillow gave her evidence, for that lady having a somewhat more lively imagination than the matron, tended to lure enterprising jurymen on to fresh indiscretions. She certainly enjoyed herself amazingly, and occupied a most unnecessary amount of time before she at length retired, dejected but triumphant, to the manifest relief of the coroner.

This brought the day's proceedings to a close. There were a few more witnesses on the list, and the coroner hoped to take their evidence and complete the inquiry on the following day. As soon as the court rose, Anstey and I with Bundy proceeded to a tea-shop hard by and, having refreshed ourselves with a light tea, set forth to catch our train at Strood Station. Thither Bundy accompanied us at my invitation, but though I suspected that he was bursting with curiosity as to the object of my mysterious journey, he made no reference to it, nor did I or Anstey.

At the barrier at Charing Cross we found Thorndyke awaiting us, and Anstey, having delivered me into his custody and seen us into a taxi-cab that had already been chartered, wished us success and took his leave. Then the driver, who apparently had his instructions, started and moved out of the station.

"I don't know," said I, "whether I may now ask what I am wanted for."

"I should rather not go into particulars," he replied. "I want your opinion on something that I am going to show you, and I especially want it to be an impromptu opinion. Previous consideration might create a bias which would detract from the conclusiveness of your decision. However, you have only a few minutes to wait."

In those few minutes I could not refrain from cudgelling my brains, even at the risk of creating a bias, and was still doing so—quite unproductively—when the cab approached the hospital of St. Barnabas and gave me a hint. But it swept past the main, entrance, and, turning up a side street, slowed down and stopped opposite the entrance of the medical school. Here we got out, and, leaving the cab waiting, entered the hall, where Thorndyke inquired for a person of the name of Farrow. In a minute or two this individual made his appearance in the form of a somewhat frowsy, elderly man, whom, from the multitude of warts on his hands, I inferred to be the post-mortem porter or dissecting-room attendant. He appeared to be a taciturn man, and he, too, evidently had his instructions, for he merely looked at us and then walked away slowly, leaving us to follow. Thus silently he conducted us down a long corridor, across a quadrangle beyond which rose the conical roof of a theatre, along a curved passage which followed the wall of the circular building and down a flight of stone steps which let into a dim, cement-floored basement, lighted by sparse electric bulbs and pervaded by a faint, distinctive odour that memory associated with the science of anatomy. From the main basement room Farrow turned into a short passage, where he stopped at a door, and, having unlocked it, threw it open and switched on the light, when we entered and I looked around. It was a large, cellar-like room, lighted by a single powerful electric bulb fitted with a basin-like metal reflector and attached to a long, movable arm. The activities usually carried on in it were evident from the great tins of red lead on the shelves, from a large brass syringe fitted with a stop-cock and smeared with red paint, and from a range of oblong slate tanks or coffers furnished with massive wooden lids.

Still without uttering a word, the taciturn Farrow swung the powerful lamp over one of the coffers, and then drew off the lid. I stepped forward and looked in. The coffer was occupied by the body of a man, evidently—from the shaven head and the traces of red paint—prepared as an anatomical "subject." I looked at it curiously, thinking how unhuman, how artificial it seemed; how like to a somewhat dingy waxwork figure. But as I looked I was dimly conscious of some sense of familiarity stealing into my mind. Some chord of memory seemed to be touched. I stooped and looked more closely; and then, suddenly, I started up.

"Good God!" I exclaimed. "It is Nicholas Frood!"

"Are you sure?" asked Thorndyke.

"Yes, quite," I answered. "It was the shaved head that put me off: the absence of that mop of hair. I have no doubt at all. Still—let us have a look at the hands."

Farrow lifted up the hands one after the other; and then, if there could have been any doubt, it was set at rest. The mahogany-coloured stain was still visible; but much more conclusive were the bulbous fingertips and the misshapen, nutshell-like nails. There could be no possible doubt.

"This is certainly the man I saw at Rochester," said I. "I am fully prepared to swear to that. But oughtn't he to have been identified by somebody who knew him better?"

"The body has been identified this afternoon by his late landlady," replied Thorndyke, "but I wanted your confirmation, and I wanted you as a witness at the inquest. The identification is important in relation to the inquiry and the possible verdict."

"Yes, by Jove!" I agreed, with a vivid recollection of the questions put to Mrs. Gillow. "This will come as a thunder-bolt to the jury. But how, in the name of Fortune, did he come here?"

"I'll tell you about that presently," replied Thorndyke.

He tendered a fee to the exhibitor, and when the latter had replaced the lid of the coffer, he conducted us back to our starting-point, and saw us into the waiting cab.

"5A, King's Bench Walk," Thorndyke instructed the driver, and as the cab started, he began his explanation.

"This has been a long and weary search, with a stroke of unexpected good luck at the end. We have had to go through endless records of hospitals, police-courts, poorhouses, infirmaries, and inquests. It was the records of an inquest that put us at last on the track; an inquest on an unknown man, supposed to be a tramp. Roughly, the history of the affair is this:

"Frood seems to have started for Brighton on the 25th of April, but for some unexplained reason, he broke his journey and got out at Horwell. What happened to him there is not clear. He may have over-dosed himself with cocaine; but at any rate, he was found dead in a meadow, close to a hedge, on the morning of the 26th. He was therefore dead before his wife disappeared. The body was taken to the mortuary and there carefully examined. But there was not the faintest clue to his identity. His pockets were searched, but there was not a vestige of property of any kind about him, not even the knife of which you have spoken. The probability is that he had been robbed by some tramp of everything that he had about him, either while he was insensible or after he was dead. In any case he appeared to be completely destitute, and this fact, together with his decidedly dirty and neglected condition, led naturally to the conclusion that he was a tramp. An inquest was held, but of course, no expensive and troublesome measures were taken to trace his identity. Examinations showed that he had not died from the effects of violence, so it was assumed that he had died from exposure, and a verdict to that effect was returned. He was about to be given a pauper's funeral when Providence intervened on our behalf. It happened that the Demonstrator of Anatomy at St. Barnabas resides at Horwell; and it happened that the presence of an unclaimed body in the mortuary came to his knowledge. Thereupon he applied to the authorities, on behalf of his school, for the use of it as an anatomical subject. His application was granted and the body was conveyed to St. Barnabas, where it was at once embalmed and prepared and then put aside for use during the next winter session."

"Was that quite in order—legally, I mean?"

"That is not for us to ask," he replied. "It was not in any way contrary to public policy, and it has been our salvation in respect of our particular inquiry."

"I suppose it has," I said, not, however, quite seeing it in that light. "Of course, it disposes of the question of his guilt."

"It does a good deal more than that as matters have turned out," said he. "However, here we are in the precincts of the Temple. Let us dismiss Nicholas Frood from our minds for the time being, and turn our attention to the more attractive subject of dinner."

The cab stopped opposite a tall house with a fine carved-brick portico, and, when Thorndyke had paid the driver, we ascended the steps and made our way up a couple of flights of oaken stairs to the first floor. Here, at the door of my friend's chambers, we encountered a small, clerical-looking gentleman with an extremely wrinkly, smiling face, who reminded me somewhat of Mr. Japp. "This is Mr. Polton, Strangeways," said Thorndyke, presenting him to me, "who relieves me of all the physical labour of laboratory work. He is a specialist in everything, including cookery, and if my nose does not mislead me—ha! Does it, Polton?"

"That depends, sir, on which way you follow it," replied Polton, with a smile of labyrinthine wrinkliness. "But you will want to wash, and Dr. Strangeways's room is ready for him."

On this hint, Thorndyke conducted me to an upper floor, and to a pleasant bedroom with an outlook on plane trees and ancient, red-tiled roofs, where I washed and brushed up, and from whence I presently descended to the sitting-room, whither Thorndyke's nose had already led him—and to good purpose, too.

"Mr. Polton has missed his vocation," I remarked, as I attacked his productions with appreciative gusto. "He ought to have been the manager of a West End club or a high-class restaurant."

Thorndyke regarded me severely. "I am shocked at you, Strangeways," he said. "Do you suggest that a man who can make anything from an astronomical clock to a microscope objective, who is an expert in every branch of photographic technique, a fair analytical chemist, a microscopist, and general handicraftsman, should be degraded to the office of a mere superintendent cook? It is a dreadful thought!"

"I didn't understand that he was a man of so many talents and accomplishments," I said apologetically.

"He is a most remarkable man," said Thorndyke, "and I take it as a great condescension that he is willing to prepare my meals. It is his own choice—an expression of personal devotion. He doesn't like me to take my food at restaurants or clubs. And, of course, he does it well because he is incapable of doing anything otherwise than well. You must come up and see the laboratories and workshop after dinner."

We went up when we had finished our meal and discovered Polton in the act of cutting transverse sections of hairs and mounting them to add to the great collection of microscopic objects that Thorndyke had accumulated. He left this occupation to show me the great standing camera for copying, enlarging, reducing and microphotography, to demonstrate the capabilities of a fine back-geared lathe and to exhibit the elaborate outfit for analysis and assay work.

"I had no idea," said I, as we returned to the sitting room, "that medico-legal practice involved the use of all these complicated appliances."

"The truth is," Thorndyke replied, "that Medical Jurisprudence is not a single subject, concerned with one order of knowledge. It represents the application of every kind of knowledge to the solution of an infinite variety of legal problems. And that reminds me that I haven't yet looked through Anstey's abstract of the evidence at the inquest, which I saw that he had left for me. Shall we go through it now? It won't take us very long. Then we can have a stroll round the Temple or on the Embankment before we turn in."

"You are coming down to Rochester tomorrow?" I asked.

"Yes," he replied. "The facts concerning Nicholas Frood will have to be communicated to the coroner; and it is possible that some other points may arise."

"Now that Frood is definitely out of the picture," said I, "do you see any possibility of solving the mystery of this crime? I mean as to the identity of the guilty parties?"

He reflected awhile. "I am inclined to think," he replied, at length, "that I may be able to offer a suggestion. But, of course, I have not yet seen the remains."

"There isn't much to be gleaned from them, I am afraid," said I.

"Perhaps not," he answered. "But we shall be able to judge better when we have read the evidence of the medical witness."

"He wasn't able to offer any opinion as to the cause of death," I said.

"Then," he replied, "we may take it that there are no obvious signs. However, it is useless to speculate. We must suspend our judgment until tomorrow," and with this he opened Anstey's summary, and read through it rapidly, asking me a question now and again to amplify some point. When he had finished the abstract—which appeared to be very brief and condensed—he put it in his pocket and suggested that we should start for our proposed walk; and, though I made one or two attempts to reopen the subject of the inquiry, he was not to be drawn into any further statements. Apparently there was some point that he hoped to clear up by personal observation, and meanwhile he held his judgment in suspense.

CHAPTER XVII

THORNDYKE PUTS DOWN HIS PIECE

The journey down to Rochester would have been more agreeable and interesting under different circumstances. Thorndyke kept up a flow of lively conversation to which I should ordinarily have listened with the keenest pleasure. But he persistently avoided any reference to the object of our journey; and as this was the subject that engrossed my thoughts and from which I was unable to detach them, his conversational efforts were expended on somewhat inattentive ears. In common politeness I tried to make a show of listening and even of some sort of response; but the instant a pause occurred, my thoughts flew back to the engrossing subject and the round of fruitless speculation begun again.

What was it that Thorndyke had in his mind? He was not making this journey to inform the coroner of Frood's death. That could have been done by letter; and, moreover, I was the actual witness to the dead man's identity. There was some point that he expected to be able to elucidate; some evidence that had been overlooked. And that evidence seemed to be connected with that dreadful, pitiful thing that lay in the coffin—crying out, indeed, to Heaven for retribution, but crying in a voice all inarticulate. But would it be inarticulate to him? He had seemed to imply an expectation of being able to infer from the appearance of those mouldering bones the cause and manner of death, and even—so it had appeared to me—the very identity of the murderer. But how could this be possible? Dr. Baines had said that the bones showed no signs of injury. The soft structures of the body had disappeared utterly. What suggestion as to the cause of death could the bones offer? Chronic mineral poisoning might be ascertainable from examination of the skeleton, but not from a mere ocular inspection; and the question of chronic poisoning did not arise. Angelina was alive on the Saturday evening; before the Monday morning her body was in the wall. Again and again I dismissed the problem as an impenetrable mystery; and still it presented itself afresh for consideration.

A few words of explanation to the constable on duty at the mortuary secured our admission, or, rather Thorndyke's; for I did not go in, but stood in the doorway, watching him inquisitively. He looked over the objects set out on the tray and seemed to be mentally checking them. Then he put on a pair of pince-nez and examined some of them more closely. From the tray he presently turned to the coffin, and, lifting off the lid, stood for a while, with his pince-nez in his hand, looking intently at the awful relics of the dead woman. From his face I could gather nothing. It was at all times a rather immobile face, in accordance with his calm, even temperament. Now it expressed nothing but interest and close attention. He inspected the whole skeleton methodically, as I could see by the way his eyes travelled slowly from the head to the foot of the coffin. Then, once more, he put on his reading-glasses, and stooped to examine more closely something in the upper part of the coffin—I judged it to be the skull. At length he stood up, put away his glasses, replaced the coffin-lid, and rejoined me.

"Has the sitting of the Court begun yet?" he asked the constable.

"They began about five minutes ago, sir," was the reply; on which we made our way to the court-room, where Thorndyke, having secured a place at the table, beckoned to the coroner's officer.

"Will you hand that to the coroner, please?" said he, producing from his pocket a note in an official-looking blue envelope. The officer took the note and laid it down before the coroner, who glanced at it and nodded and then looked with sudden interest at Thorndyke. The witness who was being examined at the moment was the pawnbroker's daughter, and her account of the mysterious man with the mole on his nose was engaging the attention of the jury. While the examination was proceeding, the coroner glanced from time to time at the note. Presently he took it up and opened the envelope, and in a pause in the evidence, took out the note and turned it over to look at the signature. Then he ran his eyes over the contents, and I saw his eyebrows go up. But at that moment one of the jurymen asked a question and the note was laid down while the answer was entered in the depositions. At length the evidence of this witness was completed, and the witness dismissed, when the coroner took up the note and read it through carefully.

"Before we take the evidence of Israel Bangs, gentlemen," said he, "we had better consider some new facts which I think you will regard as highly important. I have just received a communication from Dr. John Thorndyke, who is a very eminent authority on medico-legal evidence. He informs me that the husband of the deceased, Nicholas Frood, is dead. It appears that he died about three months ago, but his body was not identified until yesterday, when it was seen by Frood's landlady and by Dr. Strangeways, who is here and can give evidence as to the identity. I propose that we first recall Dr. Strangeways and then ask Dr. Thorndyke, who is also present, to give us the further particulars."

The jury agreed warmly to the suggestion, and I was at once recalled, and as I took my place at the coroner's left hand I felt that I was fully justifying Cobbledick's description of me as the "star witness," for not only was I the object of eager interest on the part of the jury and the sergeant himself, but also of Bundy, whose eyes were riveted on me with devouring curiosity.

There is no need for me to repeat my evidence. It was quite short. I just briefly described the body and its situation. As to how it came to the hospital, I had no personal knowledge, but I affirmed that it was undoubtedly the body of Nicholas Frood. Of that I was quite certain.

No questions were asked. There was a good deal of whispered comment, and one indiscreet juryman remarked audibly that "this fellow seemed to have cheated the hangman." Then the coroner deferentially requested Thorndyke to give the Court any information that was available, and my friend advanced to the head of the table, where the coroner's officer placed a chair for him, and took the oath.

"What a perfectly awful thing this is about poor old Nicholas!" whispered Bundy, who had crept into the chair that Thorndyke had just vacated. "It makes one's flesh creep to think of it."

"It *was* rather horrible," I agreed, noting that my description of the scene had evidently made *his* flesh creep, for he was as pale as a ghost. But there was no time to discuss the matter further, for Thorndyke, having been sworn, and started by a general question from the coroner, now began to give his evidence, in the form of a narrative similar to that which I had heard from him, and accompanied by the production of documents relating to the inquest and the transfer of the body of the unknown deceased to the medical school.

"There is no doubt, I suppose, as to the date of this man's death?" the coroner asked.

"Practically none. He was seen alive on the 25th of April, and he was found dead on the morning of the 26th. I have put in a copy of the depositions at the inquest, which give the date and time of the finding of the body."

"Then, as his death occurred before the disappearance of his wife, this inquiry is not concerned with him any further."

Here the foreman of the jury interposed with a question. "It seems that Dr. Thorndyke took a great deal of trouble to trace this man, Frood. Was he acting for the police?"

"I don't know that that is strictly our concern," said the coroner, looking at Thorndyke, nevertheless, with a somewhat inquiring expression.

"I was acting," said Thorndyke, "in pursuance of instructions from a private client to investigate the circumstances of Mrs. Frood's disappearance, to ascertain whether a crime had been committed and, if so, to endeavour to find the guilty party or parties."

"He never told us that," murmured Bundy; "at least—did you know, John?"

"I did, as a matter of fact, but I was sworn to secrecy." Bundy looked at me a little reproachfully, I thought, and I caught a queer glance from Cobbledick. But just then the coroner spoke again.

"Have you seen the evidence that was given yesterday?"

"Yes, I have a summary of it, which I have read."

"Can you, from your investigations, tell us anything that was not disclosed by that evidence?"

"Yes. I have just examined the remains of the deceased and the articles which have been found from time to time. I think I can give some additional information concerning them."

"From your examination of the remains," the coroner said somewhat eagerly, "can you give any opinion as to the cause of death?"

"No," replied Thorndyke. "My examination had reference chiefly to the identity of the remains."

The coroner looked disappointed. "The identity of the remains," said he, "is not in question. They have been clearly identified as those of Angelina Frood."

"Then," said Thorndyke, "they have been wrongly identified. I can swear positively that they are not the remains of Angelina Frood."

At this statement a sudden hush fell on the Court, broken incongruously by an audible whistle from Sergeant Cobbledick. On me the declaration fell like a thunderbolt, and, on looking round at Bundy, I could see that he was petrified with astonishment. There was a silence of some seconds' duration. Then the coroner said, with a distinctly puzzled air: "This is a very remarkable statement, Dr. Thorndyke.

It seems to be quite at variance with all the facts: and it appears almost incredible that you should be able to speak with such certainty, having regard to the condition of the remains and in spite of the extraordinary effect of the lime."

"It is on account of the effect of the lime that I am able to speak with so much certainty and confidence," Thorndyke replied.

"I don't quite follow that," said the coroner. "Would you kindly tell us how you were able to determine that these remains are not those of Angelina Frood?"

"It is a matter of simple inference," replied Thorndyke. "On the 26th of April last Mrs. Frood is known to have been alive. It has been assumed that on that night or the next her body was built up in the wall. If that had really happened, when the wall was opened on the 20th of July, the body would have been found intact and perfectly recognizable!"

"You are not overlooking the circumstance that it was buried in a bed of quick-lime?" said the coroner.

"No," replied Thorndyke; "in fact that is the circumstance that makes it quite certain that these remains are not those of Angelina Frood. There is," he continued, "a widely prevalent belief that quick-lime has the property of completely consuming and destroying organic substances such as a dead human body. But that belief is quite erroneous. Quick-lime has no such properties. On the contrary, it has a strongly preservative effect on organic matter. Putrefaction is a change in organic matter which occurs only when that matter is more or less moist. If such matter is completely dried, putrefaction is prevented or arrested, and such dried, or mummified, matter will remain undecomposed almost indefinitely, as we see in the case of Egyptian mummies. But quick-lime has the property of abstracting the water from organic substances with which it is in contact; of rendering them completely dry. It thus acts as a very efficient preservative. If Mrs. Frood's body had been buried, when recently dead, three months ago in fresh quick-lime, it would by now have been reduced more or less to the condition of a mummy. It would not have been even partially destroyed, and it would have been easily recognizable."

To this statement everyone present listened with profound attention and equally profound surprise; and a glance at the faces of the jurymen was sufficient to show that it had failed utterly to produce conviction. Even the coroner was evidently not satisfied, and, after a few moments' reflection with knitted brows, he stated his objection.

"The belief in the destructive properties of lime," he said, "can hardly be accepted as a mere popular error. In the Crippen trial, you may remember that the question was raised, and one of the expert witnesses—no less an authority than Professor Pepper—gave it as his considered opinion that quick-lime has these destructive properties, and that if a body were buried in a sufficient quantity of quick-lime, that body would be entirely destroyed. You will agree, I think, that great weight attaches to the opinion of a man of Professor Pepper's great reputation."

"Undoubtedly," Thorndyke agreed. "He was one of our greatest medico-legal authorities, though, on this subject, I think, his views differed from those generally held by medical jurists. But the point is that this was an opinion, and that no undeniable facts were then available. But since that time, the matter has been put to the test of actual experiment, and the results of those experiments are definite facts. It is no longer a matter of opinion but one of incontestable fact."

"What are the experiments that you refer to'"

"The first practical investigation was carried out by Mr. A. Lucas, the Director of the Government Analytical Laboratory and Assay Office at Cairo. He felt that the question was one of great medico-legal importance, and that it ought to be settled definitely. He accordingly carried out a number of experiments, of which he published the particulars in his treatise on 'Forensic Chemistry.' I produce a copy of this book, with your permission."

"Is this evidence admissible?" the foreman asked. "The witness can't swear to another man's experiments."

"It is admissible in a coroner's court," was the reply.

"We are not bound as rigidly by the rules of evidence as a criminal court, for instance. It is relevant to the inquiry, and I think we had better hear it."

"I may say," said Thorndyke, "that I have repeated and confirmed these experiments; but I suggest that, as the published cases are the recognized authority, I be allowed to quote them before describing my confirmatory experiments."

The coroner having agreed to this course, he continued: "The tests were made with the fresh bodies of young pigeons, which were plucked but not opened, and which were buried in boxes with loosely-fitted covers, filled respectively with dry earth, slaked lime, chlorinated lime, quick-lime, and quick-lime suddenly slaked with water. These bodies were left thus buried for six months, the boxes being placed on the laboratory roof at Cairo. At the end of that period the bodies were disinterred and examined with the following results: The body which had been buried in dry earth was found to be in a very bad condition. There was a considerable smell of putrefaction and a large part of the flesh had disappeared. The body which had been buried in quick-lime was found to be in good condition; it was dry and hard, the skin was unbroken, but the body was naturally shrunken. The other three bodies do not concern us, but I may say that none of them was as completely preserved as the one that was buried in quick-lime.

"On reading the account of these experiments I decided to repeat them, partly for confirmation and partly to enable me to give direct evidence as to the effect of lime on dead bodies. I used freshly-killed rabbits from which the fur was removed by shaving, and buried them in roomy boxes in the same materials as were used in the published experiments. They were left undisturbed during the six summer months, and were then exhumed and examined. The rabbit which had been buried in dry earth was in an advanced stage of putrefaction; the one which had been buried in quick-lime was free from any odour of decomposition, the skin was intact, and the body unaltered excepting that it was dry and rather shrivelled—mummified, in fact. It was more completely preserved than any of the others."

The conclusion of this statement was followed by a slightly uncomfortable silence. The coroner stroked his chin reflectively, and the jurymen looked at one another with obvious doubt and distrust. At length Mr. Pilley gave voice to the collective sentiments.

"It's all very well, sir, for this learned gentleman to explain to us that the lime couldn't have eaten up the body of the deceased. But it has. We've seen the bare bones with our own eyes. What's the use of saying a thing is impossible when it has happened?"

Here Thorndyke produced from his pocket a sheet of notepaper and a fountain pen, and began to write rapidly, noting down, as I supposed, the jurymen's objections; which, however, the coroner proceeded to answer.

"Dr. Thorndyke's statement was that these bones are not the bones of Angelina Frood. That the body was not her body."

"Still," said the foreman, "it was somebody's body, you know. And the lime seems to have eaten it up pretty clean, possible or impossible."

"Exactly," said the coroner. "The destruction of this particular body appears to be an undeniable fact; and we may assume that one body is very much like another—in a chemical sense, at least. What do you say, doctor?"

"My statement," replied Thorndyke, "had reference to Angelina Frood, who is known to have been alive on a certain date. Of the condition of the unknown body that was buried in the wall, I can give no opinion."

Again there was an uncomfortable silence, during which Thorndyke, having finished writing, folded the sheet of notepaper, tucked the end in securely, and wrote an address on the back. Then he handed it to his neighbour, who passed it on until it reached me. I was on the point of opening it when I observed with astonishment that it was addressed to Peter Bundy, Esq., to whom I immediately handed it. But my astonishment was nothing to Bundy's. He seemed positively thunderstruck. Indeed, his aspect was so extraordinary as he sat gazing wildly at the opened note, that I forgot my manners and frankly stared at him. First he turned scarlet; then he grew deathly pale; and then he turned scarlet again. And, for the first and only time in my life, I saw him look really angry. But this was only a passing manifestation. For a few moments his eyes flashed and his mouth set hard. Then, quite suddenly, the wrath faded from his face and gave place to a whimsical smile. He tore off the fly-leaf of the note, and, scribbling a few words on it, folded it up small, addressed it to Dr. Thorndyke, and handed it to me for transmission by the return route.

When it reached Thorndyke, he opened it, and, having read the brief message, nodded gravely to Bundy, and once more turned his attention to the foreman, who was addressing the coroner at greater length.

"The jury wish to say, sir, that this evidence is not satisfactory. It can't be reconciled with the other evidence. The facts before the jury are these: On the 26th of April Angelina Frood disappeared, and was never afterwards seen alive. On the night that she disappeared, or on the next night, a dead body was buried in the wall. Three months later that body was found in the wall, packed in quick-lime, and eaten away to a skeleton. That skeleton has been examined by an expert, and found to be that of a woman of similar size and age to Angelina Frood. With that skeleton were found articles of clothing, jewellery, and ornaments which have been proved to have been the clothing and property of Angelina Frood. Other articles of clothing have been recovered from the river; and those articles were missing from the body when it was found in the wall. On these facts, the jury feel that it is impossible to doubt that the remains found in the wall are the remains of Angelina Frood."

As the foreman concluded the coroner turned to Thorndyke with a slightly puzzled smile. "Of course, Doctor," said he, "you have considered those facts that the foreman has summarized so admirably. What do you say to his conclusion?"

"I must still contest it," replied Thorndyke. "The foreman's summary of the evidence, masterly as it was, furnishes no answer to the objection—based on established chemical facts—that the condition of the remains when found is irreconcilable with the alleged circumstances of the burial."

The coroner raised his eyebrows and pursed up his lips.

"I appreciate your point, Doctor," said he. "But we are on the horns of a dilemma. We are between the Devil of observed fact and the Deep Sea of scientific demonstration. Can you suggest any way out of the difficulty?"

"I think," said Thorndyke, "that if you were to call Mr. Bundy, he might be able to help you out of your dilemma."

"Mr. Bundy!" exclaimed the coroner. "I didn't know he was concerned in the case. Can you give us any information, Mr. Bundy?"

"Yes," replied Bundy, looking somewhat shy and nervous. "I think I could throw a little light on the case."

"I wish to goodness you had said so before. However, better late than never. We will take your evidence at once."

On this Thorndyke returned to his seat at the table and Bundy took his place, standing by the chair which Thorndyke had resigned.

"Let me see, Mr. Bundy," said the coroner, "your Christian name is—"

"The witness has not been sworn," interrupted Thorndyke.

The coroner smiled. "We are in the hands of the regular practitioners," he chuckled. "We must mind our p's and q's. Still you are quite right, Doctor. The name is part of the evidence."

The witness was accordingly sworn, and the coroner then proceeded, smilingly: "Now, Mr. Bundy, be very careful. You are making a sworn statement, remember. What is your Christian name?"

"Angelina," was the astounding reply.

"Angelina!" bawled Pilley. "It can't be. Why, it's a woman's name."

"We must presume that the witness knows his own name," said the coroner, writing it down. "Angelina Bundy."

"No, Sir," said the witness. "Angelina Frood."

The coroner suddenly stiffened with the upraised pen poised in the air; and so everyone in the room, including myself, underwent an instantaneous arrest of movement as if we had been turned into stone; and I noticed that the process of petrifaction had caught us all with our mouths open. But whereas the fixed faces on which I looked, expressed amazement qualified by incredulity, my own astonishment was coupled with conviction. Astounding as the statement was, the moment that it was made I knew that it was true. In spite of the discrepancies of appearance, I realized in a flash of enlightenment, the nature of that subtle influence that had drawn me to Bundy with a tenderness hardly congruous with mere male friendship. Outwardly I had been deceived, but my subconscious self had recognized Angelina all the time.

The interval of breathless silence, during which the witness calmly surveyed the court through his—or rather her—monocle, was at length broken by the coroner, who asked gravely: "This is not a joke? You affirm seriously that you are Angelina Frood?"

"Yes; I am Angelina Frood," was the reply.

Here Mr. Pilley recovered himself and demanded excitedly: "Do we understand this gentleman to say that he is the deceased?"

"Well," replied the coroner, "he is obviously not deceased, and he states that he is not a gentleman. He has declared that he is a lady."

"But," protested Pilley, "he says that she—at least she says that he—"

"You are getting mixed, Pilley," interrupted the foreman. "This appears to be a woman masquerading as a man and playing practical jokes on a coroner's jury. I suggest, sir, that we ought to have evidence of identity."

"I agree with you, emphatically," said the coroner.

"The identification is indispensable. Is there anyone present who can swear to the identity of this-er-person! Mr. Japp, for instance?"

"I'd rather you didn't bring Mr. Japp into it," said Angelina, hastily. "It isn't really necessary. If you will allow me to run home and change my clothes, Mrs. Gillow and Dr. Strangeways will be able to identify me. And I can bring some photographs to show the jury."

"That seems quite a good suggestion," said the coroner.

"Don't you think so, gentlemen?"

"It is a very proper suggestion," said the foreman, severely. "Let her go away and clothe herself decently. How long will she be gone?"

"I shall be back in less than half an hour,'" said Angelina; and on this understanding she was given permission to retire. I watched her with a tumult of mixed emotions as she took up her hat, gloves, and stick, and strolled jauntily towards the door. There she paused for an instant and shot at me a single, swift, whimsical glance through her monocle. Then she went out; and with her disappeared for ever the familiar figure of Peter Bundy.

CHAPTER XVIII

THE UNCONTRITE PENITENT

As the door closed on Angelina, a buzz of excited talk broke out. The astonished jurymen put their heads together and eagerly discussed the new turn of events, while the coroner sat with a deeply cogitative expression, evidently thinking hard and casting an occasional speculative glance in Thorndyke's direction. Meanwhile Cobbledick edged up to my side and presented his views in a soft undertone.

"This is a facer, Doctor, isn't it? Regular do. My word! Just think of the artfulness of that young woman, toting us round and helping us to find the things that she had just popped down for us to find. I call it a masterpiece." He chuckled admiringly, and added in a lower tone, "I hope she hasn't got herself into any kind of mess."

I looked at Cobbledick with renewed appreciation. I had always liked the sergeant. He was a capable man and a kindly one; and now he was showing a largeness of soul that won my respect and my gratitude, too. A small man would have been furious with Angelina, but Cobbledick took her performances in a proper sporting spirit. He was only amused and admiring. Not for nothing had Nature imprinted on his face that benevolent smile.

Presently Mr. Pilley, who seemed to have a special gift for the expression of erroneous opinions, addressed himself to the coroner.

"Well, Mr. Chairman," he said cheerfully, "I suppose we can consider the inquest practically over."

"Over!" exclaimed the astonished coroner.

"Yes. We were inquiring into the death of Angelina Frood. But if Mrs. Frood is alive after all, why, there's an end to the matter."

"What about the body in the mortuary?" demanded the foreman.

"Oh, ah," said Pilley. "I had forgotten about that." He looked owlishly at the coroner and then exclaimed:

"But that is the body of Mrs. Frood!"

"It can't be if Mrs. Frood is alive," the coroner reminded him.

"But it must be," persisted Pilley. "It has been identified as her, and it had her clothes and ring on. Mr. Bundy must have been pulling our legs."

"There is certainly something very mysterious about that body," said the coroner. "It was dressed in Mrs. Frood's clothes, as Mr. Pilley points out, and it appears that Mrs. Frood must be in some way connected with it."

"There's no doubt about that," agreed the foreman.

"She must know who that dead person is and how the body came to be in the place where it was found, and she will have to give an account of it."

"Yes," said the coroner. "But it is a mysterious affair. I wonder if Dr. Thorndyke could enlighten us. He seems to know more about the matter than anybody else."

But Thorndyke was not to be drawn into any statement.

"It would be merely a conjecture on my part," he said. "Presumably Mrs. Frood knows how the remains got into the wall, and I must leave her to give the necessary explanations."

"I don't see what explanations she can give," said the foreman. "It looks like a clear case of wilful murder. And it is against her."

To this view the coroner gave a guarded assent; and indeed it was the obvious view. There was the body, in Angelina's clothing, and everything pointed clearly to Angelina's complicity in the crime, if there had really been a crime committed. And what other explanation was possible?

As I reflected on the foreman's ominous words, I was sensible of a growing alarm. What if Angelina had been, as it were, snatched from the grave only to be placed in the dock on a charge of murder? That she could possibly be guilty of a crime did not enter my mind. But there was evidently some sort of criminal entanglement from which she might find it hard to escape. The appearances were sinister in the extreme; her simulated disappearance, her disguise, her suspicious silence during the inquiry; to any eye but mine they were conclusive evidence of her guilt. And the more I thought about it, the more deadly did the sum of that evidence appear, until, as the time ran on, I became positively sick with terror.

The opening of a door and a sudden murmur of surprise caused me to turn; and there was Angelina herself. But not quite the Angelina that I remembered. Gone were the pallid complexion, the weary, dark-circled eyes, the down-cast mouth, the sad and pensive countenance, the dark, strong eyebrows. Rosy-cheeked, smiling, confident, and looking strangely tall and imposing, she stepped composedly over to the head of the table, and stood there gazing with calm self-possession, and the trace of a smile at the stupefied jurymen.

"Your name is—?" said the coroner, gazing at her in astonishment.

"Angelina Frood," was the quiet reply; and the voice was Bundy's voice.

Here Pilley rose, bubbling with excitement. "This isn't the same person!" he exclaimed. "Why, he was a little man, and she's a tall woman. And his hair was short, and just look at hers! You can't grow a head of hair like that in twenty minutes."

"No," Angelina agreed, suavely. "I wish you could."

"The objection is not relevant, Mr. Pilley," said the coroner, suppressing a smile. "We are not concerned with the identity of Mr. Bundy but with that of Angelina Frood. Can anyone identify this lady?"

"I can," said I. "I swear that she is Angelina Frood."

"And Mrs. Gillow?"

Mrs. Gillow could and did identify her late lodger, and furthermore, burst into tears and filled the court-room with "yoops" of hysterical joy. When she had been pacified and gently restrained by the coroner's officer from an attempt to embrace the witness, the coroner proceeded:

"Now, Mrs. Frood, the jury require certain explanations from you, in regard to the body of a woman which is at present lying in the mortuary and which was found buried in the city wall with certain articles of clothing and jewellery which have been identified as your property. Did you know that that body had been buried in the wall?"

"Yes," replied Angelina.

"Do you know how it came to be in the wall?"

"Yes. I put it there."

"You put it there!" roared Pilley, amidst a chorus of exclamations from the jurymen. The coroner held up his hand to enjoin silence and asked, as he gazed in astonishment at Angelina.

"Can you tell us who this deceased person was?"

"I'm afraid I can't," Angelina replied, apologetically. "I don't think her name was known."

"But-er-" the astounded coroner inquired, "how did she come by her death?"

"I'm afraid I can't tell you that either," replied Angelina. "The fact is, I never asked."

"You never asked!" the coroner repeated, in a tone of bewilderment. "But-er-are we to understand that in short, did you or did you not cause the death of this person by your own act? Of course," he added hastily, "you are not bound to answer that question."

Angelina smiled at him engagingly. "I will answer with pleasure. I did not cause the death of this person."

"Then are we to understand that she was already dead when you found her'"

"I didn't find her. I bought her; at a shop in Great St. Andrew-street. I gave four pounds, fourteen and three-pence for her, including two and three-pence to Carter Paterson's. I've brought the bill with me."

She produced the bill from her pocket and handed it to the coroner, who read it with a portentous frown and a perceptible twitching at the corners of his mouth.

"I will read this document to you, gentlemen," he said in a slightly unsteady voice. "It is dated the 19th of April, and reads: 'Bought of Oscar Hammerstein, Dealer in Human and Comparative Osteology, Great St. Andrew-street, London, W. C., one complete set superfine human osteology, disarticulated and unbleached (female), as selected by purchaser, four pounds eight shillings and sixpence. Replacing and cementing missing teeth, one shilling and sixpence. Packing case, two shillings. Carriage, two and three pence. Total, four pounds, fourteen and three-pence. Received with thanks, O. Hammerstein.' Perhaps you would like to see the bill, yourselves, gentlemen."

He passed it to the foreman, taking a quick glance out of the corners of his eyes at the bland and impassive Angelina, and the jury studied it in a deep silence, which was broken only by a soft, gurgling sound, from somewhere behind me, which, I discovered, on looking round, to proceed from Sergeant Cobbledick, whose crimsoned face was partly hidden by a large handkerchief and whose shoulders moved convulsively.

Presently the coroner addressed Thorndyke. "In continuation of your evidence, Doctor, does Mrs. Frood's explanation agree with any conclusions that you had arrived at from your inspection of the remains?"

"It agrees with them completely," Thorndyke replied with a grim smile.

The coroner entered the answer in the depositions, and then turned once more to Angelina.

"With regard to the objects that were found with the skeleton; did you put them there?"

"Yes. I put in the metal things and a few pieces of scorched rag to give a realistic effect—on account of the lime, you know."

"And the articles that were recovered from the river, too, I suppose?"

"Yes, I put them down—with proper precautions, of course."

"What do you mean by proper precautions?"

"Well, I couldn't afford to waste any of the things, so I used to keep a lookout with a telescope, and then, when I saw a likely person coming along, I put one of the things down where it could be seen."

"And were they always seen?"

"No. Some people are very unobservant. In that case I picked it up when the coast was clear and saved it for another time."

The coroner chuckled. "It was all very ingenious and complete. But now, Mrs. Frood, we have to ask you what was the object of these extraordinary proceedings. It was not a joke, I presume?"

"Oh, not at all," replied Angelina. "It was a perfectly serious affair. You have heard what sort of husband I had. I couldn't possibly live with him. I made several attempts to get away and live by myself, but he always followed me and found me out. So I determined to disappear altogether."

"You could have applied for a separation," said the coroner.

"I shouldn't have got it," replied Angelina, "and even if I had, of what use would it have been? I should have been bound to him for life. I couldn't have married anyone else. My whole life would have been spoilt. So I decided to disappear completely and for good, and start life afresh in a new place and under a new name. And in order that there should be no mistake about it, I thought I would leave the—er—the material for a coroner's inquest and a will directing that a suitable monument should be put up over my grave. Then, if I had ever married again, there would have been no danger of a charge of bigamy. If anyone had made any such suggestion, I could have referred them to the registrar of deaths and to the tombstone of Angelina Frood in Rochester churchyard."

"And as to a birth certificate under your new name?" the coroner asked with a twinkle of his eye.

Angelina smiled a prim little smile. "I think that could have been managed," she said.

"Well," said the coroner, "it was an ingenious scheme. But apparently Dr. Thorndyke knew who Mr. Bundy was. How do you suppose he discovered your identity?"

"That is just what I should like to know," she replied.

"So should I," said the coroner, with a broad smile; "but, of course, it isn't my affair or that of the jury. We are concerned with this skeleton that you have planted on us. I suppose you can give us no idea as to where it came from originally?"

"The dealer said it had been found in a barrow-not a wheel-barrow, you know; an ancient burial-place. Of course, I don't know whether he was speaking the truth."

"What do you think, Dr. Thorndyke?" the coroner asked.

"I think it is an ancient skeleton, though very well preserved. Some of the teeth—the original ones—show more wear than one expects to find in a modern skull. But I only made a cursory inspection."

"I think the evidence is sufficient for our purpose," said the coroner; "and that really concludes the case, so we need not detain you any longer, Mrs. Frood. I don't know exactly what your legal position is; whether you have committed any legal offence. If you have, it is not our business; and I think I am expressing the sentiments of the jury if I say that I hope that the authorities will not make it their business. No one has been injured, and no action seems to be called for."

With these sentiments the jury concurred warmly, as also did Sergeant Cobbledick, who was heard, very audibly and regardless of the proprieties, to murmur "Hear, hear." We waited to learn the nature of the verdict, and when this had been pronounced (to the effect that the skeleton was that of an unknown woman, concerning the circumstances of whose death no evidence was available), the court rose and we prepared to depart.

"You are coming back to lunch with us, Angelina?" said I.

"I should love to," she replied, "but there is Mr. Japp. Do you think you could ask him, too?"

"Of course," I replied, with a sudden perception of the advantage of even numbers. "We shouldn't be complete without him."

Japp accepted with enthusiasm, and, after a hasty farewell to Cobbledick, we went forth into the High Street, by no means unobserved of the populace. As we approached the neighbourhood of the office Angelina said:

"I must run into my rooms for a few moments just to tidy myself up a little. It was such a very hurried toilette. I won't be more than a few minutes. You needn't wait for me."

"I suggest," said Thorndyke, "that Mr. Japp and I go on and break the news to Mrs. Dunk that there is a lady guest, and that Strangeways remains behind to escort the prisoner."

I fell in readily with this admirable suggestion, and as the two men walked on, I followed Angelina up the steps and waited while she plied her latch-key. We entered the hall together and then went into the sitting-room, where she stood for a moment, looking round with deep satisfaction.

"It's nice to be home again," she said, "and to feel that all that fuss is over."

"I daresay it is," said I. "But now that you are home, what have you got to say for yourself? You are a nice little baggage, aren't you?"

"I am a little beast, John," she replied. "I've been a perfect pig to you. But I didn't mean to be, and I really couldn't help it. You'll try to forgive me, won't you?"

"The fact is, Angelina," I said, "I am afraid I am in love with you."

"Oh, I hope to goodness you are, John," she exclaimed. "If I thought you weren't I should wish myself a skeleton again. Do you think you really are?"

She crept closer to me with such a sweet, wheedlesome air that I suddenly caught her in my arms and kissed her.

"It does seem as if you were," she admitted with a roguish smile; and then—such unaccountable creatures are women—she laid her head on my shoulder and began to sob. But this was only a passing shower. Another kiss brought back the sunshine and then she tripped away to spread fresh entanglements for the masculine heart.

In a few minutes she returned, further adorned and looking to my eyes the very picture of womanly sweetness and grace. When I had given confirmatory evidence of my sentiments towards her, we went out, just in time to encounter Mrs. Gillow and acquaint her with the program.

"I suppose," said Angelina, glancing furtively at a little party of women who were glancing, not at all furtively, at her, "one should be gratified at the interest shown by one's fellow towns-people; but don't you think the back streets would be preferable to the High-street?"

"It is no use, my dear," I replied. "We've got to face it. Take no notice. Regard these bipeds that infest the footways as mere samples of the local fauna. Let them stare and ignore them. For my part, I rather like them. They impress on me the admirable bargain that I have made in swapping Peter Bundy for a beautiful lady."

"Poor Peter," she said, pensively. "He was a sad boy sometimes when he looked at his big, handsome John and thought that mere friendship was all that he could hope for when his poor little heart was starving for love. Your deal isn't the only successful one, John, so you needn't be so conceited. But here we are home—really home, this time, for this has been my real home, John, dear. And there—Oh! Moses I—there is Mrs. Dunk, waiting to receive us!"

"What used you to do to Mrs. Dunk," I asked, "to make her so furious?"

"I only used to inquire after her health," Angelina replied plaintively. "But mum's the word. She'll spot my voice as soon as I speak."

Mrs. Dunk held the door open ceremoniously and curtsied as we entered. She was a gruff old woman, but she had a deep respect for "gentlefolk," as is apt to be the way with old servants. Angelina acknowledged her salutation with a gracious smile and followed her meekly up the stairs to the room that Mrs. Dunk had allotted to her.

I found Thorndyke and Japp established in the library—Dr. Partridge had dispensed with a drawing-room and I followed his excellent example—and here presently Angelina joined us, sailing majestically into the room and marching up to Thorndyke with an air at once hostile and defiant.

"Serpent," said Angelina.

"Not at all," Thorndyke dissented with a smile. "You should be grateful to me for having rescued you from your own barbed-wire entanglements."

"Serpent, I repeat," persisted Angelina. "To let me sit in that court-room watching all the innocents walking into my trap one after another, and then, just as I thought they were all inside, to hand me a thing like that!" and she produced, dramatically, a small sheet of paper, which I recognized as the remainder of Thorndyke's note. I took it from her, and read: "You see whither the evidence is leading. The deception cannot be maintained, nor is there any need, now that your husband is dead. Explanations must be given either by you or by me. For your own sake I urge you to explain everything and clear yourself. Let me know what you will do."

"This is an extraordinary document," I said, passing it to Japp. "How in the name of Fortune did you know that Bundy was Angelina?"

"Yes, how did you?" the latter demanded. "It is for you to give an explanation now."

"We will have the explanations after lunch," said he; "mutual explanations. I want to hear how far I was correct in details."

"Very well," agreed Angelina, "we will both explain. But you will have the first innings. You are not going to listen to my explanation and then say you knew all about it. And that reminds me, John, that you had better tell Mrs. Dunk. She is sure to recognize my voice."

I quite agreed with Angelina and hurried away to intercept Mrs. Dunk and let her know the position. She was at first decidedly shocked, but a vivid and detailed description of the late Mr. Frood produced a complete revulsion; so complete, in fact, as to lead me to speculate on the personal characteristics of the late Mr. Dunk. But her curiosity was aroused to such an extent that, while waiting at table, she hardly removed her eyes from Angelina, until the latter, finding the scrutiny unbearable, suddenly produced the hated eyeglass, and, sticking it in her eye, directed a stern glance at the old woman, who instantly backed towards the door with a growl of alarm, and then sniggered hoarsely.

It was a festive occasion, for we were all in exuberant spirits, including Mr. Japp, who, if he said little, made up the deficiency in smiles of forty-wrinkle power, which, together with his upstanding tuft of white hair, made him look like a convivial cockatoo.

"Do you remember our last meeting at this table'" said Angelina, "when I jeered at the famous expert and pulled his reverend leg, thinking what a smart young fellow I was, and how beautifully I was bamboozling him? And all the while he knew! He knew! And 'Not a word said the hard-boiled egg.' Oh, serpent! serpent!"

Thorndyke chuckled. "You didn't leave the hardboiled egg much to say," he observed.

"No. But why were you so secret? Why didn't you let on, just a little, to give poor Bundy a hint as to where he was plunging?"

"My dear Mrs. Frood—"

"Oh, call me Angelina," she interrupted.

"Thank you," said he. "Well, my dear Angelina, you are forgetting that I didn't know what was in the wall."

"My goodness!" she exclaimed. "I had overlooked that. Of course, it might have been—Good gracious! How awful!" She paused with her eyes fixed on Thorndyke, and then asked: "Supposing it had been?"

"I refuse to suppose anything of the kind," he replied. "My explanations will deal with the actual, not with the hypothetical."

There was silence for a minute or two. Like Angelina, I was speculating on what Thorndyke would have done if the remains had been real remains—and those of a man. He had evidently sympathized warmly with the hunted wife; but if her defence had taken the form of a crime, would he have exposed her? It was useless to ask him. I have often thought about it since, but have never reached a conclusion.

"You will have to answer questions better than that presently," said Angelina; "but I won't ask you any more now. You shall finish your lunch in peace, and then—into the witness-box you go. I am going to have satisfaction for that note."

The little festival went on, unhurried, with an abundance of cheerful and rather frivolous talk. But at last, like all fugitive things, it came to an end. The table was cleared, and garnished with the port decanter and the coffee service, and Mrs. Dunk, with a final glower, half-defiant and half-admiring, at Angelina, took her departure.

"Now," said Angelina, as I poured out the coffee, "the time has come to talk of many things, but especially of expert investigations into the identity of Peter Bundy. Your lead, Sir."

CHAPTER XIX

EXPLANATIONS

"The investigation of this case," Thorndyke began, "falls naturally into two separate inquiries: that relating to the crime and that which is concerned with what we may conveniently call the personation. They make certain contacts, but they are best considered separately. Let us begin with the crime.

"Now, to a person having experience of real crime, there was, in this case, from the very beginning, something rather abnormal. A woman of good social position had disappeared. There was a suggestion that she had been murdered; and the murder had apparently been committed in some public place, that is to say, not in a house. But in such cases, normally, the first evidence of the crime is furnished by the discovery of the body. It is true that, in this case, there was a suggestion that the body had been flung into the river, and this, at first, masked the abnormality to some extent. But even then there was the discrepancy that the brooch, which was attached to the person, appeared to have been found on land, while the bag, which was not attached to the person, was picked up at the water's edge. The bag itself, and the box which had been in it, presented several inconsistencies.

"They had apparently been lying unnoticed for eleven days on a piece of shore that was crowded with small craft and frequently by numbers of seamen and labourers, and that formed a play-ground for the waterside children. The clean state of the box when found showed that it had neither been handled nor immersed, and as the wrapping-paper was intact, the person who had taken it out of the bag must have thrown it away without opening it to see what it contained. The bag was found under some light rubbish. That rubbish had not been thrown on it by the water, or the bag would have been soaked; and no one could have thrown the rubbish on it without seeing the bag, which was an article of some value. Again, the bag had not been carried to this place by the water, as was proved by its condition.

"Therefore, either this was the place where the crime had been committed, or someone had brought the bag to this place and thrown it away. But neither supposition was reasonably probable. It was inconceivable that a person like Mrs. Frood should have been in this remote, inaccessible, disreputable place at such an hour. The bag could not have been brought here by an innocent person, for no such person would have thrown it away. It was quite a valuable bag. And a guilty person would have thrown it in the river, and probably put a stone in it to sink it. So you see that these first clues were strikingly abnormal. They prepared one to consider the possibility of false tracks. Even the brooch incident had a faint suggestion of the same kind when considered with the other clues. The man who pawned the brooch had a mole on his nose. Such an adornment can be easily produced artificially. It is highly distinctive of the person who possesses it, and it is equally distinctive—negatively—of the person who does not possess it. Then there was the character of the person who had disappeared. She was a woman who was seeking to escape from her husband; and hitherto she had not succeeded because she had not hidden herself securely enough. She was a person of a somewhat disappearing tendency. She had an understandable motive for disappearing.

"From the very beginning, therefore, the possibility of voluntary disappearance had to be borne in mind. And when it was, each new clue seemed to support it. There was the scarf, for instance. It was found under a fish-trunk; an unlikely place for it to have got by chance, but an excellent one for a 'plant.' The scarf was not baldly exposed, but someone was sure to turn the trunk over and find it. And at this point another peculiarity began to develop. There was a noticeable tendency for the successive 'finds' to creep up the river from Chatham towards Rochester Bridge. It was not yet very remarkable, but I noticed it, as I entered each find on my map. The brooch was associated with Chatham, the bag and box with the Chatham shore a little farther up, the scarf with the Rochester shore at Blue Boar Head. As I say, it attracted my attention; and when the first shoe was found above Blue Boar Head, the second shoe farther up still, and the hat-pin yet farther up towards the bridge, it became impossible to ignore it. There was no natural explanation. Whether the body were floating or stationary, the constancy of direction was inexplicable; for the tide sweeps up and down twice daily, and objects detached from the body would be carried up or down stream, according to the direction of the tide when they became detached. This regular order was a most suspicious circumstance. Later, when the objects were found in Black Boy-lane, it became absurd. It was a mere paper-chase. Just look at my map."

He exhibited the large-scale map, on which each "find" was marked by a small circle. The series of circles, joined by a connecting line, proceeded directly from near Sun Pier, Chatham, along the shore, and up Black Boy-lane to the gate of the waste ground, and across it to the wall.

Angelina giggled. "You can't say I didn't make it as easy as I could for poor old Cobbledick," she said. "Of course, I never reckoned on anyone bringing up the heavy guns. By the way, I wonder who your private client was. Do you know, John'" she added, with a sudden glance of suspicion; and, as I grinned sheepishly, she exclaimed: "Well! I wouldn't have believed it. It was a regular conspiracy. But I am interrupting the expert. Proceed, my lord."

"Well," Thorndyke resumed, "we have considered the aspect of the crime problem taken by itself, as it appeared to an experienced investigator. From the first there was a suspicion that the clues were counterfeit, and with each new clue this suspicion deepened. And you will notice an important corollary. If the case was a fraud, that fraud was being worked by someone on the spot. Keep that point in mind, for it has a most significant bearing on the other problem, that of the personation, to which we will now turn our attention. But before we go into details, there are certain general considerations that we ought to note, in order that we may understand more clearly how the deception became possible.

"The subject of personation and disguise is often misunderstood. It is apt to be supposed that a disguise effects a complete transformation resulting in a complete resemblance to the individual personated—or, as in this case, a complete disappearance of the identity of the disguised person. But no such transformation is possible. All disguise is a form of bluff. It acts by suggestion. And the suggestion is effected by a set of misleading circumstances which produce in the dupe a state of mind in which a very imperfect disguise serves to produce conviction. That is the psychology of personation, and I can only express my admiration of the way in which Angelina had grasped it. Her conduct of this delicate deception was really masterly. Let us consider it in more detail.

"Mr. Bundy was ostensibly a man. But if he had been put in a room with a dozen moderately intelligent persons, and those persons had been asked, 'Is this individual a man? or is he a woman with short hair and dressed in man's clothing?' they would probably have decided unanimously that he was a woman. But the question never was asked. The issue was never raised. He was Mr. Bundy. One doesn't look at young men to see if they are women in disguise.

"Then consider the position of Strangeways—the chosen victim. He comes to a strange town to transact business with a firm of land agents. He goes into the office, and finds the partners—whose names are on the plate outside, and to whom he has been sent by his London agent-engaged in their normal avocations. He transacts his business with them in a normal way, and Mr. Bundy seems to be an ordinary, capable young man. He goes back later and interviews Mr. Bundy, who is just on the point of taking him to introduce him to Mrs. Frood, when he is called away. Then, within a few minutes, he is taken to Mrs. Frood's house, where he finds that lady calmly engaged in needlework. Supposing Mrs. Frood had been extremely like Bundy, could it possibly have entered Strangeways's head that they might be one and the same person? Remember that he had left Bundy in another place only a few minutes before; and here was Mrs. Frood in her own apartments, with the appearance of having been there for hours. Obviously no such thought could have occurred to any man. There was nothing to suggest it.

"But, in fact, Angelina was not perceptibly like Bundy on cursory inspection. They were markedly different in size. A woman always looks bigger than a man of the same height. Bundy was a little man and looked smaller than he was by reason of his very low heels; Angelina was a biggish woman and looked taller than she was by reason of her high heels and her hair. Disregarding her hair, she was fully two inches taller than Bundy.

"Then the facial resemblance must have been slight. Angelina had a mass of hair and wore it low down on her brows and temples; Bundy's hair was short and was brushed back from his forehead. Angelina had strong, black eyebrows; Bundy's eyebrows were thin, or rather, cut off short. Angelina was pale, careworn, dark under the eyes, with drooping mouth, melancholy expression and depressed in manner; Bundy was fresh-coloured, smiling, gay and sprightly in manner and he wore an eyeglass—which has a surprising effect on facial expression. Their voices and intonation were strikingly different. Finally, Strangeways never saw Angelina excepting in a very subdued light in which any small resemblances in features would be unnoticeable.

"And now observe another effect of suggestion. Strangeways had made the acquaintance of Mr. Bundy. Then he had made the acquaintance of Mrs. Frood. They were two separate persons; they were practically strangers to one another; they belonged to different sets of surroundings. He would never think of them in connexion with one another. They were two of his friends, mutually unacquainted. In this condition of separateness they would become established in his mind, and the conception of them as different persons would become confirmed by habit. It would be a permanent suggestion that would offer an obstacle to any future suggestion that they were the same. That was the advantage of introducing Bundy first, for if he had appeared only after Angelina had disappeared, there would have been no such opposing suggestion. The resemblances might have been noticed, and he might have been detected.

"In passing I may remark upon the tact and judgment that were shown in the disguise. The troublesome makeup, the wig, the false eyebrows, the grease-paint, the false voice, all were concentrated on the temporary Mrs. Frood, who was to disappear. Bundy was not disguised at all, excepting for the eyeglass. He was simply Angelina with her hair cut short and dressed as a man. He hadn't even an assumed voice; for as Angelina is a contralto, and habitually speaks in the lower register, her voice would pass quite well as a light tenor, so long as she kept off the 'head notes.'

"So much for the general aspects of the case. And now as to my own position. As I had never seen Angelina, I naturally should not perceive any resemblance to her in Bundy; but, equally with Strangeways, I was subject to the suggestion that Bundy was a man. The personal equation, however, was different. It is my professional habit to reject all mental suggestion so far as is possible; to sift out the facts and consider them with an open mind regardless of what they appear to suggest. And then you are to remember that when I first met Mr. Bundy, there was already in my mind a faint suspicion that this was not a genuine crime; that things were not quite what they appeared; and that if this were the case, the clues were being manipulated by somebody on the spot.

"When I met Mr. Bundy, I looked him over as I look over every person whom I meet for the first time; and that inspection yielded one or two rather remarkable facts. I noticed that he wore exceptionally low heels and that he had several physical characteristics that were distinctively feminine. The very low heels puzzled me somewhat. If they had been exceptionally high there would have been nothing in it. But why should a noticeably short man wear almost abnormally low heels? I could think of no reason, unless he wore them for greater comfort, but I noted the fact and reserved it for further consideration.

"Of his physical peculiarities, the first that attracted my attention was the shape of his hands. They were quite of the feminine type. Of course, hands vary, but still it was a fact to be noted, and the observation caused me to look him over a little more critically; and then I discovered a number of other feminine characteristics.

"Perhaps it may be useful to consider briefly the less obvious differences between the sexes—the more obvious ones would, of course, be provided for by the disguise. There are two principal groups of such differences; the one has reference to the distribution of bulk, the other to the direction of certain lines. Let us take the distribution of bulk. This exhibits opposite tendencies in the two sexes. In the female, the great mass is central—the hip region; and from this the form diminishes in both directions. The whole figure, including the arms, is contained in an elongated ellipse. And the tendency affects the individual members. The limbs are bulky where they join the trunk, they taper pretty regularly towards the extremities, and they terminate in relatively small hands and feet. The hands themselves taper as a whole, and the individual fingers taper markedly from a comparatively thick base to a pointed tip.

"In the male figure the opposite condition prevails; it tends to be acromegalous. The central mass is relatively small, the peripheral masses is relatively large. The hip region is narrow, and there is a great widening towards the shoulders. The limbs taper much less towards the extremities, and they terminate in relatively large hands and feet. So, too, with the hands; they tend to be square in shape, and the individual fingers—excepting the index finger—are nearly as broad at the tips as at the base.

"Of the second group of differences we need consider only one or two instances. The general rule is that certain contour lines tend in the male to be vertical or horizontal in direction and in the female to be oblique. A man's neck, at the back, is nearly straight and vertical; a woman's shows a sweeping oblique curve. The angle of a man's lower jaw is nearly a right angle; there is a vertical and a horizontal ramus. A woman's lower jaw has an open angle and its contour forms an oblique line from the ear to the chin. But the most distinctive difference is in the ear itself. A man's ear has its long diameter vertical; a woman's has the long diameter oblique; and the obliquity is usually very marked.

"Bearing these differences in mind, and remembering that they are subject to variation in individual cases, let us now return to Mr. Bundy. His hands, as I have said, had the feminine character. His feet were small even for a small man; his ears were set obliquely and the line of his jaw was oblique with an open angle. His shoulders had evidently been made up by the tailor, and he seemed rather wide across the hips for a man. In short, all those bodily characteristics which were not concealed or disguised by the clothing were feminine. It was a rather remarkable fact; so much so that I began to ask myself if it were possible that he might actually be a woman in disguise.

"I watched him narrowly. There was nothing distinctive in his walk, but there was in the movements of the arms. He flourished his stick jauntily enough, but he had not that 'nice conduct of a clouded cane' that is as much a social cachet in our day as it was in the days of good Queen Anne. It needs a skill born of years of practice to manage a stick properly, as one realizes when one sees the working man taking his Malacca for its Sunday morning walk. Mr. Bundy had not that skill. His stick was a thing consciously carried; it was not a part of himself. Then the movement of the free arm was feminine. When a woman swings her arm she swings it through a large arc, especially in the backward direction—probably to avoid her hip—and the palm of the hand tends to be turned backward. A man's free arm either hangs motionless or swings slightly, unless he is walking very fast; it swings principally forward, and the palm of his hand inclines inwards. These are small matters, but their cumulative significance is great.

"Further, there was the mental habit. Bundy was jocose and playfully ironic. But a gentleman of twenty-five doesn't 'pull the leg' of a gentleman of fifty whom he knows but slightly; whereas a lady of twenty-five does. And very properly," he added, seeing that Angelina had turned rather pink. "That is a compliment in a young lady which would be an impertinence in a young man. No doubt, when the equality of the sexes is an accomplished fact, things will be different."

"It will never be an accomplished fact;" said Angelina. "The equality of the sexes is like the equality of the classes. The people who roar for social equality are the under-dogs; and the women who shout for sex equality are the under-cats. Normal women are satisfied with things as they are."

"Hearken unto the wisdom of Angelina," said Thorndyke, with a smile. "But perhaps she is right. It may be that the women who are so eager to compete with men are those who can't compete with women. I can't say. I have never been a woman: whereas Angelina has the advantage of being able to view the question from both sides.

"The *prima facie* evidence, then, suggested that Mr. Bundy was a woman. But as this was a *prima facie* improbability, the matter had to be gone into further. On Mr. Bundy's cheeks and chin was a faint blue colouration, suggestive of such a growth of whiskers and beard as would be appropriate to his age. Now if those whiskers and that beard were genuine, the other signs were fallacious. Mr. Bundy must be a man. But his cheeks looked perfectly smooth and clean; and it was about seven o'clock in the evening. My own cheeks and Strangeways' were by this time visibly prickly; and as he had been with us all day, Mr. Bundy could not have shaved since the morning. I tried vainly to get a closer view, and was considering how it could be managed when Providence intervened."

"I know," said Angelina; "It was that beastly mosquito."

"Yes," agreed Thorndyke. "But even then I could not get a chance to look at the skin closely. But when we got Mr. Bundy into the surgery, and examined the bite through a lens, the murder was out."

"You could see there were no whiskers?" said Angelina.

"It wasn't that," replied Thorndyke. "It was something much more conclusive. You may know that the whole of the human body excepting the palms of the hands, the soles of the feet, and the eyelids, is covered with a fine down, technically called the lanugo. It consists of minute, nearly colourless hairs set quite closely together, and may be seen as a sort of halo on the face of a woman or child when the edge of the contour is against the light. On the face of a clean-shaved man it is, of course, absent, as it is shaved off with the whiskers. Now on Mr. Bundy's face the lanugo was intact all over the blue area. It followed that he had never been shaved. It further followed that the blue colouration was an artificial stain. But this made it practically a certainty that Mr. Bundy was a woman.

"The question now was: If Mr. Bundy was a woman, what woman was he? The obvious answer seemed to be, Angelina Frood. She was missing; but if the disappearance was an imposture, someone on the spot was planting the clues. That someone would most probably be Mrs. Frood, herself. But if she were lurking in the neighbourhood, she must be disguised; and here was a disguised woman. Nevertheless, obvious as the suggestion was, the thing suggested seemed to be impossible. Strangeways knew both Angelina and Bundy and he had not recognized the latter; and I had a vague impression that he had seen them together, which, of course, would absolutely exclude their identity. A little judicious conversation with him, however, showed that neither objection had any weight. He had never seen them both at one time; and his description of Mrs. Frood made it clear that she had appeared to him totally unlike Bundy.

"The next thing was to ascertain definitely if this woman really was Mrs. Frood, and fortunately I had the means of making a very simple test. Strangeways had given me a photograph of Angelina bearing the address of a theatrical photographer, and from him I obtained seven different photographs in various poses. Then I received from Strangeways the group-photograph that was taken of us by the city wall, which contained an excellent portrait of Mr. Bundy. Out of this photograph I cut a small square containing Bundy's head, soaked it in oil of bergamot, and mounted it in Canada balsam on a glass plate. This made the paper quite transparent, so I now had a transparent positive. I selected from the photographs of Angelina one that was in a pose exactly similar to the portrait, of Bundy—practically full face—and treated it in the same way. Then I handed the two transparencies to my assistant, and he, by means of our big copying camera, produced two life-sized negatives, exactly alike in dimensions. With prints from these negatives we were able to perform some experiments. From Angelina's portrait I carefully cut out the face, leaving the hair and neck, and slipped Bundy's portrait behind it, so that his face appeared through the hole. We could now see how Bundy looked with Angelina's hair, and, on putting it beside an untouched portrait of Angelina, it was obvious, in spite of the eyeglass, that it was the same face. For you must remember that the Angelina that we had was the real person, not the made-up Angelina whom Strangeways had seen.

"This success encouraged us to take a little more trouble. My man, Polton, made some black paper masks, with the aid of which he produced two composite photographs, one of which had Bundy's face and Angelina's hair, neck, and bust, while the other had Angelina's face and Bundy's hair, forehead, neck, and bust. The eyeglass was the disturbing factor, though it showed very little, and Bundy managed it so skilfully that it hardly affected the shape of the eye and the set of the brow. Still, it was necessary to eliminate it, and as painting was out of our province, we invoked the aid of Mrs. Anstey, who is a very talented portrait painter and miniaturist. She touched out the joins in the composites, painted out the eyeglass in the one and painted an eyeglass into the other. And now the identity was complete. The Bundy-Angelina portrait was identical with the photographer's portrait, and the Angelina-Bundy photograph was Mr. Bundy to the life.

"However, we made a final test. Polton reduced the Bundy-Angelina portrait to cabinet size, and made a couple of carbon prints, which I brought down here and exhibited; and as Strangeways accepted them as portraits of Angelina, I considered the proof complete."

Here Angelina interrupted: "But what about that brooch? I never had a brooch like that."

Thorndyke smiled a grim smile. "I asked Mrs. Anstey to paint in a brooch of a characteristic design."

"What for?" asked Angelina.

"Ah!" said Thorndyke, "thereby hangs a tale."

"Oh! a serpent's tail, I suppose," said Angelina.

"You will be able to judge presently," he replied. "The brooch had its uses. Well, to continue: The identity of Mr. Bundy was now established as a moral certainty. But it was not certain enough for legal purposes. I wanted conclusive evidence; and I wanted to ascertain exactly how the transformation effects were worked. I had noted that Bundy and Angelina occupied adjoining houses which were virtually the two moieties of a double house with a common covered passageway. I assumed that the two houses communicated, but it was necessary to ascertain if they really did. The only way to establish the facts was to inspect the house in which Angelina had lived, and this I determined to do, in the very faint hope that I might be able, at the same time, to get one or more of Angelina's fingerprints. I made a pretext for visiting the house with Strangeways, and we had the extraordinary good luck to find Mrs. Gillow just going out, so we had the house to ourselves. But this was not the only piece of luck, for we found that Angelina had taken a drink from the bedroom tumbler and water-bottle before going out, and had left on them a complete set of beautiful fingerprints, of which I secured a number of admirable photographs.

"Examination of the basement showed that I was right as to the communication. Both houses had a side door opening into the passage-way, and both doors were fitted with Yale latches which looked as if they were opened with the same key. The passage was little used, but the gravel between the two doors was a good deal trodden, and there were numerous fingerprints on Angelina's side-door. In the kitchen was a large cupboard fitted with a Yale lock on the door and pegs inside. I assumed that when Angelina was at home that cupboard contained a suit of Mr. Bundy's clothes, and that when Mr. Bundy was in the office it contained a wig and a dress and a pair of lady's shoes.

"Well, that made the evidence fairly complete with one exception. We had to get a set of Bundy's fingerprints to compare with Angelina's. That was where the brooch came in. I knew that when Mr. Bundy saw a portrait of his former self with a brooch that he had never possessed, his curiosity would be aroused, and he would examine that portrait closely. And so he did. And on my asking him to compare the two prints, he took the opportunity to pick them both up, one in each hand, to scrutinize them more minutely, and find out who the photographer was. When he put them down, they bore a complete, though invisible, set of his fingerprints. Later, Mr. Bundy went home, escorted by Strangeways. As soon as they were gone, I took the photographs up to my room, developed up the fingerprints with powder, and compared them minutely, line by line, with the photographs of those on the tumbler and bottle. They were identical. The fingerprints of Bundy were the fingerprints of Angelina Frood.

"That completed the case; and if I had known what Angelina's intentions were I should have notified Bundy that 'the game was up.' But I was in the dark. I could do nothing until I knew whether she was going to produce a body, and if so, whose body it would be. The City wall was in my mind as a possibility, since I had noted the curious disappearance of the gate-key on that significant date and I had heard of the story of Bill the bargee and knew that Bundy had heard it, and apparently taken it seriously. But one can't act on conjecture. I could only watch Angelina play her game and try to follow the moves. When the paper-chase turned up Black Boy-lane, I knew that the wall-burial was intended to be discovered. But I didn't know what was in the wall, and I may say that I was rather alarmed. For if Angelina had taken the story of Bill as a reliable precedent and had buried a real body in quicklime, there was going to be a catastrophe. It was an immense relief to me when I got Strangeways' report that only a skeleton had been found; for I knew then that only a skeleton had been buried and that no crime had been committed. That is all I have to tell; and now it is Angelina's turn to enter the confessional."

"You haven't left me much to tell," said Angelina. "I feel as if I had been doing the thimble and pea trick with glass thimbles. However, I will fill in a few details. This scheme first occurred to me when I came down here to take over the property that had been left to me. I put it confidentially to Uncle Japp, but he was so shocked that he has never been able to get his hair to lie down since. He wouldn't hear of it. So I asked him to lunch with poor Nicholas; and after that he was ready to agree to anything. Accordingly I made my preparations. I got a theatrical wig-maker to cut off my hair and make it into a wig (I told him I had a man's part and it was expected to be a long run), got a suit made by a theatrical costumier, and down I came as Mr. Bundy. Uncle J. had already had the new plate put up. The next door offices and basement were empty, so we got them furnished for Angelina, and as soon as the wig was ready, down she came and took possession.

"Up to this time the third act was a bit sketchy. I had arranged the disappearance, and the recovery of the clues from the river, and I had a plan of buying a mummy, dressing it in my clothes, and burying it in the marshes close to the shore, where I could discover it when it had matured sufficiently. But I didn't much like the plan. I didn't know enough about mummies, and some other people might know too much. It looked as if I should have to do without a body, and leave my death to mere rumour; which would be unsatisfactory. I did want a tombstone.

"About this time an angel of the name of Turcival—he lives in Adam and Eve-street, Adelphi, bless him!—sent a Dr. Strangeways down here. He was a regular windfall—a new doctor—and I gave him my entire attention. I took him to his own proposed premises, and kept him in conversation, to let my personality soak well in. That evening I interviewed him in the office, and let him suppose that I was going to take him to Mrs. Frood's house and introduce him to her. Then, when I suddenly remembered an engagement elsewhere, I went out, and as soon as the office door was shut, down I darted into our basement, out at the side door, in at the other side door, and into Mrs. Frood's kitchen. There I did a lightning change; slipped on my dress and wig, stuck on my eyebrows, and made up my complexion; flew up the stairs, lighted the lamp in the sitting-room, and spread myself out with my needle-work. But I hadn't been settled more than two or three minutes when Uncle Japp arrived, leading the lamb to the slaughter.

"Then it turned out that I had struck a bit of luck that I hadn't bargained for. John had attended me in London and knew something of my affairs; so I appointed him my physician in ordinary on the spot. It was rare sport. The concern poor old John showed for my grease-paint was quite touching. I sat there squeaking complaints to him and receiving his sympathy until I was ready to screech with laughter. But I felt rather a pig all the same, for John was so sweet, and he was such a man and such a gentleman. However, I had to go on when once I had begun.

"But it was a troublesome business, worse than any stage job I ever had, to keep these two people going. I had to rush through from the office into the kitchen and cook things that I didn't want, just to make a noise and a smell of cooking, and listen to Mrs. Gillow so that I could pop up the stairs at the psychological moment and remind her that I lived there; and then to fly down and change and dart through into the office, so that people could see that I was occupied there. It was frightfully hard work, and anxious, too. I can tell you, it was a relief when I heard from Miss Cumbers that Nicholas was starting for Brighton, and that I could disappear without implicating him. However, there is no need for me to go into any more details. Your imaginations can fill those in."

"The man with the mole, I take it," said Thorndyke, "was—"

"Yes. I got a suit of slops in the Minories. The mole, of course, was built up, with toupee-paste."

"By the way," said Thorndyke, "was there any necessity for Bundy at all?"

"Well, I had to be somebody, you know, and I had to stay on the spot to work the clues and keep an eye on the developments. I couldn't be a woman because that would have required a heavy make-up that would almost certainly have been spotted, and would have been an intolerable bore; whereas Bundy, as you have pointed out, was not a disguise at all. When once I had got my hair cut and had provided myself with the clothes and eyeglass, there was no further trouble. I could have lived comfortably as Bundy for the rest of my life.

"So that is my story," Angelina concluded; "and," she added, with a sudden change of manner, "I am your grateful debtor for ever. You have done far more for me even than you know. Only this morning, poor Peter Bundy was a forlorn little wretch, miserably anxious about the present and looking to a future that had nothing but empty freedom to offer. And now I am the happiest of women—for I should be a hypocrite if I pretended to have any regrets for poor Nicholas. I will say good-bye to him in his coffin and give him a decent funeral, and try to think of him as he was before he sank into the depths. But I am frankly glad that he is gone out of his own miserable life and out of mine. And his going, which would never have been known but for the wisdom of the benevolent serpent, has left me free, With a promise of a happiness that even he does not guess."

"I am not so sure of that," said Thorndyke, with a sly smile.

"Well, neither am I, now you come to mention it," said she, smiling at him in return. "He is an inquiring and observant serpent, with a way of nosing out all sorts of things that he is not supposed to be aware of. And, after all, perhaps he has a right to know. It is proper that the giver should have the satisfaction of realizing the preciousness of that which he has given."

Here endeth the Mystery of Angelina Frood. And yet it is not quite the end. Indeed, the end is not yet; for the blessed consequences still continue to develop like the growth of a fair tree. The story has dwindled to a legend, whose harmless whispers call but a mischievous smile to that face that, like the dial in our garden, acknowledges only the sunshine. Mrs. Dunk, it is true, still wages public war, but it is tempered by private adoration; and almost daily baskets of flowers, and even tomatoes and summer cabbages, arrive at our house accompanied by the beaming smile and portly person of Inspector Cobbledick.